Untouched

&

Lilly Wilde

Untouched

Acknowledgments

My husband for tolerating and understanding the countless hours I spent glued to my computer, my tablet, and even my phone, and for smiling when I walked through the house screaming with excitement during each phase of this project.

My son for his critique of and enthusiasm for my promos and book cover, and his interpretation on the "select" passages I shared with him.

Of course I have to pay recognition to my already supportive group of fans who have followed me from my days of serving as admin on several Facebook pages and groups.

My Street Team, The Wilde Lillies: Jennifer, Brandie, Stephanie, Rocky, Julie, and Kelly. You ladies rocked it! Your support and enthusiasm will never be forgotten.

My fellow author and sometimes friend (smile), BS. Thank you for helping me create such a wonderful pen name.

Contents

❧Chapter One❧

"Good morning, Ms. Cason."

"Good morning, Raina," I replied, as I walked past her desk into my office.

"I'll be right in with your morning tea," she continued, as she scurried off in the direction of the kitchen.

Anxious to start another day at Raine Publishing House, I walked into my office and dropped my purse and briefcase on the meeting table. *I really love my job,* I thought, as I sat behind the luxurious Parnian wood desk, one of the many recent furnishings for RPH's new corporate offices. The company's interior decorator had made every effort to select furniture that best fit the energy and vibrancy of our individual personalities. My desk was made of six different kinds of exotic wood, including ebony and Carpathian elm, and a piece of custom glass. It suited me, as I was definitely an exotic mix of *something.*

I took in the spacious office, the lavish décor, and the breathtaking view of Boston's inner harbor, and I smiled. Hard work and a little luck had taken me from a subsidiary of Raine Industries to President of Communications of the multi-faceted publishing company.

My thoughts briefly flashed to the not-so-pleasant pieces of my life that had played a huge part in my success. My past had things I preferred to lock away, so I typically maintained focus on the present.

"Here you are, Ms. Cason." Raina's return brought me back to the day's business. "I also brought you a croissant. They're for the intern orientation, but I thought you might like to eat beforehand."

"Thanks, Raina. What time are the interns expected?"

"Nine o'clock, but Mr. Meade wants them to have a tour first. They'll assemble in the conference room for orientation at about ten o'clock and then report to their assigned departments directly afterwards."

"What's the name of the intern assigned to my division?"

"Harper Sheraton. His file is on my desk. Would you like to review it?"

"Yes, that would be helpful." I'd been in the middle of a project and hadn't been able to hand-select our intern like I normally would. "After the fiasco last spring, I have my doubts about Human Resources' assignments."

"Oh, yes. Ms. Webber. She's definitely one for the record books." Raina's beryl blue eyes sparkled as she smiled. I guessed she was reliving the nightmare of that intern in her mind as I was. "Let me grab that file for you," she said.

Raina was an attractive woman with delicate features and a

penchant for pencil skirts, which were ideal for her thin, tall frame. Sipping my tea, I watched her walk back to her desk, her auburn curls bouncing as they cascaded past her shoulders. I hoped my oversight with this term's intern didn't come back to bite me in the ass.

A few moments later, Raina returned with Harper's orientation file. "Will that be all, Ms. Cason?" she asked.

"Yes, Raina. Thank you," I replied, as she turned to leave.

Raina, having transferred to my division from editing, was an excellent executive assistant. As soon as I'd accepted this position, I'd begun looking for someone to work alongside me. I'd interviewed Raina and had taken to her instantly. She'd worked at Esquire Magazine prior to the birth of her first child, when she'd chosen to be a stay-at-home mom. Though her love and adoration for her family was apparent, I'd easily determined that she was anxious to re-enter the workforce. She'd proven to be a hard worker and a loyal employee. She also possessed a maternal warmth that I appreciated, probably because my own mother and sisters were missing from my life. In any case, I knew I'd be lost without Raina.

After skimming Harper's file, I set it aside, satisfied that he, at least on paper, had more promise than Ms. Webber. I then began reviewing the promotional campaigns that were scheduled to roll out within the next two weeks. I was so absorbed with checking and revising deadlines that I lost track of time. Thankfully, Raina buzzed my phone ten minutes before the meeting. Locking my computer and grabbing my cell, I walked out to meet Raina, discussing a minor change in my schedule as we made our way to the meeting.

We exited the elevator on the thirtieth floor and walked down the hall toward the conference room. Blake Mead, the CEO, rushed over as soon as he saw me. Raina excused herself to get a cup of tea from the buffet while I tried to interpret Blake's anxious expression. He was a good-looking man with deep set brown eyes and brown hair lightly streaked with gray. I'd always considered him a confident and capable leader, but today I saw none of his typical self-assurance.

"Listen, Aria," he said when he reached me. "Corporate is rumbling about the performance in some of our divisions, and they're in the midst of evaluating the feasibility of some of our projects. I have a sneaking suspicion they'll send someone here to analyze every aspect of our operations."

I knew why he was concerned. Our last few projects had failed expectations by a rather wide margin. "Should we meet to form a strategy?" I suggested. "We should also include Mike Ward. His division was unusually below budget projections."

"Yes, it was," Blake agreed. "I'll have Cynthia call Raina and get something scheduled for the three of us." He let out another sigh. "Well, looks like it's time. Let's get this started."

I followed him toward the front of the room and stood next to David, RPH's Marketing Director. He was tall and broad-shouldered, with a mop of dirty-blond hair and thick, solemn brows offset by a boyish grin. Greenish-blue eyes gleamed behind rectangular-framed glasses that sat at the very tip of his nose.

David and I began discussion of his many deadlines, one of which was for my division. He confirmed that he would have the final prints ready for my approval later this afternoon, and we talked about a business lunch if my schedule permitted, which I needed to verify with Raina. I glanced toward the buffet, but she was gone. I scanned the room in search of her, but stopped short at the gloriously handsome man standing near the door.

He appeared remarkably confident, browsing the room as if assessing it before making a decision to enter. I was practically gaping at him when his eyes finally connected with mine. Was it possible for the heart to skip a beat? Because mine certainly had. His eyes traveled the length of my body, and then he nodded a hello. I smiled, unable to tear my eyes away. Whoever he was, I quickly surmised that he was an unadulterated orgasm in a suit. Virginia gently throbbed as my mind instantly ventured to dark, naughty places. Oh, fuck me…please!

Blake interrupted my mini daydream; based on his expression, he'd called my name more than once. Embarrassed by my slip, I turned toward Blake with feigned interest, hoping he didn't realize that I was going goo-goo over Mr. Fuck Me.

"Yes?" I replied.

"Would you like to begin the meeting and let me finish up or would you prefer I start?" he asked.

He *consistently* made this offer and I *consistently* accepted. I really didn't understand why he didn't just make it the standing protocol. "I can start," I replied, hoping I could maintain focus despite my derailed thoughts.

"Good, I was hoping you'd say that. It takes the pressure off of me to set the tone. I seem to always make people nervous," he replied.

"I wonder why that is," I said dryly. Blake was a very astute, very staid businessman. He often came across as intimidating, despite his efforts to appear otherwise.

I faced the interns and other staff members and took a seat near the head of the conference table. "Good morning, everyone. If you will all be seated." Everyone moved toward the chairs situated around the table. I would have preferred Blake open the meeting because I was still rolling in the aftershocks of Mr. Fuck Me. I took a deep breath and focused on the agenda, although I would have preferred to focus my attention on the hot sexy stranger in the dark gray suit.

Once everyone was seated, I began the introductions. "My

name is Aria Cason, and I am Raine Publishing House's President of Communications. I'd like to welcome you and present you with a brief introduction to the company and the agenda for our meeting today. I'd first like to introduce some of the key RPH staff who'll also be speaking this morning. Starting clockwise, this is Adam Shelton, Senior Editor; David Shaw, Director of Marketing; Kent Richmond, Director of Finance; and last but certainly not least, Blake Meade, our fearless President and CEO. We've also invited a few RPH staff who will serve as your mentors during your next few months with us. We're all extremely pleased that you've chosen RPH as your intern site this summer..."

The remainder of my briefing detailed the different areas of the company, devoting a great deal of time to specifics of my department. I went on to inform them of the success of previous interns, some of whom had been offered positions at RPH. It was very difficult to concentrate and present the information as I normally would, due to my fleeting thoughts. I had to continuously remind myself not to hone in too much on one particular individual.

Blake and Adam were next in line, offering their views from the perspectives of CEO and editor. At the conclusion of the departmental introductions, Blake asked each of the interns to introduce themselves and provide details of the path that led them to RPH. When it was Mr. Fuck Me's turn, as I would expect, all of the women's eyes were glued to him. I smirked to myself. Surely these Bland Betties didn't think they stood a chance with a man like him. I was by no means an uppity type, but I was a realist. And realistically speaking, there was not a chance in hell of any of them hooking up with this guy. He seemed above it all — above the frivolities of the hunt and the seduction.

He scanned the others around the table, giving direct eye contact as he spoke. His relaxed, confident vibe bordered on smugness, but it easily commanded the attention of everyone in the room — he was utterly captivating. He had *cool* written all over his face, and he radiated a calm control that sent his sex appeal through the roof.

As it turned out, his name was not Mr. Fuck Me; it was Aiden Wyatt. He was a Harvard graduate, having earned multiple degrees — one of which was a Masters in Business. As he spoke of his education and work experience, my attention was fragmented by the intoxicating combination of his face and his voice. He was exceptionally attractive, but more than that, he had that *something* about him that was more appealing than his looks. It immediately drew you in — as if he had glamoured you. Yes, I was a fan of a certain HBO series, and just like those fictional magical creatures, he had me absolutely spellbound. I didn't typically pay attention to a man's mouth unless he was doing something intimate with it, but I found myself watching his lips. The words dripped from them like warm honey. Was he aware of the heat he was creating? I could have literally reached an orgasm from just hearing him speak.

After having received his business degree, he'd attended Harvard Law School—where he completed his law degree—but upon graduation, he opted for a different career. I was perplexed as to why he would consider an entry-level position, with such an impressive educational background. He was, in a word, amazing. I would love to have met him under different circumstances. He appeared to be damned near perfect! Why did he have to be an intern? And an even better question: why was he interning here? With his level of education, he had endless career possibilities.

Aiden had been the last intern to speak. The director of Human Resources, Lorraine Atchison, entered to officially announce the department assignments. I assumed Aiden would work within the finance or legal department since he had a background in both. *Good luck, ladies.* I couldn't imagine how difficult it would be to work closely with him for a day, let alone the next four months.

With the meeting finished, I walked to Harper, our assigned intern, just as Lorraine approached Aiden. I overheard the word *transfer;* obviously they were in conversation regarding the departmental assignments. I glanced toward the two of them. Lorraine was eyeing him as if she wanted to rip his clothes off.

Not that I couldn't see why.

The room slowly emptied as everyone returned to their respective departments. Raina and I were exiting with Harper when Lorraine asked to speak with him

"Aria, can you give us a moment? We'll walk down to your office shortly," Lorraine said.

"Of course," I replied. Raina and I left the three of them in the conference room.

"Ms. Cason, it seems you have an admirer," Raina said as she pressed the button for the twenty-fifth floor.

"What?"

"Don't tell me you didn't notice the way Aiden was staring at you?"

"No, I can't say that I did," I replied.

"Hmm..."

"What is it, Raina?" I asked, since she obviously had more to say about the intern.

"Ah, nothing. I was just thinking it's a good thing he's not working in our department. It would be difficult to work with someone as appealing as he is."

"Appealing?" I asked, smiling and feigning disinterest. "Is that what he is?"

"So you *did* notice how handsome he is. I knew you were as affected as the rest of the women in the room," she accused.

"Affected? Interesting choice of words."

"Interesting and accurate," she added with a laugh.

Seemed we both felt we had dodged a very hot and sexy bullet. "Raina, if you would, send Harper to my office when he arrives," I said, as I walked past her desk.

"Of course, Ms. Cason."

Raina and I had previously selected the projects that I would assign our intern. We actually needed some additional research on the new marketing concepts for RPH's e-publishing division. We needed a campaign to break into the fortified position Amazon had in this arena. I sat at my desk and woke my computer to locate the list of preliminary action items that Harper would need.

"Ms. Cason."

"Yes," I replied, still looking for the file. "What is it, Raina?"

"Our intern is here and chomping at the bit to get started," she stated. I looked up from the screen with a welcoming smile that quickly faded as I found myself staring into the gorgeous green eyes of Aiden Wyatt.

❧Chapter Two❧

He proffered a smile, which I was unable to return. This couldn't be correct. What the hell happened? Surely he'd been misdirected.

Of course, that must have been it. The thought calmed my frantic nerves so I was able to reply. "Not that we wouldn't welcome you with open arms to our team, but I believe Harper Sheraton was assigned to my division. What department are you looking for? Perhaps Raina can escort you," I said.

He casually stepped into my office, his smile accompanying his overly confident disposition. What a gorgeous smile. *Could he be any sexier?*

"Ms. Cason… It is *Miss* Cason, isn't it?" he probed.

"Well, yes it is," I replied, surprised he would request the distinction.

"Ms. Cason, obviously Ms. Atchison failed to alert you of the changes, but she spoke with me a few moments ago. Due to my various credentials and work history, HR deemed I would be more of an asset to your division. I hope that doesn't pose a problem."

Fuck yes it poses a problem.

"Of course. It's no problem at all," I said aloud. "We're lucky to have you. I mean, someone with your diverse and impressive background."

Why the hell wasn't I informed?

"Please, have a seat," I said, motioning him toward the meeting table. I stood and walked over to sit across from him, wondering if he could sense my unease.

"Ms. Atchison asked that I give you this." He passed a folder to me as I took a seat. Glancing at him before reviewing the file, I forced a smile, hoping my irritation wasn't apparent. I made a pretense of looking over his qualifications; I could feel his eyes on me, and it was extremely uncomfortable.

I had to look up eventually. *Damn, damn, damn.* Direct eye contact had never been a problem for me, but I found it difficult to look at him without feeling it was inappropriate for the work place. I took a breath and looked up to meet his eyes.

My prolonged gaze was almost involuntary, as it was somewhat impossible to look away. He had the greenest eyes I'd ever seen. Now that I was closer, I could see a speck of gray around the edges. It was more than the beauty of his eyes that held me captive, though. It was as if I were being compelled to expose myself, enabling him to view a part of me that was meant only for me, the part I tried desperately to keep hidden.

I blinked, severing the connection. "I apologize. My mind was a million miles away. Can you excuse me? I need to speak with

Raina for a moment."

"Yes, of course," he answered, though obviously confused by my abruptness. Standing quickly, I walked out of my office in search of Raina. I found her in the reception area talking to Zoe, our publicity assistant, and Bailey, our receptionist. I asked them all to join me in briefing Aiden. I needed someone in the room to dilute my unease.

Leading them back to my office, we all took a seat around the table. Aiden glanced at each of them before returning his gaze to me. "I thought it best if we each briefed Aiden on our individual roles with the upcoming campaign," I said. "Each of you will provide him with the particulars, and we'll develop an agenda for separate meetings as necessary. Some of the meetings will be with the staff outside the communications division, so we'll need to identify the points of contact and begin scheduling appointments."

We spent the first half of the morning reviewing the ad campaigns to which Aiden was assigned. We also continued the discussion of his credentials. His education was extraordinary: having earned his initial degrees in business and political science. He later obtained a law degree from Harvard and a medical degree from Emery—which I found odd. He detected my curiosity and further explained that he graduated high school at age thirteen and pursued dual undergraduate degrees, which he completed when he was eighteen. In view of his youth, and his interest in both law and medicine, he'd decided to obtain degrees in both, and upon completion of his education, he would decide his long-term career. In the end, he reverted to the business field. From what I gathered, the decision was spearheaded by Aiden's father, an unyielding businessman, who'd urged Aiden to follow in his footsteps.

His intelligence was quite disarming; I was extremely impressed. As he spoke, I unwillingly studied his features. His skin was slightly tanned, which I attributed to some time on the beach—I couldn't see him as the tanning booth type of guy. He had thick dark hair that curled at the ends, resting right above his collar. His nose was straight and distinguished, and his lips, flawlessly sculpted, were full and kissable. I couldn't determine which aspect I wanted to fixate on more. Not only did he look unbelievably perfect, he sounded like a talking orgasm. His voice was deep and extremely sexy. I'd never heard a velvet timbre like his before, one that made you squeeze your thighs together and think naughty thoughts. The entire package was overwhelming.

He couldn't possibly be single. He wasn't wearing a wedding ring, but that meant very little these days. I didn't know how anyone could work alongside this man without routine bathroom breaks to do you-know-what! I'd read about this in books— encountering a sinfully gorgeous man whose overpowering sensual appeal caused you to think of nothing less than hard-core sex. But never had I come face-to-face with a man like that in real life — until now. I didn't realize until he smiled at me that I had actually stopped breathing. I took a breath and returned his smile, then directed my attention to Raina.

"That will tie everything up for phase one, and I'll email each of you a copy this afternoon," Raina said, in reference to the upcoming agendas.

"That sounds perfect. Thank you, Raina. It would appear we're done, unless someone has questions." I glanced at each of them, hoping to prolong the meeting, but everyone was silent. I then thanked Raina, Zoe, and Bailey for their contributions. They extended pleasantries to Aiden and fell into conversation as they exited my office.

Although I no longer had a crutch in the room, my focus somehow remained solely on work. As I reviewed previous related campaigns and project details with Aiden, I was acutely aware that his disposition had shifted, also. Perhaps his change was what actually enabled me to divert my attention from Virginia and her whorish tendencies to the task at hand. Whatever the reason, most of the tension had disappeared — and for that I was grateful. I wasn't familiar with the vulnerability of losing control, and I didn't want to be.

"You'll also collaborate with Josh Landry. He's our division's research assistant, and then there's River Duncan, our graphic designer."

"And I'll be meeting them when?"

"Tomorrow. This should give you an idea of what we're striving for." I passed the portfolio to him. "You may want some time to review it later."

"If it's okay, I'll take a look at it now."

Well damn. "Okay, sure."

He was a very quick study, taking in every aspect of the diverse campaign elements, asking questions that were rather notable, given his limited exposure to this area of work.

"I think you may have a problem here and here." He pointed out the sections listed in the disclaimer.

I reviewed the information he'd referenced. "I'm sure it's fine. Legal signed off on this weeks ago," I said, sliding it back over to him.

"Either they were looking over it after a long lunch or they simply didn't know what they were looking at, but this will not work."

Meeting his unwavering gaze, I knew he'd be more than just a challenge for my libido. "Let's have you meet with legal. Just have Raina set it up."

"Sounds good. Thank you, Ms. Cason."

Given our recent marketing failures, he understood the

necessity of this campaign being a success. I could see that he and I could work extremely well together if I could place my earlier reservations aside.

"Ms. Cason."

We were so deeply engrossed in work that I was startled when I heard Raina's voice on the telephone intercom.

"Yes, Raina?"

"It's nearly time for lunch, and you've not informed me of your plans. Shall I order in or did you plan to go out today?"

"Thanks for checking on me, Raina. I think I would wither away to nothing if you didn't save me from my workaholic propensities."

I sensed Aiden's eyes on me, easily altering the aura of the room in one short measure. I shifted my gaze to meet his and smiled to ease the awkwardness. He returned my smile, his glance falling to my lips. I swallowed and shifted uncomfortably in my seat. I raised my brows slightly, questioning if there was a problem. His response was a darkening of his irises. His lustrous green stones locked with my sunlit drops of honey. Desperate to escape his penetrating gaze, I stood and returned to my desk. I could work with him, but I sure as hell couldn't handle being near him when he looked at me like that.

"I had a feeling that you'd lost track of time," Raina said.

"Guilty as charged," I stated, glancing nervously at Aiden. "I think I'll grab lunch at the bistro on the corner. I need a break from the office for a while." Aiden's focused gaze had captured Virginia's full attention. Yes, I needed to get away for a few moments to clear my head of this potent thing I had going on with him.

"Yes, ma'am," she replied.

"Thanks, Raina. I'll be leaving out shortly." I waited for her reply, but there was silence. I looked up from my calendar to see she was now standing in the entrance to my office. She passed a fleeting look between Aiden and me, clearly noting something in the atmosphere.

I turned off the speakerphone and looked up to see Aiden's eyes dart from Raina to me. I smiled politely, although there was nothing polite about the thoughts racing through my head. "I think I've overwhelmed poor Aiden already. I would hate to scare him off his first day."

"You couldn't scare me away, even if you tried, Ms. Cason. I've seen enough to know with certainty that I'll enjoy my time at RPH far more than I'd anticipated."

Was it me, or did his reply have a mixed meaning? From the way he was eyeing me, he was referring to something more than his internship.

I cleared my throat as I reminded myself to provide an appropriate response.

"I'm pleased that you're excited, Aiden, but you may wish to reserve your judgment until you've experienced a few more days at RPH. I'm known to be very challenging. I'm certain that after you've become more familiar with my demands on your time, you'll want to run out screaming."

"Honestly, I don't think that will happen," he replied. "As a matter of fact, I have a strong sense that I'll enjoy every minute, and that I'll acquire a wealth of knowledge under your excellent tutelage."

Again, I wondered if his statements had hidden meaning. "Well, that's very flattering, Aiden. Be sure to pass that on to Mr. Meade when you meet with him for your exit interview. It never hurts to have someone remind him of my importance."

"I wouldn't think that anyone would need to be reminded of your obvious attributes, Ms. Cason."

Okay, time to change the subject. "Thank you, Aiden. I'm going to head out for lunch. I'm not sure if you have plans, but we have a cafeteria if you would like to eat in the building. If you prefer to eat out, Raina can provide you with a list of the local restaurants." I stood and walked over to grab my purse and jacket, trying desperately not to show the effect he had on me. "I'll see you in about an hour."

"Yes, you will," he replied as he stood and followed me out of my office.

"Raina, can you assist Aiden with some lunch options? I'll see you two in a bit."

I walked past Raina's desk and headed for the elevators. After pressing the down button, I reached inside my purse to grab my phone just as the elevator doors opened and I stepped inside. As the doors closed, I glanced up to see Aiden standing beside Raina's desk, and wondered how I would manage this interesting development.

I'd decided to have lunch at Grotto, an Italian restaurant that I frequented when I needed a small break from the office scene. The hostess greeted me as I walked in and quickly led me to a booth. My time here was always the same. I always sat in a booth near the window to watch the passersby, and I always ate the same lunch.

I ordered my usual—the zuppa, a garlic soup. I thought better of it for a second, until I remembered that Aiden would be working with Raina the remainder of the day. I definitely didn't want to be near him while reeking of garlic.

Thankful to have some time to myself, I started to replay the morning's events. I felt disoriented, as though everything had been thrown out of whack, and I knew I'd handled it poorly.

Where did things go wrong? I did expect an intern this morning, and I knew the first half of the day would be devoted to him or her. What I didn't know was how I allowed that intern's presence to affect me in just a matter of hours. And even more, I didn't know how the hell I'd be able to work alongside him for the next several weeks.

Lunch ended much too soon. I did, however, manage to give myself one of my famous pep talks, reminding myself of my professionalism and my personal policies — there were certain things I absolutely wouldn't do. And I refused to let Mr. Fuck Me send any more of his subliminal messages to Virginia. I smiled to myself, wondering if any other women named their lady parts. I knew men did, although some packages didn't measure up to the names. Did Aiden have a name for his? I wondered if it was a *huge* package. Virginia twitched at the thought, and I quickly reprimanded myself for yet again veering mindlessly into a sexual lane in which Aiden was driving.

Usually after lunch I was raring to go, but for obvious reasons, I was hesitant to return to my office. Aiden and Raina were talking at her desk when I exited the elevator on our floor. They noticed me almost immediately, and I smiled in their direction as I walked toward my office. This was going to be next to impossible. I couldn't work so close to that man; I simply couldn't. I mulled over some possible excuses to reassign him to a different department.

Before I went into my office, Raina stopped me. "Ms. Cason, I know I was to work with Aiden the remainder of the day, but Mr.

Richmond has requested my assistance in Editing. It seems Mr. Nelson had to leave on an emergency, and Mr. Richmond asked if I could orient the intern since that was one of my duties when I worked in that department."

, *Fuck.* I was counting on having her work with Aiden. *I can do this. I can do this. I can do this.*

Who the hell was I kidding? I couldn't do this. If I was having this much trouble on day one, how the hell was I supposed to handle this over the course of the next few months?

"That's fine, Raina. I can finish bringing Aiden up to speed. Did you have a chance to show him his office?"

"I was just about to when Mr. Richmond came down," she replied apologetically.

"No problem, Raina. If you'll walk him there on your way out, that would be great."

"Yes, ma'am. I'll see you first thing tomorrow."

I turned to Aiden, bracing myself. "Give me a minute to put my things down and I'll be right there."

"Sounds good," he said, as I walked into my office. I placed my phone in my desk, checked my voicemail, retrieved my laptop, and then headed to meet with Aiden for what was sure to be a torturous few hours.

Aiden was seated at his desk and looked up as I walked toward him. He looked good behind that desk; it fit him. The elitist air I'd noticed this morning when he entered the conference room was there again. I felt as though I were his subordinate, not the other way around. I took a seat in one of the two chairs near his desk and opened my laptop in search of Raina's orientation list. My plan was to review the items and get the hell out of there as quickly as possible.

As we talked, I primarily focused on my computer screen, giving him the occasional eye contact to create the façade of a normal business conversation; when in actuality, I felt nothing close to normal. He didn't have access to two of the servers so I needed to enter my passwords to open the files. I walked around his desk and leaned toward him to reach his keyboard.

I felt unusually self-conscious. "I had garlic for lunch; I hope I don't smell as though I did," I said, embarrassed.

"No. On the contrary, you smell wonderful."

No. *He* smelled wonderful — a strong, earthy, and seductive scent. I could breathe him in all day. I had to actually restrain myself from leaning in closer and inhaling.

The next several hours were a mix of tension, awareness, and restraint. I'd dated hot guys before, but this was on a completely different level. It was as though I was looking at a photoshopped picture on the cover of a magazine. It was terribly difficult to avoid staring. It took everything in me to maintain my professionalism when what I would have loved to do was jump his bones. This was the first time in an extremely long time that I had thought of reconsidering my *Fuck Rule*. Well, more like Fuck Rules—one of which was that I didn't date co-workers; least of all subordinates.

I showed him the files he would need to access on the servers in order to complete his projects. I explained that the passwords were changed every quarter for security purposes, so he would be given new passwords before he completed his internship. There were other files and instructions that he would need, but Raina would work with him tomorrow to assist with those minor details.

I was relieved when I noticed how quickly the hours were passing. Towards the end of the day, I received a call from Raina notifying me that she had arranged a meet-and-greet for Aiden with the television and print marketing divisions. Thankful for the reprieve, I jumped at the opportunity to show him some other parts of the building, killing time until the meet-and-greet.

We toured the editing and e-publishing departments. As I expected, everyone stared—even the men. Aiden was just that overwhelming. The ladies were either blushing or too nervous to make direct eye contact, and the men appeared slightly intimidated by him. I was delighted that he didn't seem the least bit affected by any of them. Then I scolded myself because it shouldn't matter one bit to me, right?

After the introductions, I excused myself and headed back to my office. I was free to resume my normal day to day routine without any further distractions, since Aiden would be leaving after his meetings. Around five o' clock, I sighed, relieved that I had survived the day—barely, but still—with my sanity and professionalism intact.

ꔮ   ꔮ   ꔮ   ꔮ

I was glad to finally be home, putting an end to the day and escaping Aiden's presence, although I couldn't escape my thoughts. My mind wandered…a lot. I thought back to the moment our eyes first connected, and how he looked so impossibly gorgeous as he stood in the doorway of the conference room. I remembered the way he studied me during our conversations, and the slow curl of one side of his mouth when he smiled, showing a glimpse of his perfect teeth. I thought of his deep green eyes, glimmering as though sparkling in the light of the morning sun. He possessed so many disarming attributes, even his scent. He had the sexiest smell imaginable. I could still smell him on my clothes after three hours leaning over his desk. I changed out of my work clothes, hoping it would help me stop thinking about him.

I donned my workout clothes and trotted downstairs to my home gym. It was a fair sized room that consisted of a treadmill, stationary bicycle, tread climber, Bow Flex, and some free weights. The building's gym included most of the same equipment, plus a couple of saunas and swimming pools, but I usually preferred to exercise in the privacy of my home.

After a thirty-minute run and thirty minutes on the bicycle, I grabbed a bottle of water and went back upstairs for a shower. As I dried off, the rumbling in my stomach reminded me that I hadn't eaten since lunch, so I made a sandwich and salad for dinner and watched some TV before calling it a night.

My mind was running to and fro, and I couldn't fall asleep. It was almost midnight and I was still awake. It was time for my insomnia cure-all. I opened the drawer of my nightstand and pulled out one of my favorite toys.

On nights like this, my imagination and battery operated boyfriend were all I needed to fall fast asleep—a play date for Virginia with one of the many friends who occupied my nightstand. The star of my fantasies this particular night was, no surprise, none other than Aiden Wyatt.

๑Chapter Three๑

The next morning I awoke refreshed and ready to tackle the day, resolved to keep a level head around Aiden. I was sure that last night's release would reduce his sex appeal. I'd convinced myself that yesterday's weakness could have been attributed to my sexual deprivation; after all, it had been a few months since I had sex. Six months to be precise, on a vacation to Belize with my best friend, April Jensen—which reminded me we needed to schedule another getaway soon.

I arrived at the office at exactly a quarter after seven, hoping to have a few moments to myself before Aiden's arrival. As I walked past Raina's desk, I noticed that her computer was off, which meant she had not yet arrived. Raina was consistent. Upon arriving to work, she went to her desk to flip on her computer, and place her purse in a locked drawer. She then walked into my office, said good morning, and offered my morning tea.

I'd beat her to the punch this morning. I wanted to get settled before the staff arrived, so I went for tea before diving into my work day. As I neared the kitchen, I heard voices coming from behind the door. I opened it to meet the gazes of six people seated at one of the tables; all eyes were on me as I approached, but the ones that I immediately connected with were the color of dark emeralds.

Fuck, he was already here. My steps faltered. I hadn't expected to see him for at least another forty minutes or so. I quickly recovered and glided past them with a civil "good morning." I busied myself with getting tea and found myself wondering why he'd arrived so early. Was he as obsessed with work as I? And if so, why was he sitting here shooting the breeze with the administrative staff? I didn't want to admit it, but the fact that they were sharing a cozy cup of coffee with the man who'd recently starred in my sexual fantasies bothered me.

Tossing my foolish annoyance aside, I eavesdropped on their conversation. Kiersten from marketing said how much she enjoyed meeting him yesterday, and that if he ever needed a lunch date, she was his girl. *Ugh!* Aiden thanked her for her offer just before Jennifer from the legal department said she'd be joining him and the head counsel when they met to discuss the legal facets of Aiden's marketing campaign. *Of course* she was looking forward to his take on things.

Gag me. I turned to leave before hearing any more. They were pathetic. "Hope you all have a great day," I said, as I moved past their table.

They chimed, "Thank you, Ms. Cason. You too," and I listened for Aiden's voice but he said nothing. I heard a metal-legged chair slide across the floor as I reached for the door.

"Ms. Cason, since we're headed in the same direction, I'll walk back with you, if that's okay," Aiden said. I smiled, and when I looked over my shoulder, once again all eyes were on me. *Who has his attention now?*

Ugh! Stop it Aria. This was beyond childish.

"No need to rush, Aiden. You have about thirty minutes before your day begins."

"Yes, but I'm anxious to get started. I trust that's all right?"

"Of course," I stated, turning to open the door.

"Allow me to get that for you." He brushed past me, and his seductively hypnotic scent penetrated the space around me. I nearly moaned aloud. Obviously last night's playtime with Virginia hadn't lessened this man's effect on me at all.

The remainder of the morning was damned near a carbon copy of yesterday. Regardless of the many times I told myself to stop, I somehow managed to fall into one sensuous daydream after another. I imagined Aiden's beautiful lips entangled with mine in a heated embrace while his hands slowly caressed my body, melding me into him. I pictured him fully naked, glorious like an Adonis standing before me, eager to ravage me. I thought of how his skin would feel next to mine. I was enjoying my naughty reverie when Raina's voice recalled my attention to the matter at hand. Both she and Aiden were staring at me. I was utterly embarrassed and attempted to fall back into the meeting.

Although I'd exhausted great effort to remain professional, Raina knew me well enough to know something was off.

Aiden's presence was just too much. I was appreciative that the majority of his time was spent with Raina. I had to assist her and Aiden with some minor details, but fortunately Raina was able to provide him with the particulars on other key components of RPH: the IT infrastructure, key vendors, and business associates with whom we often collaborated on particular campaigns. Since Raina was aware of my expectations for this project, they only had to check in with me occasionally for input.

By lunchtime, I was so consumed with inappropriate thoughts that I rushed out of the building without informing either of them. I needed a view that didn't include Aiden. I needed routine, so I escaped to a place that would offer that—the Grotto. I ordered my usual lunch entrée, and I sat at a booth near the window. I was so out of sorts that I ordered a drink. I'd given up on this workday. My only concern at the moment was calming my nerves. Or maybe it was the hormones that needed some level of calm. Whichever it was, one drink quickly became two. I emailed Raina, indicating that I had an out-of-office meeting I'd forgotten about, and that I would see her tomorrow morning. Tomorrow would be a better day. It had to be.

The next day actually *was* better, as were the next several days. It appeared I had worried for nothing. I rarely saw Aiden; he was in meeting after meeting, learning the ropes. He spent a great deal of time with Josh, who was serving as his division mentor. Aiden was so busy that he barely had time to greet me in the halls. The way his gaze combed over my body when we passed each other was difficult to ignore, but it was tolerable. If we were able to keep that up, I would make it through the next few months. The trick was to avoid him, and so far that was working.

Late Friday, I was preparing to leave for the day, flipping off the lights in my office before I walked to the elevators. The doors opened to a crowd of lively employees ready to start the weekend. We stopped at the twentieth floor, and I was surprised to see Aiden and Jennifer step in to join our decent. He smiled and said hello. I returned the pleasantry as I slid to the left, giving him ample room. This was the closest I'd been to him since Tuesday, and it was too damned close. When the doors opened, I stepped out and walked briskly to my car.

I spent the majority of the weekend working, so when Monday rolled around it was as though I hadn't really had a weekend at all. I arrived at my office, and Raina reminded me of a department meeting at nine o'clock. I was anxious at the thought of being in a room with Aiden, but his closeness shouldn't pose much of a problem since there would be several other employees in attendance.

The meeting was very interesting and quite productive. It would appear that Aiden had soaked in every detail of our division, and several others, last week. He was commenting and arguing points that required an abundance of RPH information. I was impressed but curious as to his newfound knowledge, which seemed broader than an intern's usual scope. Thanks to Aiden's contributions, the session ended with a full list of action items for our next meeting, and before I realized it, everyone except Aiden had left the room.

"Ms. Cason, I would like to schedule some time with you to review the last quarter's numbers in e-book sales."

"Is this something we can add to next week's agenda?" I asked, hoping to avoid any one-on-one time with him.

"Possibly, but we'd accomplish more without the excess."

"Okay, sure. Can you check with Raina and see when I have an opening?"

"Will do," he replied.

"Is there something else?" I asked, when he didn't leave.

"Do you have lunch plans?" he asked.

Why would he ask that? "I'm having a working lunch," I replied.

"You're quite the busy bee, aren't you?" he asked.

"Well, it's the only way to make the honey," I said.

"I'd have to disagree. It's not the only way," he replied, a ghost of a smile on his beautiful lips.

Was he starting this again? I could only maintain my resolve with minimal contact and zero innuendos. If either one of those moved too far out of balance, I was screwed.

"You're quite the worker bee yourself. I was very impressed with your input during the meeting."

"Thank you. I do what I can," he replied.

I'm sure you do. The intensity of his gaze was unbearable. I needed to get him away from me.

"Well, I have a very full day, so if you can check with Raina on your way out, that would be great," I said.

"Maybe you and I can schedule a working lunch soon. I'm interested to see you outside the walls of this building," he said.

"Well, that's not going to happen," I quickly replied.

"Oh, why is that?" he asked.

"I don't typically have lunch with my—"

"Your what? Subordinates?"

"No. I was about to say coworkers," I replied.

"Because...?" he asked.

Because none of your business Mr. Fuck Me! "Just one of my rules."

"Rules are made to be broken," he challenged.

"Not my rules." If I didn't end this conversation, who knew where it would lead. I wasn't about to find out. "As interesting as this topic is, I really need to get busy."

"Of course, Ms. Cason."

I exhaled, watching him walk out of the room. I still wanted him, and if I was reading the signs correctly—and I was confident that I was—he wanted me, too.

There. I finally admitted it. I wanted him; I wanted him to fuck the hell out of me. But regardless of my desire for him, I absolutely refused to succumb to anything more than a professional relationship with that man.

I made it through the rest of the week with little to no direct contact with Aiden. The next day would mark two weeks since Aiden entered the doors of RPH. Yes, I was counting down the weeks until he left. It was the only thought that gave me solace with this situation.

I left shortly after lunch for a dental appointment and headed home afterwards. I grabbed my phone as I walked through the door.

"Raina, there's been a change in my schedule, I won't be returning to the office."

"Legal sent up some documents that require your signature, and they were supposed to go out in the mail this afternoon. And the Spectrum mock-ups need your approval before the presentation tomorrow."

"Can either of those wait?"

Her voice was apologetic. "Not really. They need to go out first thing tomorrow morning. I can have them messengered to you this evening."

"That works. Thanks, Raina."

I grabbed a bottle of wine and sunk into the couch to watch television. Two glasses of wine later, I was fast asleep.

The sound of my phone ringing awakened me. I looked at the time. It was five o'clock and the phone ID showed the call was from RPH.

"Hello," I answered, getting up and walking to the kitchen for some water to help me wake up.

"Hello, Ms. Cason."

I stopped dead in my tracks at hearing the very sexy voice I'd been trying to avoid. "Is there a problem, Aiden?"

"Only if you say no."

"Excuse me?" I asked, confused.

"I would like to take you to dinner."

"Er…I don't think so, but thank you for asking," I replied, ill-prepared for his invitation. I grabbed a bottle of water from the fridge.

"Why?" he asked.

I took a seat at the counter. "The same reason I declined the invitation for lunch. And not that I owe you any further explanation but I'd prefer to stay home and have something delivered. It's been a long day," I replied.

"Have you ordered?" he asked.

"No." I glanced at the drawer that held menus from various local restaurants.

"What will you order?"

"Hmm…the house special," I answered automatically, not sure why I was giving him more information than I intended.

"From?"

"The Brewer's Art. Why?" I opened the bottle of water and looked at the cap, spinning it over and over between my fingers.

"It's on North Charles Street, right?" he asked.

"Yep, that's the place."

"I have a suggestion," he said.

"Okay," I replied, knowing full well where this was leading.

"You have to eat, and so do I. Let me pick up the food, and we can eat together at your place. You're already home and hopefully done with work for the day. Get comfortable, and by the time you've detoxed from work, I'll be at your door."

"I don't know," I said, my voice still throaty from my nap. I took a long swig of water as he went on.

"What's not to know? Besides, I have to stop by either way to drop off the papers and marketing props."

"And why is it that you have to do that?" I asked.

"Raina was in the process of calling a messenger and I volunteered to deliver them. She thought it was a good idea due to the time limits," he said.

"Oh, she did, did she?"

"Yes. So let me do this. I want to do something nice for you. You've been so welcoming, and I want to return the gesture."

I paused, considering his offer as I moved my hand over my stomach, hoping to suppress the growling.

"Let me feed you." The words smoothly flowed from his mouth.

And that's where I lost my grip on logic. The way those four words practically dripped from his lips sent a signal straight to my lady parts.

"Okay," I agreed before I could stop myself.

I could practically hear the slow, sexy smile forming on his lips. "Great. I'll be at your place in no time."

"I live in Silo Point. Do you know where that is?" I asked.

"Just another quick GPS entry and I'll see you shortly," he replied.

"Okay," I whispered.

A bizarre feeling surged through me as I ended the call and placed the phone on the counter. I felt wired and nervous, like a schoolgirl who had just spoken to her first crush. I was suddenly parched. I downed the bottle of water before hopping into the shower—a very *cold* shower.

An hour later the intercom buzzed, alerting me to Aiden's arrival. A sense of foreboding pulled me from the sofa, warning me of all of the ways the evening could go wrong. As I walked to the door, I took a deep breath and told myself that this was merely two coworkers having dinner, nothing more. I reached for the knob to open the door and there he stood, bags in hand, looking like the hottest delivery guy in the world.

"Hi," I said, taking him in. Every time I looked at him felt like the first time, and it was always overwhelming. He was still wearing his work attire: a shirt and tie, but the tie was loosened and he had unbuttoned the top three buttons of his shirt.

"Hi. Isn't this better than some random stranger showing up at your door?" he asked, assessing my appearance.

Uh, hell no.

"I even picked up a bottle of wine," he said.

"Oh, how kind of you."

"I do what I can, Ms. Cason."

Yeah, don't you though? "Why don't you come in?" I asked.

"I suppose I should, being that you are a woman in need."

I stepped to the side, allowing him to enter, and directed him to the kitchen. His sexy smell was still there, leaving a trail that flooded my senses. I gazed appreciatively at him as I followed his lead. *What the hell was Raina doing to me?* This was the one safe place I'd counted on. Yet here he was, in my home. This was bad.

"In need?" I asked.

"Well, aren't you?" he asked, staring playfully at me. I didn't know how to respond. He must have sensed that I wasn't going to reply, because he laughed. "In need of food, Ms. Cason. What else could you possibly be in need of?"

Bastard. Him and his damn wordplays and double meanings. He did this every time an opportunity presented itself. Two can play that game.

"You're absolutely right, Aiden. I am in need of food, which seems to be something you're pretty efficient at delivering. Perhaps you missed your true calling."

He chuckled at my comeback. "Where are your plates?" he asked.

"You can actually have a seat," I said, motioning toward the table.

"As can you. I much prefer to be the one serving."

"I'm sure." The words escaped my lips before I realized. "I meant—"

"No need to explain. I'm pretty sure we both know what you

meant," he murmured.

I directed him to the cabinet with the plates and the wineglasses and watched him as he moved around in my kitchen. He opened the bags, removed the containers, and placed them on the counter.

"Silverware?" he asked, looking up at me. I pointed to the drawer below the cabinets.

"Why don't you have a seat? It's not as if you're doing much beyond staring, anyway," he said.

I couldn't help but laugh. Grabbing the bottle of wine and wineglasses, I walked toward the dining table. I placed the glasses on the table and took a seat. He was behind me within seconds, placing a plate in front of me.

"Why?" he asked, as he sat.

"Why what?" I asked.

"Why were you staring?"

"I wasn't."

He smiled, knowing I was lying. "Oh, my mistake. I was preparing myself for a compliment, but apparently you don't toss those out too often," he said.

"Just eat," I replied.

"We need music. I noticed the speakers; where is your control center?" he asked.

"On the wall near the bar," I answered.

He stood and walked to the bar and pulled out his phone. "So you aren't married, but you never did say if there was a significant other in the picture. Is there?" he asked as he fidgeted with the controls.

"I never said I wasn't married."

"You aren't," he said matter-of-factly. "Is there a boyfriend?"

"I'm not going to answer that."

"So no, then." He smirked as he docked his phone. "That would explain why you're so uptight."

"Excuse me?" I asked, startled by his directness.

"Just an observation. I apologize if I offended you."

As if he gave a damn about offending me. He'd been offending me since our first day working together. And stupidly enough, I'd let him. I'd never allowed anyone else to get away with stepping out of line, *ever*. So what the fuck? Maybe it was because he was so fucking hot. That face, that body, and the way he spoke—it was sensory overload! Each time I looked at him all I could think of was sex.

To add to the forbidden allure, his choice of songs was the icing on the cake. I was being seduced by the soft sounds of Ed Sheeran's *Kiss Me*.

I glared at him, and his overconfident smirk pissed me off. I realized that the problem wasn't his hotness. It was the fact that I couldn't seem to maintain my footing with him. Everything I said, he somehow twisted it.

"I don't think I've ever come across anyone as audacious as you in my life," I said. "Especially considering our working relationship."

"And there it is — the fact that you're technically my boss and I'm the lowly intern. I was wondering when you'd bring that up. Ms. Cason, those are just titles. They are of no significance to this conversation." He returned to the dinner table, opened the wine, and poured a glass for each of us.

Was he the guest here or was I? "Do you always just assume control of things?" I asked.

"When I see the need, yes."

"So you saw the need in this case?"

"When it comes to you, I see a need for much more than dinner plates and music," he said.

I avoided his gaze and picked up the glass of wine to take a sip. "And that would be?" I asked.

"I think we both know what you need."

The boldness of his words sent a shiver through me. Images of his cock stroking deep inside me flashed through my mind. I squeezed my thighs together so tight that they hurt.

"Oh really? And what about you? What do you need?" I asked, holding his gaze.

His eyes darkened, and his voice lowered. "Why? Are you

volunteering?"

Holy shit! I swallowed the lump in my throat and stared into his eyes, mesmerized as the color shifted. His presence alone was overkill, but when he said things like that, it was enough to make me unravel, and Virginia was pulsing so hard I think she came a little.

He smiled, fully aware of the effect of his words.

I took a deep breath. "I didn't see the papers that Raina sent," I said, after taking another sip of wine.

Grinning at my not-so-subtle redirect, he replied, "They're in the messenger bag on the counter."

"Thank you for bringing those over, by the way. I'm sure you know you didn't need to do that."

"It wasn't entirely selfless, actually," he said.

I looked at him, questioning his statement.

"I wanted to see you," he said, gauging my reaction.

"You refuse to stop, don't you?" I asked.

"I have no intention of stopping," he replied.

"Well, you're wasting your time," I said.

"Am I?" He looked at me with so much arrogance that it practically oozed from his pores. "Eat before your food gets cold," he said.

I reached for my wine and took a gulp. He explained some of the issues he saw with the mock-ups that Raina sent over, not that

I heard much of what he was saying. My attention was diverted by the seduction of his deep voice. It was alluring and sensual, like diamonds dipped in chocolate. I looked at his lips as he spoke; they were that sexy pinkish color that made you want to suck on them. As for his eyes, I could have stared into those sparkling emeralds forever.

He was right; I was in need. I needed to be fucked — rough and deep. So rough that I could feel it for days.

He became quiet and looked at me as if awaiting a response. *What the hell? Had he asked me something?*

"I appreciate your feedback. I'll consider that when I review them," I said, hoping my reply made sense.

We finished the meal in silence. He cleared the table, thanked me for having dinner, and he left. There were no further innuendos, not even a hint of his cocky self-assuredness. I wasn't prepared for that.

Closing the door behind him, I rushed to my bedroom, and opened my favorite drawer, frantically searching for my double bullet dildo. Tonight I definitely needed the forceful vibrations of its dual bullets. I tugged my pants and panties off and hopped into bed, moaning as I plunged the huge dildo inside my aching cunt. I didn't tease myself as I normally would to prolong the time with my B.O.B. Instead, I started ferociously pumping it inside me as thoughts of Aiden flashed behind my closed lids, the way he looked at me and the words *we both know what you need* spinning in my head.

Oh fuck! How could a piece of silicone feel so fucking good? I gyrated on the dildo with the vicious need to come. It didn't take long before I felt the tightening of my core and a deep orgasm flowing through me, the spasms so hard that I cried out. I slowed the thrusts, but continued sliding the jelly material in and out of me as I relished the remaining pulses of my sex. That was the best faux fuck I'd ever experienced.

My senses slowly returned as I lay there, partially sated. I wondered what Aiden would think if he knew the effect he had on me. I had very little doubt that every scorching glance, every suggestive word, every indecent gesture was calculated to yield the result he wanted. He was taunting me. He dangled the salacious bait with every opportunity, and like a starved animal, I bit, fully aware of the risks.

My breathing slowed and I went to the bathroom to wipe myself and was astounded at just how much wiping I had to do.

I walked to the kitchen to retrieve the messenger bag and a glass of wine. After reviewing the material and notating some changes, which I emailed to Raina, I started another bottle of wine. I was restless, and I didn't want to think of Aiden or why he left so abruptly, but that was precisely where my thoughts wandered. Did it sink in when I told him that he was wasting his time? I should have been relieved he left the way he did, but I wasn't.

Wandering, back to the kitchen, I loaded the dishwasher. I later watched a couple of episodes of *The Mindy Project* between texting April about our upcoming vacation plans.

Sounds good. I'm so excited!

Me too. I miss you so much, April. This is long overdue.

Miss you more!!! You have no idea! Work is kicking my butt, too. So, yeah the timing is perfect!!!

More problems with your boss?

Yeah, she's being a royal biatch. Oops gotta go, my new guy is calling. I'll text you tomorrow. Love ya.

Love you too, April… and what new guy?

She didn't reply. I couldn't recall her mentioning she'd met someone new. Not that it mattered very much, because she wouldn't keep him around long. She tended to start out with a bang, but her interest quickly fizzled and somehow it was always the guy's fault. I let out a sigh. I hope this one didn't let her down too badly.

I finally decided to call it a night and climbed into bed. My head was spinning from all of my ponderings about Aiden — and from all of the wine. The last vision before I dozed off was of Aiden's face, his emerald gaze penetrating mine.

I awoke the next morning with a horrible headache and an upset stomach. I didn't think I'd consumed enough to suffer a hangover. The motion of my stomach told me otherwise. I rushed for the toilet to divest my stomach of the unwanted substance, then I sank to the floor near the bathtub, contemplating my present state.

Well, I wasn't going to work today; I felt like crap. After coaxing myself from the floor, I grabbed my phone to email Raina, informing her of my intent to work from home, and that I would have the papers messengered to the office. I felt another urge to throw up so I hurried back to the bathroom.

Missing work because I was having difficulty controlling my libido…that was so not me! I'd always prided myself on being the consummate professional, never mixing business and pleasure. I'd always upheld my policy to avoid socializing with coworkers outside of work functions. I often got invitations to lunch or to a girls-night-out, which I politely and consistently declined. It had gotten to the point that no one bothered to ask me anymore because they knew the answer would be no. That's who I was, the loner, the person who kept business and personal *very* separate. Yet, here I was on the floor of my bathroom, hungover and ashamed that in a mere two weeks I'd started to wreck the image that I'd worked years to build.

I'd completed my education at Boston State University and started working at Raine Publishing House as a Publicity Assistant right after graduation. A few years and a few promotions later, I was the President of Communications. I loved my job and I loved to work. Although considered successful in the publishing industry, I always strived for more and had a tendency to place work before everything else — but you wouldn't know that judging by the last two weeks.

April constantly berated me for not having a personal life. My reasons for not having one were valid enough that I didn't pay attention to her rants. I admitted that my life was a bit dysfunctional, but whose wasn't? It was structured in just the way that fit *me*.

The need to maintain control in my life was as necessary as breathing for me. I didn't want to rely on anyone for anything, because the disappointment that could accompany that reliance could be disastrous. That's why I'd decided long ago that no one would be in charge of my happiness, love, money, or even my orgasms.

I was actually quite happy. I had the love of a best friend who was more like a sister and I had a high-level position with a very generous salary. I didn't want for anything except maybe a stiff dick every now and then. But that tended to come with complications, which I chose to avoid.

It was very rare that I came across the right caliber of man, and even then I kept him at arm's length, which meant that most of my pleasure was self-induced. It was my preference and for the most part, it got the job done. I had a plethora of toys, books, and naughty video links that helped maintain my sanity. I'd actually learned quite a few tricks from a book series that I'd read a few months ago, which had opened my mind to several things, some of which I hadn't had the opportunity to experience, but to which I was certainly game.

Perhaps one day I would finally admit that I should be in counseling and commit to a more normal path...whatever that was. For now, I knew that the type of personal life April wanted for me could lead to the type of heartbreak some people don't come back from. I was the result of that kind of relationship. My mother had a *personal* life once, which fucking annihilated the lively person I had once known and loved.

Not that I didn't still love Mom, but after Dad left something inside her wilted and died. My spirited and loving mother vanished. She tried and failed miserably to maintain a sense of stability in the lives of her children. It was horribly painful to watch. In the end, I left Dayton, Ohio, as soon as I had the chance, and never looked back.

I graduated from high school and received a full academic scholarship to Boston State University. Initially I visited home for the holidays, if I managed to save enough money from my part-time job to cover the airfare. Eventually, I began saying I didn't have the money to visit, which was logical given my college student budget. To this day I still made excuses to stay away, although I knew it hurt Mom that I didn't return home. Maybe one day I would. Maybe. Going back to Dayton seemed impossible to me. The mere thought of home slapped me with every memory I was desperate to forget.

The stroll down memory lane stirred up emotions from which I'd extricated myself years ago. I didn't want to think about any of this. I needed to redirect my attention to me, something that typically required little to no effort. I was unable to do that today. It was because of him. Why did my determination seem to dissolve in the presence of Aiden Wyatt? It wasn't as though he was attempting to do anything more than get me into bed — no love and trust complications involved. So why the internal struggle with this? What puzzled and frightened me was how much this situation with him somehow felt out of my control.

Men had been useful for one and only one purpose in my life thus far — to fill in from time to time when B.O.B. couldn't quite get the job done. Some may have considered it harsh, but I considered it necessary. I simply chose to use them before they had the chance to use me. Although I'd encountered a few stumbling blocks, the ends more than justified the means. Was I at fault if one of them fell for me? Especially when I'd made it crystal clear that all I wanted was sheet-ripping sex? What man wouldn't love sex with a beautiful woman who wanted nothing in return other than orgasm after orgasm?

If I encountered complications, as with a guy I'd met a couple of years ago, I handled it. He wanted more than sex; he wanted *me*. When I noticed a change in the relationship, I mentioned it and he denied it. He claimed that I misread his comments. Eventually he began with gestures that were impossible to misread. I severed that relationship immediately with no intention of giving him a second chance.

There was another instance with a guy where I was basically stalked. He somehow learned where I worked, had flowers delivered—even dropped by RPH. Not wanting to bring any attention to my private life, I consulted security, and the next time he attempted to visit, he was quickly apprehended and removed from the building. After that, I decided my only fun times would happen far from the city limits of Boston, which was why I had such an immense need to make plans with April for our next girls' excursion. It was a matter of my sanity and Virginia's well-being!

The next weeks at work were all business when it came to interacting with Aiden. I made sure of it. I wouldn't allow myself to be pulled into any more of his overtures. I scheduled our meetings such that Raina or other staff members were present, thereby lessening Mr. Fuck Me's amorous pull. On the rare occasion he and I were alone, Aiden would slip in a sexual innuendo, which I redirected into a business discussion. Surely he would grow bored of this game once he realized it wasn't getting him anywhere.

Well…anywhere but my fantasies. He was the inspiration for several of my B.O.B related orgasms on an almost nightly basis. I had recently invested in a Blue Dolphin, which was waterproof and even warmed up. It ensured that bath time was the best part of my day.

We'd successfully launched two campaigns, and there was an upcoming company party in celebration of that feat—a casino cruise that would also serve as a fundraiser for the writing scholarships at Boston State University. As with all company parties, my position required that I at least make an appearance, say a few polite hellos, and give my speech. I always left shortly thereafter, but I wouldn't be as fortunate this time, however, because we were scheduled for a four-hour cruise.

In honor of the campaign's success, we decided to afford the staff a four-day weekend with the party on Wednesday and the offices closed on Thursday and Friday. I was heading to St. Barts with April on the last flight out Wednesday night. I was so anxious to get away that I was about to pull my hair from the roots. I needed a pair of strong hands on my bare skin. Working with Aiden had made it nearly impossible to think of anything else. I was counting the days I'd have to endure this torture. Only eight weeks and then I could move on from this daily denial of a man whom I wanted so badly that I could taste him.

Wednesday before the party, Aiden, Raina, and I met to discuss the preliminary details for Aiden's third and final campaign. I sent a silent thank-you to Raina for being present. My silent thank-yous to her had become a mantra of late. I honestly didn't think I was capable of abstaining if left alone with him. When we finished our meeting, Aiden and Raina left the conference room, and I stayed behind and jotted some notes on my tablet.

Walking back to my office, I saw Aiden at Raina's desk. Raina looked up as I approached them. "Ms. Cason, I've confirmed your itinerary for St. Barts this weekend. Shall I email the details or would you prefer a hard copy?"

Raina, lifesaver that she was, had completed my travel plans. With preparations for Aiden's follow-up campaign and other project deadlines, I had been using every extra minute in my schedule to mark items off my work checklist.

"If you'll send both to me Raina, that would be great. Thanks."

I looked at Aiden and noted his probing glare, but I quickly turned away. *Yes, Mr. Fuck Me, I'm getting the hell out of Boston. I'll be far away from you and I'll finally get fucked.*

After lunch, I left Aiden in Raina's capable hands, freeing the remainder of my day for meetings with Blake, RPH's CEO, to discuss the direction of our e-publishing division. It was growing at an unexpected rate, and we were considering delegating some of the departmental goals to my section

My final meeting was with Adam, the director of finance. He was on the same page as Blake with the e-marketing development, as it would afford the company a wider revenue stream. After reviewing my department's budget, we were done for the day.

It wasn't quite five o'clock, but I needed to get home to finish packing. I entered my office unnoticed, grabbed my purse and computer bag, and made a dash to the elevator. I was relieved that I was out the door without an Aiden encounter. One more company function and I was off to St. Barts. I let out a sigh of relief as the elevator doors opened but quickly inhaled as I came face to face with the man I was hoping to avoid.

❧Chapter Four❧

I couldn't move. His eyes traveled slowly down my body and back up again. "Going down?" he asked.

Going down? On this gorgeous man? Just the thought of him in my mouth made it water. And of course Virginia was always ready to play when it came to Mr. Fuck Me.

When I didn't reply, he asked again. "Ms. Cason, care to share the elevator with me?"

Duh…so he wasn't being inappropriate. *Or was he?* With him, it was hard to tell.

"Yes." I stepped in, yet he didn't move. He was too close. His scent was too potent. My breathing accelerated. *Damn.* Was he going to move?

"Do you mind?" I asked.

He smiled that panty-dropping half smile and moved marginally as the elevator doors closed. I turned to face the doors and stepped as far to the side as possible. There was so much sexual tension in the small compartment that I could smell it. Why, oh why, had I stepped into this elevator? I should have made an excuse to rush back to my office.

"I'm actually glad we have a moment alone," he stated.

I swallowed and turned, slowly meeting his gaze. The

luminous green of his eyes captured and held mine.

"And why is that?" I asked, hoping he didn't notice my nervousness.

"You've been very remote with me of late, and I would like to know why."

"Uh…I don't know what you mean," I replied, shifting uncomfortably. I definitely should have pretended that I'd forgotten something.

"Are you sure about that?" he asked, stepping closer to me.

"Yes," I replied defensively, making an involuntary step backwards only to realize my back was to the wall.

"Hmm."

That was all he said. What was he doing?

Finally he said, "I can't help but think that your distance is due to what I said a few weeks ago over dinner."

"I have no idea what you mean."

"Sure you do. Either I really did offend you, or I was correct in my assessment. I'm leaning more towards the latter."

I gaped at him, incredulous at his boldness. "Your opinion of me means next to nothing."

"Are you saying I'm wrong? Because I'd be more than happy to provide you the means to take the edge off."

I instinctively reached up to slap him but he quickly grabbed my hand.

"You need to unwind," he said, releasing my hand and stroking my cheek with his fingertip, leaving a path of fire in its wake.

I looked up and saw that the elevator was still on the twenty-fifth floor. He followed my glance and turned back to face me.

"May I ask you something?" he asked.

"I'd rather you not, but I'm sure you will anyway, so what is it?" I replied, preparing for his next unseemly inquiry.

"Would it be inappropriate if I were to tell you that I find you incredibly attractive?" he asked.

He stepped closer, so much so that I was only breathing his minty breath and that amazing cologne that had to have been made just for him. I literally felt weak in the knees. My eyes zeroed in on his lips. I wondered how it would feel to kiss him.

"Aiden, I'm not sure what your end game is here, but yes, I think this conversation is very inappropriate, and I want you to stop. Now."

"I wasn't aware that coworkers were frowned upon for simply paying each other compliments," he countered, a hint of a smile around his lips.

"There's nothing simple about anything you're doing, now or any time up to this point. You know damned well that I'm referring to something much more discouraged amongst coworkers than compliments," I retorted.

"Are you seriously unaware of the way you look at me when we're in a room together? Or the body language? Or the sexual tension when we're near each other, such as now? Is that something that should be discouraged, also? If so, how would you recommend we do that?"

I stared at him, dumbfounded.

"Exactly. You have no suggestions, nor do I. I look at you and my mind goes crazy. I want to touch you, to relish the feel of your skin beneath my fingertips. I want to taste you and I want to explore you. I've thought of little else since meeting you, and you'd be lying if you said you hadn't thought the same."

I wanted to say something to reject his truth, but quite frankly I was so fucking hot for him at that moment, I couldn't. My chest began to rise and fall rapidly as the excitement of the situation pulled me savagely to him. Virginia was immediately filled with an intense throbbing and longing that she needed satisfied.

He stepped toward me, and then his body was on mine, my back pressed solidly against the wall. I couldn't move; I didn't want to. He lowered his mouth to mine and I inhaled, absorbing the fullness of his unique scent. He slowly parted my lips with his, and softly tugged my bottom lip. I moaned into his mouth as his tongue slipped between my lips. He placed his hands on either side of my face, pulling me deeper into his mouth. I surrendered my lips to him—my tongue was his as he pulled and sucked on the tip. He sealed his mouth over mine, starting a skilled, sensuous exploration. I was so lost in him. My purse and bag hit the floor as I grabbed the back of his head, pulling him closer still. Our teeth clashed as our kiss morphed into uncontrollable lust.

His hands moved slowly down my neck to my shoulders. He palmed my breasts, a low growl moving through his chest as he groped them fully, pinching my nipples and sending a sensation to Virginia that she had long been missing. He began unbuttoning my shirt as he planted wet kisses along my neck, nipping the skin at the hollow. Freeing my breast, he lowered his head to my nipple, licking before taking it into his mouth and then gently suckling. I had totally lost my bearings until I heard the ping of the elevator. Aiden immediately severed contact with my breast. I frantically reached for my buttons in a futile effort to reassemble my clothing. He pushed my trembling hands away and buttoned my shirt.

"Your lipstick is smeared. Use this." He pulled a handkerchief from his jacket pocket. Did men still carry those? I grabbed the handkerchief and started to wipe my lips as the elevator began to move.

I was a nervous mess, which he noticed when I couldn't even manage to wipe my fucking mouth. He took the handkerchief from me and fixed my lipstick. His eyes lingered on mine and then returned to my lips as he placed the handkerchief in his jacket and bent to retrieve my purse and bag. I took them from him and looked at the needle on the elevator as we approached the twenty-second floor. The elevator doors opened and three men stepped in.

I recognized one of them, from the legal department. He smiled at me and I smiled in return. My heart was pounding so rapidly I would have sworn he could hear it. He pressed the button for the parking garage and exchanged pleasantries with Aiden. I looked at Aiden, but he seemed unaffected. You would think the last several minutes hadn't occurred. I shifted a few steps toward the door and to the left in an attempt to move away from him, but he shifted almost as quickly as I did, moving with me. I slowly shook my head signaling that he shouldn't do that, but he showed no signs of acknowledging my silent plea.

The elevator stopped at the next floor and four people joined our descent, headed for the eighteenth floor. The others shifted back, allowing them room. Aiden in turn moved behind me. Although we weren't touching, I could feel him. Suddenly, his hand was at my waist, pulling me back toward him, unnoticed by the others. I attempted to free myself, but his grasp was unrelenting. I tried once more, and his fingers dug into my waist, causing my sharp intake of breath. The others were chatting amongst themselves, unaware of this little tug of war.

Leaning toward my ear, Aiden whispered, "My dick is so

fucking hard for you." Virginia twitched at his shameless revelation as he pushed his erection toward me. He released my waist and grabbed my hand, pulling it behind me. I tried tugging it away to no avail. He moved my hand until it was on his hardness. I didn't know what shocked me more—his girth or the fact that he had pulled his cock out in an elevator full of people. I made an attempt to jerk my hand away but he would not release me.

He leaned down towards me again, his breath warm and sultry in my ear. "Feel what you do to me. What you always do to me." I knew I shouldn't have, but I couldn't help myself; I allowed my fingers to rest around his dick. My eyes widened and Virginia was jumping with wet excitement at the discovery of how huge and how fucking hard he was; I didn't think I'd ever felt a man as hard before.

His hand covering mine, he guided my fingers back and forth along his manhood, a low moan escaping him. I closed my eyes, imagining this massive hardness inside my wet and wanting cunt. I wanted him to fuck me! I wanted it with everything in me. *Fuck! I needed to get out of this damned elevator.* He directed my hand toward the head of his cock, where my fingers encountered light moisture.

My hand froze as the elevator door opened at the tenth floor. Three ladies entered the confined space as one of the men from the eighteenth floor exited. The doors closed as my fingers moved along the head of his dick. What was I doing, and why did I not want to stop?

His lips at my ear, he whispered, "Taste me. Place your fingers in your mouth." He released my hand and as if spellbound, I did as he told me, slowly moving my hand up to my lips and slipping the tips of two fingers inside my mouth. *Mmm*...I loved the taste of pre-come, and he tasted especially good—like sweet fruit—and I wanted more. I wanted his cock in my mouth. I wanted to greedily lick and suck him. I wanted to feel the hot, thick fluid slide down my throat, and milk him until he had no more to give.

He pulled me closer, his cock poking my back. I tensed, wondering what was next. "Relax. You're so rigid. I can help you with that, you know." He nipped my earlobe and slipped his tongue in my ear, driving me insane; my body was starting to feel limp. I was oblivious to my surroundings until the elevator doors opened, alerting us to our arrival on the fifth floor. Two additional people entered. As the doors closed, I jerked away from his touch and collected myself as well as I could in preparation to exit the elevator. My body had betrayed me so much in the past few minutes that if my legs moved upon command, it would be a welcome surprise.

The doors opened to the first floor. As everyone began

moving out of the elevator, I summoned every ounce of composure I had and rushed out without looking back. I was damned near running. I didn't know if Aiden was following me, and I didn't care. If I could just make it to my car, I would be free of the insane effect that man had on me. I hurried past the security desk to the turnstile and was outside. My phone was ringing but there was no fucking way I would stop to answer it. Damn, I was supposed to get off on the ground floor to access the garage and get to my car. Was this what I had to look forward to over the next few weeks? Poor self-control, poor decision making, and wet panties?

I started walking. I wouldn't chance going back into the building. I would take a cab home, wait until I was certain Aiden had left the building, and return later for my car. I spotted a lady exiting a cab a few feet in front of me, and I started to walk faster in hopes of grabbing it before someone else. "Miss, can you hold that cab for me?" I shouted. She nodded and said something to the cab driver. "Thank you," I said once I reached her.

"No problem," she replied.

I jumped into the cab, announced my destination, and we were off.

I glanced over my shoulder as we drove into traffic, and saw Aiden in an embrace with who appeared to be the lady who'd held my cab.

❧Chapter Five❧

Settling in the cab, I exhaled what seemed like two months' worth of emotions. I was a wet, horny, trembling mess. What just happened? What did I just do? Who was the cab lady, and why was Aiden hugging her? Why did I care? Did anyone notice what we were doing in the elevator? Fuck, I could lose my job over five minutes of lust-filled insanity!

My phone rang again, and I looked down and saw that it was Adam, RPH's finance director. What could he want? I briefly considered sending him to voicemail but thought better of it on the off chance that his phone call was related to what had just occurred in the elevator. I'd much rather know now than to be caught off guard, face-to-face, at work. I slid my finger across the screen to answer.

"This is Aria."

"Aria!" He sounded winded and anxious.

Adam was renowned for his calm demeanor; to hear him sound anything but composed was cause enough for alarm. This call clearly signified that he knew.

"Yes?" I replied hesitantly.

"Aria, I apologize for contacting you at the last minute, but I had several unexpected interruptions today, and I fell behind schedule," he explained.

Turned out he'd called because he needed my e-publishing marketing information for a presentation later that night. I breathed a sigh of relief as I ended the call. My respite was short-lived as I considered the location of the marketing information— my work computer.

My remote connection from home wasn't working, which meant I would need to return to RPH. I figured I should be safe from a run in with Aiden, since he had left the building behind me. Besides, I didn't have another option. I had to get those files to Adam. It would only be a quick dash back to my office. This would give me the chance to retrieve my car before rushing home to get dressed.

I asked the cabby to turn around, hoping upon hope that I was correct about Aiden not being there. My heart was still racing when the cab stopped in front of RPH. I paid the cabby, and as I emerged from the cab, I quickly scanned the passersby, praying that I wouldn't spot Aiden. I entered the building and scurried past security to the elevators. It seemed I hadn't been the only one in a rush to start the evening's activities, because the elevator made no stops, getting me swiftly to the twenty-fifth floor.

Stepping out of the elevator, I noticed Raina was gone, her computer powered down and her desk lamp off. I walked past her desk and opened my office door. I crossed the room and sat at my desk, powered on my computer and located the file that Adam needed. As I composed the email, I called him to let him know that he should receive it within the next few seconds. He apologized for the inconvenience and said he would see me later in the evening. I closed the file and shut down my computer. Rising from my chair, I looked up to see Aiden leaning casually against the door.

"Well hello, Ms. Cason."

What the fuck is he doing here? "Uh, hello." I cleared my throat, sitting back down. "I thought you'd left for the day."

"Something unexpected turned up, and I had to return to my office. I was actually headed back out when I noticed your door was open. Fortunate for me," he said as he walked in, closing the door behind him.

Damn. I should have closed it.

As if reading my mind, he continued. "Had your door been closed, I would have missed the pleasure of seeing your gorgeous face before tonight."

"Fortunate for you? Why is that?" I asked, my heart rate accelerating as he stalked closer.

"Oh, I don't know. A number of reasons, several of which occurred in the elevator."

"Yes, about that..."

He interrupted me. "Yes, about that. It was nice, much more

than nice actually, especially the feel of your hand around my cock," he replied, his gaze smoldering.

That was all it took, and Virginia was throbbing. *What a weak whore of a cunt!*

He took a few steps towards me, stopping in front of my desk. I rose from my chair to leave. No way was I going to allow him to get any closer. I walked around my desk, and he stepped in front of me, not allowing me to pass.

"Aiden, please." I looked at him, hoping he wouldn't push this, but I saw no signs of retreat in his eyes.

"Please what? I never imagined you to be one to beg, but there's no need to do that. I would think you'd know by now that I'm willing to give you whatever you want," he purred, his voice sending shivers through me.

"I'm not begging, you sarcastic ass. I'm saying, don't do this," I pleaded.

"Do what?" he asked, with a pretense of misunderstanding.

If I were being honest, I wanted to fall into his arms and let him have his way with me, but I knew it would only be an even bigger mistake than my previous lapses in judgment with him. We were standing extremely close to each other, so close that I could feel the heat radiating from his body. *I wanted him. Damn, I wanted him!*

He leaned down and kissed my cheek, and I closed my eyes,

relishing the warmth and softness of his lips. He planted a sweet, chaste kiss below my chin and lightly swept his lips back and forth across my jaw, moving toward my ear. He reached for my arms, sliding his hands up to my shoulders, and I fell into his chest, relenting to his heated touch. His lips were on my neck, planting soft, sensuous kisses at the nape and slowly moving his hand upward, reaching my hair and gently pulling, forcing my head back, fully exposing my neck. His touch had weakened me to gentle whimpers. I should've fought him. I knew it with everything in me, but I couldn't, and at that moment I didn't want to.

He turned me away from him, and with his hands resting on my shoulders, he walked me to the side of my desk.

"You didn't answer me, Ms. Cason. Exactly what would you like me to *not* do? I would like to think I would do anything for you, with one exception, and that's letting this go before we have a chance to see where it takes us. I won't do that," he said, his smoky voice hypnotizing me.

I turned to face him, desperate for a way out of this, but I saw no indication of him relenting. I was fucked because there wasn't a chance in hell that I would be able to avoid what I knew was inevitable.

"You *won't* do it? It's not as if I don't have a say in this. You will only do what I allow you to do, and nothing more," I said.

"Oh, so are you saying you *allowed* me to kiss you in the elevator? And I assume you *allowed* me to unbutton your shirt and grab your breasts and tug on your perfect nipples? And I am pretty certain you *allowed* me to place your hand on my cock and taste me?"

"Fuck you."

"That's what I'm hoping you will allow me to do—fuck you."

Virginia was throbbing, filled with want for this man whom she and I both knew was off-limits.

"I want you to feel me deep inside you. Give me that. *Allow* me that, Aria."

He'd never called me Aria before. It was the most beautiful and provocative thing I'd ever heard.

"Yes," I whispered, and he took me into his arms and gently kissed me. His kiss was soft and deep before evolving into a heated, fierce feast as we tasted each other. He abruptly pulled away and turned me so that I was facing my desk. His manhood was erect—prodding my back as he leaned down and touched his lips to my neck.

"Mmm. Your skin is so soft and sweet," he murmured, his voice smooth as velvet.

I moaned as he cupped my breasts, and traced the wet heat of his tongue along my neck. Pinning me against the desk, he positioned me so that I was only able to move my upper torso. He then guided me to lean over the side of the wooden frame while he slowly raised my skirt.

I heard his sharp intake of breath as he took in what was on display for him. He spread my legs and quickly slid my panties to the side. A condom wrapper fluttered to the floor, and before I could object, he was inside me, filling me.

Holy fuck. He was huge. My mind went someplace else as I relished the heated lust of this man easing his dick out of me. I savored every thick, hard inch until he was back in again. Only this time, he didn't slide slowly into my pussy. He plowed into me with such fierceness that my body bolted forward. Damn, he was so deep. He pulled out and slammed into me again.

"Fuck, you feel even better than I imagined," he growled, moving faster, his balls slapping against my ass. He was so huge that his repeated thrusts were almost painful, but it was a deep, satisfying pain that made me ache for more. My body responded, wanting to meet his thrusts, but I couldn't because I was pinned firmly between his body and the desk. I could only lie there as he continued his delightfully painful plunges into me. He felt my small push toward his dick and his grip tightened, forcing me flush with the object that was supporting his assault.

"What a tight, greedy, pussy you have, Ms. Cason," he whispered between thrusts. I understood—he wanted to be in control of my body and in control of my pleasure—and he was. I absorbed each forceful thrust, wanting to cry out, but I couldn't because his hand was covering my mouth. I wanted to have some type of bodily response but he had me positioned in such a way that I could only take what he was giving.

"I'll remove my hand, but if you utter one sound I'll stop fucking you. Then, I'll gag you and fuck you so hard that you'll be glad your screams are muffled," he warned, his voice deep and menacing.

His salacious threat made me even hotter for him. I wanted this; I needed this. I was afraid to reply aloud, so I only nodded. He removed his hand from my mouth and my head continued to buck forward as the force of his pelvis took me to places I didn't think possible. I couldn't decipher which was greater: relief that he'd removed his hand, fear that he'd threatened to be rough with me, or carnal pleasure as I took delight in everything he was making me feel.

He circled his hard length inside me, teasing and stretching. "Do you like this?" he asked.

"Mmm hmm," I moaned.

"Do you like the way my dick feels inside your tight pussy?"

He slammed into me, bolting me forward. I bit my lip to avoid screaming.

"Then tell me," he demanded.

"I like the way your dick feels inside my pussy," I whispered, panting.

"You feel so fucking good. So tight and wet." He leaned over me, placing his hand on my chin and pushing his finger in my mouth.

"Suck," he commanded. I greedily sucked his finger as he plunged into me. "Slowly," he murmured.

I did as he instructed while he continued his circular motions inside me, filling me and driving me wild. He pulled his finger from my mouth and slowly trailed down to my chin. He stopped the circular torture and rammed into me; he was so hard. His hands were suddenly gripping my shoulders, pulling me towards him, as he pumped harder, forcing his cock deeper inside me. Oh shit! I could barely take it all.

He continued his rhythm with each hard forceful plunge, and I took in each one, desperate for the next. My pussy responded, wanting to come apart and release months of pent up arousal. He felt it too, because he slowed and lifted my upper body slightly from the desk, sliding his hands down, finding my breasts, which he cupped and kneaded with gentle, dexterous fingers. He was slow and tender at first and then he began grabbing and squeezing. He pinched my nipples and twisted as he pulled through the fabric. I cried out as the exquisite pain flowed through me.

"Seems you can't follow instruction, sweetheart," he said as he forced a deep thrust into me and then another.

"I'm sorry," I said between breaths. "I didn't mean to—"

"Quiet. You know what's coming next, don't you?" he demanded, his voice low and ominous. With his hardness still inside me, he took the sides of my blouse and quickly pulled it apart, the buttons scattering onto the desk and floor. Untucking my blouse from my skirt, he yanked it off. Oh, what the hell was he doing? With deft fingers, he quickly unclasped my bra and removed it as well.

He reached up to my mouth. "Open," he ordered, and I quickly complied. He took the sleeve of my blouse and forced a portion of it into my mouth and then he tied it in place with my bra!

Oh fuck! He was really gagging me! I didn't resist. I let him do as he pleased—whatever it took—as long as it meant he would continue giving me this insane pleasure.

He resumed his relentless pounding, and I took in each deep invasion. Unable to move, unable to speak, and barely able to breathe, I slipped into a place that I couldn't comprehend. I moaned each time he shoved his big dick inside me. I didn't ever want it to stop.

"Isn't this what you wanted?" he asked, but I was too lost to respond. "My dick inside you? Filling your greedy pussy," he grunted.

He lifted me and stepped back, pressing his back to the wall. "Lean into me," he murmured.

His large hands gripped my hips, guiding me to the root of his thick cock as he began thrusting upwards, bolting into me in fierce, rapid succession while pushing me down harder to meet him.

Fuck, I felt him in my stomach.

"Ahh, shit," he breathed. "I could be inside you all day and never get enough."

I was in a lust-filled daze as my senses flowed further away. On his last thrust, my core tightened and weeks of pent-up frustrations unraveled as I came, my body jerking, my muscles contracting and expanding, releasing my juices on his still-hard cock. My body relaxed as I gradually fell back down to earth, my moans of pleasure muffled by my shirt.

"Oh, shit. I'm gonna come. Ahh… fuck," he growled, pumping into me, still pushing my hips down to meet his brutal thrusts. I felt him growing harder, and then he exploded, spilling inside me as he claimed his release, his breath harsh against my cheek. He held me tightly to his chest as our breathing slowed. It was quiet. He finally lifted me off of him and gently placed me on my feet.

Oh, so now he could be gentle?

He untied my bra and turned me to face him. Slowly he

pulled my sleeve out of my mouth as our eyes met for the first time since he'd entered me. I noticed the small beads of perspiration on his forehead. And his eyes—they had slightly changed color to a light fern green.

He stared at me intently, searching…for what? A sign that I was okay with what just happened? I didn't know. I stared, too, fascinated by his eyes as they darkened. They became the shiny darkness of emerald stones, the deepest green with the longest lashes I'd ever seen. I didn't want to move, I wanted to stare into his eyes and watch them dance.

"Hi," I whispered, for lack of anything better to say.

A slow smile crossed his lips, and he touched the tip of my nose with his finger. "Hi yourself. Are you okay? I didn't hurt you, did I?" he asked, with perceptible concern in his beautiful eyes.

I was still in shock and unable to assess if he actually had hurt me or not. I shook my head. Damn, where was my voice? Had he fucked me into silence? I didn't know what to say. This had never happened to me before, and I wasn't sure how I should feel or respond to him. I didn't like this feeling of being exposed and vulnerable.

"What's wrong?" he asked, lightly tracing my cheek with his fingertips, leaving a trail of heat where his fingers had touched.

I felt an overwhelming need to escape his entrancing gaze. I looked away, staring past him. He gently guided my chin so that I was again facing him, staring into his warm, emerald eyes.

"Aria. Please say something. I haven't known you very long, but I know enough to say that it's unlike you to be this quiet."

A reluctant smile touched my lips at that truth. I swallowed and attempted to find my voice. "Nothing's wrong. I'm just a little out of sorts. Er...this is a first for me."

His brow furrowed as shock and confusion crossed his handsome face.

"Not a *first* in regard to sex, of course, but here, in my office, with a, uh, coworker," I explained, embarrassed at my current state.

"A *coworker*? Is that what I am?" he questioned.

"Aren't you?" I snapped as I reached for my bra; he passed it to me as I pulled down my skirt.

"I was under the impression that we were slightly more than coworkers, Aria. Apparently I was mistaken. Guess it's a good thing you don't make a habit of fucking coworkers in your office, huh?"

"What's your fucking problem?" I demanded.

"No, what's *your* fucking problem?" he countered.

"Do you really want to know?" I asked.

"Yes, please enlighten me," he replied, his jaw clenching.

"You!" I nearly shouted at him. "Since the day you darkened

my door, you've been my fucking problem." I turned abruptly to gather my purse. I didn't bother putting on my shirt and bra. I slipped on a jacket from the coat rack near my door, buttoned it, and without looking back, stormed out of my office.

❧Chapter Six❧

I rushed to the elevator and jabbed the call button impatiently as I glanced over my shoulder. The doors opened, and I stepped in and pushed the button for the parking garage. The elevator began to close just as Aiden stepped out of my office. You would have never known from looking at him that he had just fucked his boss senseless. His demeanor was cool and aloof, which I had come to recognize as one of his many masks. I took him in from the tips of his shoes upward, stopping my appraisal once I saw the look on his face. *Anger?*

The elevator doors closed, bringing finality to the scene. What the fuck was *he* angry about? I was just fucked and gagged in my office by my fucking intern. Just saying that in my head sounded all sorts of wrong! *I had sex in my office.* With my subordinate, no less. But damn, it was so amazingly hot! Remembering him inside me, I touched my nipples, which were sore from his sensuous abuse. Truth be told, Virginia was sore also. Very sore!

I buttoned the skipped buttons of my jacket and made a futile attempt to smooth my hair as I waited to exit the elevator. I shoved my shirt and bra into my purse just before the doors opened. Looking downward, I hurriedly made my way to the parking garage. I wondered what I would see if I were looking at the security cameras. Would I see a woman who had been shamelessly ravaged? I silently prayed not. I hoped I would see a woman who worked late and who had a lot on her mind as she rushed to get home in preparation for the evening's company party.

Nearing my car, I quickened my steps and then pressed the unlock button on the key fob. After taking one last look over my shoulder, I slid inside the car, wincing as I pushed through the discomfort—I was a lot sorer than I thought. My phone rang, but I decided to let it go to voicemail. The last time I left work and answered my phone, I opened a door to disaster. This time whoever was calling would have to wait. I secured my seat belt and started home. For the second time today, I was in the busy Boston traffic headed to the safety of my condo. The difference was that I was leaving work after an extreme orgasm, courtesy of Aiden Wyatt, whereas on my first attempt to leave, I was only guilty of stroking his cock and tasting his come. Either way, I was fucked. Literally and figuratively.

Entering my condo, I began undressing, leaving a trail of clothing to the bathroom. After starting the water, I went to the kitchen for a bottle of wine. A hot, relaxing bath and a couple glasses of alcohol would do much to soothe my thoughts. Heading back to the bathroom, I grabbed my phone, placed it on the docking station and launched an upbeat playlist. I appreciated the speaker system throughout my home as the room filled with the cheery rhythm of Katy Perry's *Roar*. Katy was one of my favorite artists; I was drawn in the moment I heard the chorus of her massive hit, *I Kissed a Girl*, which I still loved.

I dimmed the lights in the bathroom and stepped into the tub. Settling in, I closed my eyes and allowed the music to flow over me. Music was my cure-all. It made happy times happier, and other times, like now, it offered a much-needed distraction.

After a few songs and a glass of wine, I was actually in a much calmer place. I prepared myself to replay today's events and evaluate my predicament. I needed to know at which exact point had I lost control of the situation with Aiden.

When I emerged from the tub thirty minutes later, I'd determined that I never really had control over the situation with Aiden. The only reason I hadn't given in to him weeks ago was because he hadn't made a serious attempt. The moment I saw him, it was inevitable. What happened today was trouble on many levels, the most important of which was my job. I needed a way to silence this and to ensure it would never happen again.

I had formed a couple of logical conclusions. First, there was no way anyone could have seen us in the elevator; as far as I could tell, no one ever looked at us. If they had, I would've noticed. But then again, there were a few moments when my eyes were closed. And — oh, shit — I wasn't completely sure there wasn't a security camera in there. I'd never noticed one, but...

How was it fucking possible for anyone to have that type of effect on me? I could barely recall the details of what happened exactly.

Second, in regard to the sex, my office door had been locked and we were actually pretty quiet while he was fucking me, thanks to the gag. Who would have thought there would come a day in which I would be thankful for being gagged?

But the point was, I was pretty sure that what occurred between us was just that — between us. No one knew.

Third, I needed to make sure it stayed that way if my career was going to remain intact.

The way I saw it, I had only a couple of choices — pretend the office sex never happened and hope that Aiden would do the same, or confront him, ask him to keep his mouth shut, and make certain that it never happened again.

There was actually a third option. I could do what I really wanted — let him fuck me as hard and as often as possible. After all, the damage was done. The indiscretion in the elevator alone was enough for me to lose my job and taint my career. Sexual harassment — that's what they would label it. Forget that he was the one harassing *me*! I would be the one to take the fall, since I was his supervisor.

So if I was going to get the boot over sexual harassment, I

may as well make it worth it and have as much mind-blowing sex with him as my cunt would allow, which may not be very much considering how sore I was from just one romp. But he'd be worth the delicious pain. I could definitely suffer through it. Of course, that was Virginia talking. Virginia was a lot like April. Always up and ready for some hot, scandalous sex, consequences be damned.

Totally ignoring Virginia, I finished packing. After the party, I planned to change clothes, grab my luggage, and head to the airport. I only packed a carry-on because most of my time there would be in a bikini, so extra clothes weren't a necessity. I would buy whatever else needed once I landed.

After placing my luggage near the door, I sat at my bureau to fix my hair. I added a few braids on the sides and at the nape, gathered them along with the loose hair, pulling it all to meet in the back in a knotty woven mass. I'd left out my bangs and pulled them back over the top to create a little extra volume. After deciding I'd done a pretty good job, I applied my makeup and entered my closet to select my attire. I decided on a Vera Wang cocktail dress. It was a silver satin strapless dress with tiered layers that stopped a few inches above the knee. There was a triangle cutout that revealed my upper and lower mid back, and it put the girls on display, making it more revealing than what I would normally wear to a company function, but I loved this dress on me — it accentuated everything I loved about my body. It was daring, slightly understated, and sexy. Foregoing a necklace, I donned my favorite diamond earrings and matching bracelet. I grabbed my silver clutch and slipped on a pair of silver Christian Louboutin peep-toe pumps and exited my bedroom.

April called earlier, beyond excited to begin our four-day weekend. I filled her in on a few of the details regarding my situation with Mr. Fuck Me in hopes she would, perhaps, just this once, understand my plight. But true to form, she didn't see the problem. She thought it all sounded amazingly hot. The fact that it involved a level of risk was all the more attractive to her. I never said that it wasn't hot, because the mere thought of this afternoon with him made me desperate to pick up where we left off, but it was also dangerous, and it violated my Fuck Rule. Most importantly, it violated a company policy that I'd desecrated in damn near every way possible.

I'd done just enough to both get fired and involve RPH in a sexual harassment scandal. Aiden must be aware of the legal ramifications, given his background in law. I couldn't simply disregard what happened; I would talk to him and ask that he ignore my lapse in judgment and continue our professional relationship. Simple enough. I suspected Aiden would still push the envelope with this. I just couldn't predict how far he would push it.

The missed call earlier was from him—more than likely an

effort to initiate another seduction and conquest. Maybe, just maybe, I was jumping to the wrong conclusion, but after replaying the afternoon, I doubted it. Judging from the way Aiden looked at me when the elevator doors closed, he wasn't finished with me. Not nearly. If only I hadn't gone back to the office for Adam, I wouldn't have ended up giving Aiden exactly what he'd wanted.

What's done, is done. Straightening my shoulders, I grabbed my clutch and gave myself a pep talk for what was sure to be a tumultuous evening.

My anxiety amplified as I drove along Route 93 toward the docks. I neared Atlantic Avenue, following the signs for Rowes Wharf and the Boston Harbor Hotel, my palms sweating. Turning toward the Wharf, I arrived at the docks, following the line for the valet attendants. Stopping beside the attendant, I noticed the steady stream of people crossing the access ramp to board the Odyssey. I took one last glance in the mirror and then opened the door to an evening that was certain to be a turning point. As to the direction of the turn, well, that depended on Aiden, and the thought of him having that type of control was terrifying and angered me to no end.

I gradually made my way aboard the Odyssey, my heart in my throat. Reaching the main deck of the yacht, I inconspicuously eyed the partygoers in search of Aiden. I didn't see him, but I spotted Raina. *Wow!* She looked really pretty in her smart short black organza cocktail dress. It had a soft neckline adorned with shiny sequin motifs, and a white bow tie at the waist. I'd never seen her dressed in anything like this before. She was usually ultra-conservative. But perhaps, like me, she was feeling risqué tonight.

"I love your dress," I said, reaching her.

"Thank you, Ms. Cason. It's not too much, is it?" she asked nervously.

"I think it's perfect. You look beautiful," I mused.

"Thank you. This isn't something I would normally wear, or even buy, but it was a birthday gift from my sister. When I told her about tonight's party, she insisted that I wear it."

"Well, I think it was an excellent choice."

She smiled, noticeably relaxing. "Look at you! You look like a runway model. Then again, you always look so gorgeous."

"I seriously doubt I have any resemblance to a runway model, but thanks for saying it all the same," I replied, smiling. I wondered how Aiden would respond when he saw me this evening. Would he still find me appealing or would he treat me as he did the other women at RPH? He was cordial, sometimes witty, but it was obvious he had no real interest in any of them. Although I should be comforted by the thought of him finally treating me like a colleague, part of me relished the attention he couldn't seem to help but bestow me. I knew that was contradictory, but in some ways he was someone I could seriously fall for, given a different set of circumstances. If he weren't a coworker, for instance. I'd never felt that before—the feeling that I wanted something more than sex from a guy. I never allowed myself to feel that way. But Aiden...he made me do things and think things that were outside of my control. That was the part of this I didn't like.

"Aria, would you like to play blackjack with us?"

"Hmm?"

"I was saying that Bailey and I were going to try our hand at blackjack and wanted to know if you would like to join us," Raina said.

"Sure, that sounds like fun," I replied. I had been too lost in my Aiden induced daze to notice that Bailey had joined us, but I greeted her now. "You look ready for a night out on the town. That dress looks amazing on you."

"I was just thinking the same thing about your dress, Ms. Cason. You look incredible," she added, quickly lifting her eyes from my boobs. I hoped that wasn't an indication that I was revealing too much.

"Thanks."

"Where did you find your dress?" Raina asked Bailey as we turned to find the blackjack table.

"I actually bought this last season from Barney's. You wouldn't believe the deals you can get at the end of the season, and my husband told me long ago that if I wanted designer dresses like this, I'd have to shop the sales," she said, laughing.

It was a black silk crepe sleeveless tulip dress with a box pleated bubble skirt and a perforated hem. It was extremely fitted at the waist, accentuating her slim figure. The high-backed four inch pumps were perfect for the dress, giving the appearance of super long legs. Unlike Raina, Bailey was more than confident in both her appearance and in her ensemble.

As we entered the relaxed and festive atmosphere of the Odyssey's game room, I found myself excited for the first time this evening. There were gaming tables dispersed throughout the room—blackjack, roulette, poker, baccarat, and my favorite…craps! I wasn't an exceptionally good player, but I loved the anticipation and excitement that coursed through me when I grabbed the dice, everyone anxiously waiting for me to throw the number that would help them "buy baby a new pair of shoes".

Scantily dressed waitresses busied themselves taking orders and distributing drinks. I hoped they weren't the usual watered-down alcohol served in most gambling arenas, because I would need less dilution if I were going to make it through this night in one piece.

Cheers erupted in the crowded area that held the slot

machines. We followed the sound of the merriment to see a large group of RPH employees congratulating a lucky winner, who appeared to be Jennifer. In that dress, I couldn't be sure, because she wasn't the same Jennifer I saw within the walls of RPH.

Bailey led us to a table with three empty stools, two of which were situated side by side. Bailey and Raina selected those two, leaving me to sit at the end. Taking our seats, we passed the dealer some bills in exchange for chips. Since I was seated at the end of the table, I would be the person relied upon for a payout. I hated sitting here because if you caused the entire table to bust, you got nasty looks thrown your way like knives.

The first two hands were easy wins, not requiring any type of strategy due to the cards being dispersed in favor of the table. I'd play a couple more hands and stop before I caused anyone at the table to lose and toss the blame my way. Besides, I wanted to play craps. Blackjack was my second favorite table game, but the exhilaration factor was missing. Jackpot winners at the slot machines may be the loudest people in the house, but nothing was quite like the collective excitement that builds at a craps table.

Another bout of cheers erupted to the right of the blackjack table. I glanced over and immediately found Aiden standing beside the bar, speaking with Adam and Blake. He was his normal gorgeous self, although there was nothing normal about his level of hotness. He was dressed in white slacks, white dress shirt — top buttons undone with no tie — and a sky blue dress jacket. He looked perfect, casually standing with his arms crossed. Obviously uninterested in the conversation with Adam and Blake, he cast his gaze about the room. When he finally reached me, our eyes were momentarily glued to each other. No doubt about it — he was off-the-charts hot. I could seriously eye-fuck this guy all night, but I reluctantly severed our connection and grabbed my chips. Without a word to Bailey or Raina, I made a beeline for the bar. I knew I needed to talk to Aiden, but I needed a drink to calm my nerves — and my libido — before approaching him.

Three drinks later, I was standing at the craps table — another delay of the inevitable. After four lucky rolls of the dice, I'd started to relax and enjoy myself again, until an unwelcome player joined the opposite end of the table.

He tossed several bills toward the pit, and the dealer shouted, "Check change one thousand." He waited on approval from the pit boss then slid Aiden's chips to him. How did an intern have money to toss around like that? I was fully aware of his mediocre salary, and he didn't earn nearly enough to risk one thousand dollars of it. But maybe he was the type that saved every dime for those times when he wanted to throw caution to the wind.

I was still the shooter, and the stickman slid the dice back to me as he announced that the point was nine. I grabbed the tiny, red cubes and placed them side by side with the four and the three facing up, then tossed them to the end of the table.

"Nine. Shooter rolled nine."

The players quickly scooped up their winnings as the stickman pushed the dice to me again. I repeated my normal setup of the four and the three and tossed the dice again toward the opposite end of the table. They bounced off the back wall and landed on nine again. Cheers erupted around me. I would have enjoyed this much more had Aiden not been there, watching me. His eyes lingering on mine, he told the dealer to place all of his chips on the point everyone was hoping for. *What was he doing?* I grabbed my drink from the waitress and absorbed the enthusiasm around me. The stickman hadn't passed the dice to me yet because of all of the new bets that were being placed. This was the part where I would usually crap out—everyone upping their bets based on a few lucky rolls. I decided to stop while I was ahead—I hated when such a huge build-up resulted in a massive disappointment. After the dealer stopped taking bets, the stickman pushed the dice towards me, and I shook my head and motioned for him to pass them to the person beside me.

"No, you should finish your roll, you're on a hot streak," said the person to my left.

I shook my head and looked over to see it was Greg, from the legal department. "Too much pressure," I told him.

A familiar voice spoke on my other side. "Ms. Cason, I have a lot of money on you, and from what I've seen, you perform extremely well under pressure."

Aiden had walked around the table to stand beside me. I looked at him, then glanced at the expectant faces circling the table, and finally, I reached down to grab the dice.

I sighed. "Okay, but this is the last time. Whatever happens, you asked for it."

I was about to toss the dice when Aiden stopped me. "Wait, aren't you forgetting your ritual?"

Huh? Oh, yes. I had forgotten, because his closeness was driving me mad! Damn, he smelled so good. I smiled as I pictured a mindless cartoon character involuntarily floating as her nose led her to the most exquisite of smells. That's exactly how my responses had been for this man: mindless and involuntary.

I situated the dice with the four and three on top, tossed them, and closed my eyes, awaiting sounds of disappointment. I was relieved and shocked when I heard cheers instead. I opened my eyes to the excited faces around the table.

"Nine! We have a hot shooter tonight folks," the dealer announced as he began swiftly distributing the winnings.

"I knew you could do it," Aiden whispered in my ear.

Just like I'm sure you knew you were going to fuck me.

I turned toward the table. "Okay, that was the last roll for me, everyone," I said, as I reached over the top of the table to collect my winnings.

As my tablemates shouted compliments — *Good shoot*, and *Don't go*, and *One more roll* — I stepped back and walked away, relieved that I made that last nine...and that I was placing some distance between Aiden and me.

I grabbed an agenda from one of the hors d'oeuvre tables and saw that it was almost time to assemble on the upper deck for dinner. Entering the sky lounge, I found a very different venue. The lighting was not as bright as on the main deck, allowing the moonlight to spill into the space. Massive windows encircled the room, providing a fantastically calming view of the moonlit water. Dining tables were arranged around a recessed stage. On the left edge was a lectern embossed with the Odyssey's logo. I looked for the table designated for RPH executives, only to discover we were to be seated by departments.

Damn. I hurriedly scanned the room for my departmental staff in hopes of manipulating the seating arrangement. I spotted Raina and Bailey walking in, and I was about to approach them when Adam appeared, asking me to start the evening's festivities, as he had decided to present the closing statements. Before I could object, I saw that Zoe, Raina, and Bailey had taken their seats at our table, as had River and Josh. There were only two chairs left, leaving Aiden and I sitting beside each other. *Damn! Was Adam determined to keep getting me fucked?*

❧Chapter Seven❧

I half-heartedly walked to the lectern and asked that everyone take their seats. My part was brief—a welcome, a statement of purpose, and applause for a job well done. Blake followed my introduction with details on the company's growth and the overall progress of the year's strategic plan.

I ultimately returned to my table and saw that Aiden had been seated. Reluctantly, I assumed the available chair. The waiters began circling the room and commenced with drink and dinner orders. As our waiter detailed the preparation for the veal francese, Aiden leaned toward me and I stilled immediately.

"I didn't have a chance to tell you that you look absolutely gorgeous tonight," he whispered.

"Thank you," I replied, relaxing marginally. I was expecting something much more overt, given today's indiscretions. I removed my phone from my handbag and checked that it was on vibrate before I placed it on the table. I wanted to keep in close contact with April until we had both reached St. Barts. I also wanted to be aware of any last minute flight changes. Hopefully the app for the airline was no longer having update issues, and I would be able to receive up-to-date information without calling the airline directly.

I noticed Aiden fidgeting with his phone as the waiter approached to take my order.

My phone flashed a notification. After giving my order to the waiter I saw that I had received a text. It was from Aiden.

As beautiful as you are in that dress, what would it take to get you out of it?

And so it began. So much for my miniscule hope that he would back off now that he had gotten what he wanted.

Let's not start this again.

Is that an order or just a suggestion from one coworker to another?

I waited a few minutes and decided to reply.

I'm not interested in playing games with you. Today was a mistake. You should forget it happened. I have.

The only mistake was not fucking you harder.

I dropped the phone in my lap and shifted nervously in my chair. My hands intertwined repeatedly as I attempted to think my way out of my predicament. I browsed the room, corner to corner, as if something — or someone — would give me a clue.

The only thing I came up with, was to just ignore Aiden and not encourage his wayward thoughts. As I placed my phone on the table, his hand found my thigh and I gasped. Bailey looked towards us, I smiled at her, and thankfully she redirected her attention to the center of the room.

I was on edge as it was, and the heat from his hand sent a stream of suggestive sparks directly to Virginia. She was such a traitorous bitch! I struggled to adjust my leg away from Aiden, hoping to remove his hand without the others noticing the impish exchange. Aiden replied by holding tighter, his fingers firmly grasping my thigh. I hurled a warning glance at him, which he coolly ignored as he directed his attention to Raina and Bailey.

"Are you ladies enjoying the evening?" he asked, casually sliding his hand higher, pushing my dress up. I was absolutely fuming but had no idea how to free myself of this position. I picked up my phone and sent him a text.

You are seriously pushing it! Remove your hand from my fucking thigh!

A few moments later, he checked his phone and replied.

If I were pushing it, you would know. That was made fairly obvious earlier. Besides, my hand is very comfortable. I think I will keep it where it is.

Bastard!

Bailey, Raina, and Aiden dove into a conversation about the party, gambling, and the yacht. I reached down to pry his hand from my thigh but there wouldn't be a way to budge him without my jerking it away and causing the others to notice. What had happened since yesterday to cause him to be so unrelenting and forceful with me? I reached down and pinched him, surprised when he responded by pinching my thigh in return. I jerked my leg slightly at the unexpected sting and realized he would not release me until he was good and ready. I nervously surveyed the room to determine if anyone had noticed the weirdness at our table. There was obviously nothing discreet I could do about it. I had to endure the irritation and deal with him later in private.

I turned to face the others, defeated. I placed both hands on the table and joined the conversation. Raina was filling us in on her plans for her upcoming vacation to Hawaii with her family. After five minutes or so of idle chatter, our drinks arrived and I immediately took a sip of my vodka cranberry. The waiters brought our meals a short time later, and I was offered a refill, which I gladly accepted.

The alcohol was beginning to lessen my anxiety about Aiden's nearness, so I continued drinking and enjoying the meal. Aiden's hand stayed on my thigh, and occasionally he made soft, circular motions. I pretended not to notice, hoping he would see that he was having no effect on me and remove his damned hand. No such luck.

Dessert was served, and Aiden began his ascent up my thigh. I drew in a quick breath and slowly exhaled as his hand slid over my thigh and between my legs. I nervously looked around the room, terrified that someone could see what was going on. Everyone was oblivious, including the five people at our table. He gently pushed my legs apart, allowing him access to his target. He slid my panties to the side and began slowly circling my clit just as I was removing the fork from my mouth. I bit down, hard. I let out a gentle whimper and five sets of eyes landed on me.

"This is very good," I said, hoping to cover my blunder.

"I'll bet it's delicious," Aiden said. He leaned over and whispered, "I would love a taste."

He continued circling and teasing; I was soaked. So much for my wackadoodle plan to show him that he wasn't getting to me. I clenched my thighs, and he responded by pinching my clit. I looked at him, pleading, hoping he would stop. He obviously took mercy on me and slowly removed his finger as I placed a bite of my Frozen Haute Chocolate onto his plate. Everyone was too engrossed in conversation to notice when Aiden slipped his finger into his mouth.

"Delicious. Tastes even better than I imagined."

I was too turned on to give his impudence the attention it deserved. Virginia's muscles tightened as the thought of Aiden's tongue doing unimaginable things to me flickered in my head. Before I could reply, Adam's voice came over the speaker system, detailing the events for the remainder of the evening: dancing, drinking, and more gambling for the next two hours as we headed back to the port. He rambled a few closing statements and everyone applauded as the lights lowered, transforming the room into a dance club, complete with pulsing music and illuminating flashes of light that swirled on the ceiling.

The urgency of my dilemma dissipated as the sounds of

Maroon 5's *Maps* filled the room. I loved Maroon 5; they were an amazing band and made for some great music therapy. I envied musicians with their ability to create something that was somehow good for both the body and soul. Although not musically inclined, I had always wanted to try my hand at playing an instrument.

I wistfully glanced at the excited dancers making their way to the floor, then I noticed someone approaching our table. That had been Jennifer at the slot machine after all. She had certainly embellished her day-to-day look.

"Hi, everyone." Although she said *everyone,* she clearly intended her greeting for Aiden. Her overly cheery smile and sparkling eyes never left his face.

"I seem to recall you mentioning that you loved to dance. How about you show me what you can do?" she asked him.

Aiden's head fell back slightly as he laughed. "I would love to," he replied, rising from his chair. He grasped Jennifer's hand without as much as a glance at me. I watched as they reached the dance floor. Aiden was already moving to the beat, his confidence in his ability apparent. He whirled her out and rolled her back into his chest. I was instantly filled with an irrational surge of jealousy. I wanted to look away but I was unable to tear my eyes from the two of them.

They danced well together. Although their bodies were not

touching, they were too close for my liking. Aiden's dance moves were suggestive and sexy, which was something he apparently couldn't turn off. They both moved with slight sexual overtures in time to the beat.

Jennifer leaned in to say something at which they both laughed. She was enjoying herself. She didn't mind that people were watching. She was just being herself. I envied that; I'd never been able to distance myself from my anxieties long enough to let loose and enjoy, unless it was on vacation. But that was *planned* enjoyment. Everything about me was planned, organized, and analyzed. I sighed as I wondered how it would feel to break away from those shackles.

Two other ladies joined Jennifer and Aiden, each taking her turn for some one-on-one with him. I watched how he maneuvered with each of them, giving each one just enough to pant for more. I hated to watch them drool over him, even though I was sure the desire was one-sided. Besides, while they were relishing this moment, my pussy was just on his finger and hopefully the taste was still in his mouth.

I glared at them, anxious for the song to end. I understood it was difficult to avoid having eye-sex with that man, but I didn't wish to see them do it. Eventually I forced myself to look away and face my tablemates, who were also focused on the dance floor. I turned back, casually glancing at Aiden and his groupies just once more, I told myself.

Damn… He caught me staring. I gazed around the room in an effort to appear indifferent. I heard clapping and looked to see the women with whom Aiden was dancing applauding him. Had they never seen a good-looking man dance before? He was smiling as Jennifer said something funny and casually touched his arm. He leaned down slightly to whisper in her ear, and then he sauntered towards our table. I practically screamed at myself to look away, but I couldn't. It was as if he'd silently willed me to keep my focus on him. I swallowed and my heart rate accelerated. What was he doing?

He stopped directly in front of me, presenting his dazzlingly perfect smile. "Ms. Cason, would you do me the honor?" he asked, his hand extended to me.

Before a reply could even reach my lips, I'd lifted my hand to his and risen from my seat. His touch was as magnetic as his face. A current flowed between us as his skin touched mine, further compelling me to do anything he asked. It was that spellbound pull that had caused me to submit to him in the elevator and again in my office. That undeniable power allowed me to sit surrounded by colleagues and endure his delicious torment at the dinner table. Was this how all women responded to him, and how often did he take advantage of our weakness?

His smile faded as he appraised my expression. He couldn't

possibly know what I was thinking, but if his gaze was an indication, he was privy to my inner most thoughts. As was typical with him, I felt exposed, even more so because of an audience that had never seen this kind of thing from Aria Cason.

This was not something I did. I attended these events as professional etiquette. I mingled enough to be cordial, and I left. I never engaged in any overtures that did not relate to business. But here I was now, on exhibit for my entire company. This was a huge mistake. Just as I was about to extract my hand from his, he led us away from the table.

The music changed as we reached the edge of the dance floor. The Latin beats pulsing through the speaker system were exceedingly familiar—salsa! I took salsa lessons as a prelude to one of my many vacations with April. She and I were great together on vacations—sometimes too great, which was another story. We had actually developed into quite skilled salsa dancers. I was convinced that our aptitude stemmed from the fact that it was an insanely sexy dance, and for a woman who didn't have routine access to it, anything involving sex was enticing.

He placed his hand at the small of my back as he leaned down and whispered, "Are you ready?"

"As I'll ever be. I hope you can keep up," I replied, confident of my abilities.

"I can if you can," he challenged.

The feel of his hand against my exposed skin sent tingling sensations throughout my body. Before I could respond, he was spinning me out, away from him, and I immediately fell into character. I lifted my right hand flamboyantly as he held tightly to my left, pulling me back to him, my right hand landing on his firm chest. Our eyes connected, and his hands slid down both sides of my body and back up again. He pulled me closer, our bodies becoming one as we moved to the seductive beat.

Our hips were doing a dance that could only be interpreted as a prelude to sex. Everyone else in the room faded into the background; all I could see was Aiden. I was overwhelmed by his touch, his smell, the heat radiating between our bodies, the slick sweat gliding down our skin, and the way our bodies moved in sync. Each dance step rendered me breathless. He turned me, my back to his chest, and we swayed in time to the lustful beats, his pelvis rotating seductively as he pulled me closer.

His movements mirrored mine — very fluid and smooth. He grabbed my hand and turned me; we were once again facing each other, our bodies stuck together as we spun around so fast the floor came with us. As the song neared its end, he grabbed my waist and lifted me from the floor. He looked up at me, his eyes smoldering, his breathing harsh. I stared back into the dark jewels of his eyes as he slowly guided me down his chest, forcing us closer, our breathing ragged, and our lips almost touching. The music stopped.

We stood, lost in each other's eyes, until the applause reminded me of my surroundings. Embarrassed, I skimmed the crowd, noting the cheers from the men and the glares from the women. I motioned for him to release me and took several steps back. *Oh, what did I just do?*

I shifted my gaze, taking in the insanely hot man standing before me, and was instantly furious. I turned away and hurried from the dance floor. My closeness to this forbidden man had affected me, and I wouldn't allow an audience to witness any more than they already had. Damn him.

I made a beeline to the deck, which was as close to an escape as was possible. I spotted a lighted gazebo off to the side. I exhaled deeply as I reached the steps, attempting to rid myself of…what? Attraction? Passion? I didn't know. I shook my head in utter confusion. Why was this happening?

I peered into the darkness stretched out before me, taking in the night, and appreciating the way the moonlight shone on the water like a pale band of silver. The waves and the night air began to relax me, at least marginally. I was relieved to breathe air that was untainted by him. His presence had done what I'd come to expect—overtaken my willpower. Only a couple of hours more and I would be able to break away from him completely, if only for a few days.

"Why did you run away?" Aiden's sudden appearance both startled and aggravated me. Why, oh why, had he followed me out here? He placed his hands on either side of my shoulders and turned me to face him.

"Why did you run?" he asked again, bewildered. I made several attempts to speak but no words would come. Me. The person who had to constantly remind herself to put on a muzzle. "Did you not enjoy our dance?"

He paused for my answer, which didn't quite formulate in my brain. I enjoyed it much more than I should have. I was angry with him for that, and with myself for the weakness he caused in me.

I shrugged his hands from my shoulders. He cocked his head as though assessing his own question. "No, that can't be it, because you were meeting me step for step, which suggests you enjoyed yourself—more so than you care to admit, I would wager. I also think you enjoyed watching me dance with Jennifer." His lips twitched in an attempt to hide his amusement. "You *were* watching rather intently," he added.

So he'd noticed. Had he been putting on a show for me?

"I know you liked it," he said, assessing my reaction. I lowered my gaze to his mouth, appreciating the way his lips formed as he spoke.

Without warning, his mouth was pressed against mine. His

touch was ferocious, yet tender and sweet as he cupped my jaw, drawing me closer. His hand on my hip, he guided me back alongside the gazebo. I responded instantly to his touch, to that undeniable pulse of heat that I felt earlier. His mouth moved urgently on mine, parting my lips and stroking deeply. My body melted into his; I was once again lost. I pressed closer to him, my hands behind his neck, working my fingers into his hair. We were so close, connecting in a way I couldn't understand, fitting perfectly as he lavished deep, lingering, soft licks into my mouth.

He gently broke our kiss. I looked up at him, meeting the tender softness of his green eyes. He cupped my chin in his hands, holding my gaze, the mutual intensity building as the silence of the dark waters floated around us. With a soft smile, he licked his lips and pulled me to him again; I gently pushed him back, trying to clear the last few heated moments away.

"I'm sorry. I don't know —"

"No, don't," he said. "Don't apologize. This was amazing. It was —"

"It was a mistake. Another fucking mistake," I said. "This shouldn't…this can't happen."

"Why not?" he asked

Why not? I looked at him as though he was suffering from a case of idiocy. As intelligent as he was, he clearly possessed tunnel vision when in pursuit of pussy!

"What do you mean *why not*? You know why," I said.

"No, quite frankly, I don't. What? Are you going to say it's because I work for you? Is that the best you can come up with? Give me a fucking break. This is insane! You want this as badly as I do," he stated.

"I can see how you would think that, given recent events but—"

"The problem here is that it's not on your terms. You analyze everything. Don't you think I saw that in your eyes when I asked you to dance, or when I ask you anything that isn't business related? Are you literally unable to refrain from being such a self-contained perfectionist that you can't just go with what makes you feel good? Simply let yourself feel something?"

"How dare you! How dare you sum me up in that way! You don't know a damn thing about me. Oh, so you think just because we danced to a song that quite frankly would have made anyone a little flushed, that it meant something? Well, just to set the record straight, it didn't. It was a dance, nothing more. And this," I motioned with my hands, indicating the two of us, "absolutely should not have happened."

We stood in silence, glowering at each other; it appeared he was as offended as I. Why the fuck was he offended? I had been embarrassed and treated like a common whore! I was the victim here, not him!

"What would you have me do at this point, Ms. Cason? Apologize? Agree?" he asked flippantly.

"No, I don't expect you to apologize, because that would require something that you obviously don't possess. The only thing you can do for me from this point on, Mr. Wyatt, is your fucking job. And just to clarify, that doesn't include fucking the boss."

I turned toward the bench in the gazebo. I sat down and saw that he hadn't moved. "Is there something else?" I demanded.

"No, I was merely giving you a moment. You know, in case you change your mind. Women are known to do that from time to time, and we both know that you have a time or two. At least recently, anyway," he said.

Asshole. What was I thinking, dancing with him that way? It was blatantly obvious that I was as affected by our recent jousting as he was. If I'd had the remotest chance of convincing him that this afternoon was meaningless, I certainly didn't now.

"We both know what your problem is."

"I don't have a problem, Aiden," I countered.

"Sure you do," he replied matter-of-factly. "It's the fact that someone else is in control of something that you enjoy. You can't stand it."

"Go to hell." I stood to walk past him, attempting to step around him and leave the gazebo, but he blocked my exit.

"Why would you let your control issues deprive you of something you want?" he asked, his eyebrows knitted in confusion.

"I find it amusing that my refusal of your services equates to deprivation. Your arrogance is very unflattering, but I'm sure you're aware of that."

"I'm positive that you were quite pleased with my services and my demeanor earlier. This is the first I've heard of it described as arrogance."

"What I would find *pleasing* at the moment, is having you out of my sight, so please move," I said.

"You really aren't capable of appreciating pleasure unless you're in control, are you? If it makes it easier, I'm willing to let you dominate me once or twice," he replied, smirking.

My mouth dropped open. The audacity of this guy knew no bounds. I honestly had no words. I mean none!

"You want everything to be controlled and planned. That's not how the world works, Ms. Cason."

"Oh, so you think you have me all figured out? I don't give a damn what you think of me. You don't know a fucking thing about me. You think that you can sum me up in one or two sentences, but you don't know a fucking thing about yourself. You bolt from career to career and city to city trying to find yourself. You don't even know *you*! How the fuck can you know me?" I snapped.

He frowned. "You have quite the foul mouth," he replied, totally unaffected by my assertion.

"Foul mouth? Me? As if nasty little words have never trickled from your tongue. I distinctly recall several explicit terms dripping from your lips when you gagged me in my fucking office! If I want to say fuck, I'll say fuck. Fuck, fuck, fuck! What the fuck are you going to do about it?"

We stared at each other for an eternity, and a smile gradually crossed his lips. I finally smiled, too, biting my lip to avoid laughing.

"What are we doing, Aria?" he asked in a soft whisper. It almost sounded like a defeated plea, one I struggled not to give into. "Why are we making this so difficult? Let's not try to define it or struggle for control. Just go with it. Can you do that?" he asked.

I could see the desire in his eyes, which made me want to give him what he wanted — what I also wanted — but knew was wrong for me. I sighed. "Aiden, to be honest, I can't see it causing anything but trouble. I know you must see that, too. I just don't understand why you're pushing this. Why can't you just leave it alone?"

"Haven't you ever been inexplicably drawn to something or someone? When I walked into that conference room that first day, the instant you turned and our eyes met, that was our defining moment. I'll admit that I initially brushed it off as merely a sexual attraction, but once I witnessed the many facets of your beauty, your intelligence, and your passion, I knew it was more. I wanted to get to know you. I wanted you. I still want you," he said, his voice a deep, sexy whisper.

He had the same effect on me, but unlike him, I knew that if we succumbed to this, disaster was inevitable. We needed to resolve whatever this was now, because I couldn't take it anymore. His relentless pursuit, his unwavering stance, just…him! It was too much!

"Do you realize that your behavior screams sexual harassment? Is that what you want? To be fired for something as mundane as getting another notch on your belt?" I asked.

His gorgeous eyes, initially pensive, immediately clouded with anger. With practiced calm he asked, "Is that what you want? Do you really want me out of your life in that way?"

"Yes, I do. If that's what it takes, then yes."

"Really?" he implored.

Unfortunate for me, my resolve was at level zero. I sighed in defeat. "No, it's not what I want, but I can't keep doing this with you. Please. You've got to let this go," I pleaded.

"That's not what you want. If you did, you would have made that clear long ago. So let's forgo that discussion and come up with a way to make this work."

No matter what I said, he wouldn't believe me. I mean, given everything that had happened, why should he?

"You're struggling with this; I can see that. Obviously part of your hesitation is the nature of our professional relationship. I understand your position, and I appreciate your being cautious. However, I'm confident that we can be mature and keep this to ourselves."

He was right. Part of my trepidation was due to our business relationship. But even more of it had to do with feeling powerless in this situation. I didn't have an answer for him. At least not one that I was prepared to reveal.

"As entertaining as this stop-and-go scenario has been thus far," he continued, "I would like to suggest we take a different route. Since you find me arrogant, I will preface this by saying that I by no means intend to come off that way. But I know you want me."

"Look—" I started.

"Before you get defensive, I know that it's intense on *both* sides; I can admit that."

He took a step closer to me. I closed my eyes and inhaled, which was a very bad idea because I was breathing in more of him.

I watched his eyes darken as they darted from my eyes to my

lips. "What?" I asked.

"How long are you going to make me wait to fuck that hot, tight cunt of yours again?"

I would have normally been offended if a guy said some shit like that to me, but coming from him, it was such a turn on, and Virginia didn't want him to wait, she was ready to give him everything he wanted.

"You already know we can be good together. Let me show you how much better it can be," he coaxed. "My internship ends in, what, two months? Just give me the next two months."

I shook my head.

"Okay, one month, and if you still have objections, I'll drop it."

"Just like that?" I asked.

"Just like that," he replied.

Could that work? *No. Hell no.* I shouldn't...I *couldn't* consider this ridiculousness. "I want this to stop now, not in two months, not in one month. Why aren't you grasping that?"

He sighed and glanced at the evening sky. I followed his gaze and was amazed at the magnificence above us. The stars were extraordinarily bright, twinkling back and forth, much like my conversation with Aiden. It was an exceptionally beautiful evening, a night that lovers would find romantic as they moved on the liquid darkness, while the subtle breeze stirred the scent of love. But Aiden and I were not lovers, we were coworkers. Not even that, in fact; he was an intern who would be leaving my company in the very near future. I lowered my gaze to reach his beautiful face. He closed his eyes, inhaled deeply and then looked back at me. He seemed…defeated? That couldn't be right.

He leaned in toward me, so close his lips almost touched my ear, and whispered, "I know you liked it. All of it."

Right on cue, Virginia clenched. He was right. I completely identified with his desire for this, because I felt the same. I could sense myself drawn uncontrollably to him. And I knew that if I didn't come up with something to stop myself, I would be lost in him. I could feel it happening already. This was the one thing that I had been truly afraid of, the one thing I had run from for years. It was much more than the sexual appeal. It was him. Everything about him pulled me in. I was terrified. He didn't want me to fight this, but I knew that if I didn't, I would be opening a door to heartache and suffering…and possibly the same fate as my mom.

"I never said that I didn't like it. I said that it should stop."

"I told you, and I will continue telling you until you accept it, I want you."

"Well, what if I don't want you? Are you planning to force yourself on me?"

"That's too ridiculous of a question to warrant a response, Aria."

I opened my mouth to reply but I panicked at the sound of voices nearing. He grabbed my hand. "Come with me." I followed as he led me into a corridor. We approached a closed door. He looked around, I assumed to ensure we weren't seen, and then pulled me inside the dark vacant room. Without looking for a light switch, he grabbed me in his arms and pressed my back firmly to the door. In one fluid movement, he was on his knees in front of me and sliding my dress up over my thighs. I didn't object as he pushed my thighs apart and slid a finger under my panties, pulling them aside. Then his mouth was on me. I leaned my head back, panting as his tongue opened the soft wet folds. My urge to resist vanished as his warm tongue began expertly massaging my pussy. I melted into his mouth.

"You taste so good," he whispered between long deep licks.

My moans of pleasure reverberated throughout my body as he lifted my leg over his shoulder, opening me wider for him.

I didn't know what was going on with me, but I'd have to figure that part out later — for now, I was giving in.

❧Chapter Eight❧

I arrived at Boston Logan International and strolled directly to airport security. I was pleasantly surprised to see a line that moved relatively quickly. I made my way to the terminal, but not before a stop at Starbucks to grab a Chai Tea Latte. I reached the US Airways gate, took a seat, and grabbed my phone to check in with April. We had planned to arrive at St. Barts as close to the same time as possible. I was scheduled to arrive around three o'clock in the morning and she at eight o'clock. Soon after I talked to April, there was an announcement of a short flight delay, which ultimately became a long delay of four hours due to mechanical issues.

Later, when I boarded my flight, I was embroiled in thoughts of Aiden and his proposal. Indecent? Maybe. Sexually satisfying? Most definitely. Dangerous? Extraordinarily so. More than I should entertain. I backtracked to see how I'd gone from a resounding no to giving that man parts of me that I never allowed anyone to access. That damned dance—it was the final piece that drove me directly into his arms...or onto his cock was a more apt phrase.

That was the second time salsa dancing had led to something *beyond* unexpected. The difference being that the first time it happened, it was with someone I trusted to *not* hurt me. April and I were on our trip to Venezuela, headed back to our hotel room; it had been an amazing night filled with hot guys, strong drinks, wet bodies, and salsa dancing. It had gotten pretty late and the club was about to close when April and I said good night to our dance partners, much to their disappointment. After we left, we took a cab back to the hotel and staggered up to our room, loud and giggling like two school-aged girls. We were so wasted that it took nearly five minutes to place the hotel door card the correct way in the key slot. We finally stumbled into the room, shoes in hand.

"Tonight was a blast, Aria."

"Yeah, it was, huh? I can't remember the last time I had so much fun. But you know, I think one of us had too much to drink, though," I added, giggling.

"Wow! That's a shock. I usually have to listen to you go on and on defending yourself before you admit anything. I really didn't want to say it, but you did go way overboard."

"Me?" I asked.

"Yes, you."

"Uh, I was referring to you, April. You could barely stand toward the end of the night, let alone dance. That's why I had the remarkable idea to leave before your salsa dancing took a turn for the worse."

"*My* salsa dancing? I'm such an awesome dancer that I could do it in my sleep, so no doubt I'm equally awesome under the influence of a little alcohol. You, on the other hand, lose judgment and go a bit far on the sexy part of the dance. That's why *I* had the remarkable idea to get out of there before that guy lost control and tried to fuck you right there on the dance floor."

"What are you talking about? I didn't do anything that you, or any of those other women, weren't doing. And by the way, I had the idea to come back to the hotel, not you. See, you're too drunk to remember what happened even thirty minutes ago," I teased.

"Do you remember how he responded when you went down on him?" she asked, laughing.

"What? I did no such thing."

"Yep, you kinda did," she replied.

She opened her purse and pulled out her iPhone and located a salsa tune, then grabbed my hands and pulled me to the center of the room. "Dance with me, and I'll show you. You are him and I'll be you."

She began moving like a sultry exotic dancer closing the distance between us. She turned around and gyrated her butt so that it was touching me.

"I did not do that."

"Uh, yeah, you did. But wait, there's more."

She turned and placed her hands on my shoulders, sliding them down as she moved towards the floor, her face in front of Virginia and her hands on my ass as she rubbed her lips in my pelvic area. She lost her balance on the way back up and fell into me, pushing me back on the couch, and we both erupted into drunken laughter, our faces mere inches apart.

"I'm so glad we're best friends. I love you, Aria."

"I love you too, April."

April kissed me briefly on the lips and we started giggling again, and before I knew it, we were engrossed in a deep kiss.

"What are we doing?" I asked, laughing.

"I don't know, but I think I like it," she replied and grabbed my hand, pulling me towards the bedroom. We were standing near the bed staring at each other. We both giggled and somehow a sultry kiss erupted, one that made me feel things I'd never felt before.

I grabbed her breasts as her tongue caressed mine—a kiss that became increasingly sensual with each stroke. Leaning down to catch the hem of my dress, she lifted it over my head and then removed my bra. When I reached to unbutton her dress, I discovered she wasn't wearing a bra at all. Her breasts were achingly swollen—her nipples erect and eager. Grasping them both in my hands, I leaned closer and softly kissed her still blossoming buds. A low moan escaped her as I circled my tongue around one tip before pulling it between my lips, sucking. She pulled me closer and our lips met again as we lay on the bed, our bodies writhing.

As we kissed, my hand trailed down her body and I eased two fingers inside her, stroking her hot flesh. She began grinding, urging me to pump harder, so I pushed a third finger inside her and probed deeper. When I felt the walls of her sex tighten, I eased my fingers out of her and moved them over her lips. She licked her juices from my fingers and then pulled me into a kiss as her hands moved to my shoulders, urging me downward. I followed her prompting and positioned myself between her thighs, and softly kissed the tip of her clit—licking and sucking on the sensitive bud as she moaned and grinded on my face.

She sat up, her elbows supporting her upper body as she watched me. "Let me taste you," she said. "Sit on my face." I licked her slick flesh once more, and then facing her feet, I positioned myself atop her mouth. She grabbed my ass, pulling me down, burying her face in my sex. Her tongue eased inside me, and I nearly convulsed. It felt so good, so soft and sensual.

She passionately licked and sucked as I leaned over and slid my tongue between her slick folds, lapping at her clit as I twirled my fingers inside her. She was so wet—my fingers were soaked. I pushed in deeper, moving harder and faster. Her hands clamped down on my ass, pulling me downward as I writhed shamelessly on her mouth, our moans in unison as we approached a climax. I felt the tightening of my core and cried out, the vicious orgasm flowing through me. Her deep moans vibrated into me as she shivered, her climax claiming her as she suctioned my clit, sucking so hard that my body trembled over her. Her tongue laced over my sex one final time before releasing me. Breathless and exhausted, I fell on the bed beside her. Our breathing slowly calmed, and we drifted off to sleep.

The light of the morning sun shone brightly in the bedroom, inviting me to join the new day. I slowly opened my eyes, which sent a direct message to my head, reminding it to throb mercilessly from the overindulgence of alcohol the previous night. I turned over in bed, coming face to face with April. She was asleep and practically uncovered, revealing her breasts. I found it odd that she was in my bed and even more so that she was naked. I realized my own state of nakedness, and memories of the previous night came rushing back.

She and I had never done anything like that before. Yes, we had kissed, goofing around after having too many drinks, but who hasn't kissed their best girlfriend in this day and age? But to go as far as having sex with her? The thought had never crossed my mind.

I quietly slipped out of bed and walked to the bathroom to take a shower. Stepping in the steaming hot flow of water, I closed my eyes and allowed the water to caress my body as my mind drifted to my unexpected jaunt with April. I was alarmed when I felt soft hands on my shoulders, and turned to see she had stepped in the shower behind me. We exchanged knowing smiles, and I turned back to face the water. After showering and washing our hair, we dried ourselves and stepped out of the bathroom to start our day. Not a word was spoken about the previous night's events.

ھ   ھ   ھ   ھ

The pilot announced that we had reached cruising altitude and could use approved electronics. I'd forgotten to set my out-of-office message, so I reached for my laptop to check my work email. Skimming the list of new messages, I didn't notice anything too pressing, but one name seemed vaguely familiar. Since I didn't fully recognize it, I decided to wait and check it once I was back at the office. I set my automated reply and then checked my personal email. I froze when I saw a message from Aiden. How did he get my email address? I stared at the subject line, wondering if I should delete it. After a minute or so of internal debates, I clicked to open it.

Aria,

I hope you enjoy your vacation, but not so much so that you forget your promise. I'm anxiously awaiting your answer. Your delicious smell is still on my lips. I've licked them so much in the past hour that they are damn near chapped.

I want you.

A.

Virginia, although sore, immediately tightened. Did she ever get enough? I clicked reply.

It's only been a few hours. Wasn't twice today enough to sate your appetite? One would think so, but obviously not when it comes to you.

I smiled and clicked send.

His response.

How is the flight?

I typed a reply.

The flight is great, except for a minor annoyance that I can't seem to escape, even at forty thousand feet!

I opened his next email.

Oh, so you've got jokes? I don't recall your finding anything remotely annoying when I was fucking you. If memory serves, I rendered you speechless.

I didn't reply.

A few moments later, another email.

Are you ignoring me?

I didn't answer. I powered off my computer, placed it in my

bag, and reclined my seat to get some rest. I wanted to enjoy the next four days. But how could I do that when the very reason I needed the escape was lurking in the shadows?

ॐ   ॐ   ॐ   ॐ

In what seemed like minutes, the voice of the airline attendant awakened me.

"Ladies and gentlemen, as we start our descent, please make sure your seat backs and tray tables are in their full upright position. Make sure your seat belt is securely fastened…"

I adjusted my seat in preparation for landing. I was once again mentally exhausted, which had become the norm as of late. I'd slept the entire flight and didn't have a chance to sort out my feelings about Aiden's suggestion. In the small amount of time in which I had thought of him, I'd been distracted by memories of the elevator, my office, and the dark room on the yacht. I wanted to accept his offer, but it was on his terms, not mine. That was atypical for me; I set the terms, and the other party agreed — even if he had been expecting more, he always agreed. Now the tables had turned and I was being propositioned. I felt cheap. I wondered if this was how the men in my past had felt. No, I doubted that. What was I thinking? I laughed to myself as I walked through the US Airways air bridge.

Thankful that I only had a carry-on, I took the escalator down one level and found the sign for ground transportation. We were staying in Pointe Milou at the Mirande Villa, a short ten minutes from the airport. Although exhausted, the excitement of beginning my vacation overshadowed my need for sleep. I sighed happily. This beautiful paradise offered all the ingredients for a successful holiday with my best friend, and I couldn't wait to get started.

As I exited the cab, a valet secured my bag and led me to the welcome center concierge. I noticed April sitting near the indoor fountain talking to a handsome stranger. Well, I assumed he was a stranger, but with April you never knew. She was a hot-guy magnet. She never kept any of them around for any measurable amount of time, she always found fault with them.

April was a gorgeous brunette, slightly taller than me and with a few more curves—her boobs and ass were a little more accentuated than mine. She practically lived in the gym and was actually the ideal weight, not like those skinny girls who starve to stay in a size two. It was her laugh that had caught my attention; she had a very distinct, contagious laugh. I completed the check-in process and rushed over to say hi to the one person who truly felt like family to me. She glanced up in time to see me approaching and jumped from her seat, squealing as she rushed to meet me, and hugging me so hard I started to laugh.

"Finally," she said.

"Finally what?" I asked.

"You're here, silly!"

"I'm glad to see you, too," I replied smiling. "So, who's your friend? Wait—you didn't bring your *new guy* on *our* vacation, did you?" I asked, referring to the handsome man with whom she was engrossed in conversation a few seconds ago.

"Oh, hell no—that *new guy* is old news," she said, waving him off.

I smiled at her, shaking my head. *Another one bites the dust. That's my April.*

"And this guy," she motioned with her head towards the fountain. "He's just someone I was sitting beside on the plane. We struck up a conversation and ended up sharing a cab here. Isn't he hot?"

April walked over to him and introduced us. He was actually even more appealing up close. We exchanged friendly conversation until the concierge notified us that the ferry shuttle to the villa had arrived. We said our good-byes and headed outside—both of us anxious to get to the villa and start our vacation.

The shuttle ride revealed the breathtaking luxuriousness of the beach-fringed volcanic isle. It was a virtual paradise of exotic colors and clear tranquil waters. I was disappointed at the thought of only having a few days here. Our itinerary consisted of snorkeling, soaking up the tropical sun, clubbing and shopping the local boutiques. Oh, and of course the hot guys — the main reason I initially booked this trip, even though recent events had made that motive pointless.

The ferry attendant grabbed our luggage and assisted us off the boat, leading the way once we were safely on the deck. Arriving at the villa, we opened the door to the spacious living room, which revealed a welcome bouquet of flowers in the center of the room. After bestowing the attendant a very generous tip, he wished us a great time on the island, and then he was off.

I darted across the room to the sliding glass doors out onto the patio, which offered a breathtaking view of the Caribbean Sea. The reclining beach chairs were so inviting that I plopped down onto one and sighed. This was just what I needed — the serenity of the water gently splashing on the beach, the coconut palm tree framed view of the sea, the gentle warm breeze washing over me. For the second time in minutes, I longed for an extended vacation here.

"This is beautiful," April breathed. She had walked past me to the edge of the deck, taking in the view of our paradise.

"Let's get showered, changed, and get this vacation started."

"My thoughts exactly," April agreed and we started back inside.

We quickly showered, changed into our bikinis, and walked back out to the patio, enjoying the beautiful view. I looked out at the water, taking note of the sailboats, swimmers, and beach loungers, eager to join them. We grabbed our beach bags and stepped off the deck into a warm and sandy tropical day.

ک ک ک ک

The next morning, as we dressed and began discussing our plans for the day, my phone chimed. I checked it to see a text from someone named Kellan.

Good morning beautiful. Hope you can join us for breakfast before we head out to Lorient Beach. We're downstairs near the pool.

I was confused. *Who the hell is Kellan?*

"What's wrong?" April asked.

"What?" I looked up from the phone.

"I was asking what's wrong?" April walked over and sat down beside me. "Something bad in that text?"

"Oh, no. I guess not. I'm just a little hazy on the details of last night." I scanned my phone for any other strange texts. "Did we make plans to go to the beach with anyone last night?"

"Umm. Yup!" She searched my face, and her brow furrowed. "Don't you remember? We're going with Kellan and Blaine."

"Damn, how much did I drink last night?"

"A lot," April added with a giggle.

"Obviously. Well, Kellan just texted, asking if we want to join them for breakfast. They're out by the pool. I guess I'm game if you are."

"Did you even need to ask? I'm in." April sprang from her seat. "I'll be ready in just a sec. I need to toss some sunscreen and an extra cover-up into my bag first."

"Okay, I'll let him know that we're headed down. Grab my bag from the bed and I'm ready."

I replied to Kellan's text just as April was entering the living room. Grabbing our bags, we exited the patio to start our new day in St. Barts. The instant my feet touched the sand, I sighed, reveling in the beauty of the island. I looked at the sand shimmering in the sunlight like thousands of tiny jewels. The sound of the seagulls directed my attention toward the water; the distant waves were like white horses galloping in unison. The sky was a brilliantly bright baby-blue with white silvery clouds gliding almost imperceptibly against it, the sun shining approvingly on the beautiful scene. This was definitely not a place one should go for just four days.

We were approaching the outdoor dining patio when I caught a glimpse of a man walking toward a group seated near the outer tables. An undeniable familiarity caused me to squint and focus in a little closer.

"That guy looks like..." I didn't finish my statement because he looked back toward the waiter and I saw that he was exactly who I thought he was.

"Who?" April asked.

I didn't answer and took a closer look; there was no way that he could be here. But he was!

"Who?" she demanded, more anxiously this time.

"It's Aiden!"

"What? Where?"

"There! Sitting with those people near the pool," I whispered, motioning slightly with my head in his direction.

"Fuck!" she exclaimed.

"What?" I asked, looking at her.

"He is fucking gorgeous. That's the guy that you're unsure of? Are you crazy? Hey, if you don't want him, I'll gladly take him off of your hands."

"Why does that not surprise me?"

"But wait, what is he doing here? Do you think he's here because of you?" she asked.

"I... I don't think so." He didn't know I was coming to St Barts...or did he? I certainly didn't tell him.

But if he's not here because of me, what are the odds of both of us being in St Barts this weekend? Oh, but Raina had mentioned my itinerary right in front of him. Maybe he did follow me here. But how did he arrange it so quickly? Had Raina helped him?

My shock morphed into anger as the realization hit me. This jerk followed me nearly twenty-four hundred miles!

"Let's go before he spots me. Let's find the guys, have breakfast, and get off this island."

"Are you sure, Aria? I mean, if he came all this way, it would be pretty fucked up if you avoided him," she said, obvious disapproval in her voice.

"Look—what's fucked up is the fact that he followed me here," I said, angry at myself for not being more careful with my plans.

"Actually, you don't know why he's here," she replied.

"You know what? You're right. I don't know, and I don't want to know, so let's go."

"I hope you're not leaving on my account," came a voice from behind me. Not just any voice—*his* voice. The voice that could make me do just about anything. I closed my eyes, attempting to stake claim on some patch of calm. I turned nervously to rest my eyes upon the beautiful man. His dark brown hair was slightly tousled from the gentle breeze, his eyes alive with excitement. He had a bit of stubble. He was usually clean-shaven, but this look suited him. It was incredibly sexy—more so than usual, if that were remotely possible. I unwillingly took him in and realized that my imagination hadn't done him justice. I found myself in awe of his hard, lean frame as he stood before me, shirtless and barefoot. I tried to tear my gaze from his magnificent form, but it was no use. My visual perception was on overload, darting all over his exposed torso, unable to decide which part I appreciated more. Sculpted shoulders accentuated perfectly toned arms, his veins pulsing under the taut skin of his biceps. His muscular chest revealed pecs that begged for my touch. My gaze lingered on the sexiest abs I'd ever seen. The icing on the cake was a defined V, visible thanks to his trunks hanging loosely at his waist. My eyes rested there much longer than they should have. I forced my glance upward. His devilishly handsome features shifted into a knowing grin as he watched me staring. He was flashing that panty-dropping smile that made me weak in the knees, so I could only imagine the effect it had on April.

"Hello, Aria." I loved the way my name slipped from his lips. Actually, I loved the way anything slipped from his lips…hell, I loved his lips.

"What are you doing here?" I demanded.

"Why did you ignore my email?" he countered.

Was he fucking kidding me?

His eyes skimmed my chest. My cover-up was open—exposing my barely-there bikini top. "You're looking well," he said, his eyes flashing back to mine. "I was sitting with my family and noticed you, so I decided to come say hello," he said.

"Oh, so you just happened to notice me? Like you just happened to be here in St. Barts?"

"I would like to introduce you to my family," he replied,

disregarding my questions.

"Why?" I asked.

He smiled and took hold of my hand, lifting it to his lips and planting a soft kiss, his mesmeric touch momentarily interrupting my anger. "Because it's the polite thing to do…especially since they're boring holes into my back, staring over here."

I glanced around him and noticed that all eyes were on us. They didn't look very friendly. Curious, yes, but definitely not friendly. "I don't think so. We have plans."

"It will only take a moment." He glanced at April, as if suddenly aware of her presence and reached out to shake her hand.

"Where are my manners? Hi, I'm Aiden Wyatt."

April stared at him as if he were the only man on earth. Quite frankly, she looked dumbfounded.

"This is April Jensen," I butt in, sparing her the appearance of idiocy.

"Hi, Aiden. It's nice to meet you," she said.

Well, what do you know. It talks.

"It's a pleasure to meet you, April," he said, then immediately returned his attention to me.

"So, my parents…will you walk over to meet them?" he asked.

"Well, we sort of have people waiting for us, and if we don't hurry we'll miss the ferry."

"It will only take a second." He turned to April. "You wouldn't mind would you?" he asked.

"Uh, no. It's no problem," April said.

I glanced at her and mouthed *traitor*. She looked at me and shrugged apologetically. She was such a sucker for a good-looking guy.

A man's voice came from behind me. "Ladies, are you still up for breakfast before we head to Lorient?" I turned to see that Blaine and Kellan had joined us. So these were the guys April and I met at the bar last night? Hot! Seeing them without the veil of alcohol jarred my memory, at least in small increments. After April and I left the villa yesterday, we had walked along the beach. During the course of our island exploration, we followed the lure of loud music and came across a club where we met these two guys. After a few drinks and some dancing, we agreed to hang out with them today. Actually, it was a much-needed distraction for me. For April, it was probably something entirely different.

"Hi guys. We were actually planning to join you for breakfast but we were, uh, detained," I replied.

"No problem. We haven't ordered anything. It was starting to get a little noisy so we decided to come up closer to the villas. Are you ready?" Kellan asked, glancing at Aiden. "We're not interrupting anything, are we?"

I looked up at Aiden whose expression had totally frosted. The twinkle in his eyes had disappeared.

"Of course not, this is my…er…we work together. This is Aiden. Aiden, these are Blaine and Kellan."

Aiden subtly nodded hello and then directed his glare at me. *Oh shit. What is it now?* It wasn't like we were an item; at most we were fuck buddies, plain and simple. We really hadn't established even that much, to be honest.

"Can you excuse us for a second?" Aiden asked, pulling me away without awaiting a reply.

"So is this why you rushed out of town?" he asked, gesturing toward Blaine and Kellan, his temples throbbing.

"What?"

"I think you know what I'm asking," he said.

His reaction caught me off guard. "Aiden, I don't know what you mean. I'm on vacation with a friend—not that I owe you an explanation. So whatever else you are insinuating—don't!"

"You're absolutely right; you don't owe me an explanation," he stated, his calm resurfacing. "I would still like for you to meet my family, and then you can return to your friends."

I turned to look at April, but she was engrossed in conversation with the fellas, so I complied. "Sure, I'd love to," I lied.

"Thank you," he said as our eyes locked. I started to feel that familiar heat that consumed me whenever I was near him. I knew he felt it, too, because that hungry look was back. I wouldn't do this here — especially not with an audience again.

"Shall we?" I motioned toward his parents.

He stared at me, his eyes narrowing. He didn't move. I started walking toward his family and he followed, catching up with me in two short strides.

"We need to have a talk," he stated.

"You're certainly right about that," I retorted.

As we neared the table with his family, I felt extremely self-conscious. They were smartly dressed, even for the beach. And here I was bursting forth with my boobs flashing. These people had a look of affluence and arrogance, much like the look I sometimes saw on Aiden.

"I would like for you all to meet Aria Cason. Aria, this is my mother and father, Sienna and Connor, and my sister and brother, Sloan and Nicholas."

"Hello. It's nice to meet you," I said.

"Lovely to meet you, Aria," his mother said, smiling at me. Maybe I was wrong. She seemed nice, actually. "Aiden, don't be rude, invite her to sit," she instructed.

"Yes, Mother," Aiden replied, offering a seat to me.

"Thank you, but I have plans with some friends, and we're

slightly behind schedule. We were actually about to have breakfast when Aiden spotted me."

I looked over at Aiden; his temples pulsed as he eyed me.

"This is a beautiful island. Are you all here for a family vacation?" I asked. Perhaps this would tell me if Aiden really *had* followed me here.

"It's actually a mixture of business and pleasure," said Connor. "I'm here on business, and we decided to make a vacation of it, as well. Aiden had initially declined our invitation, but surprised us yesterday when he called saying he would join us after all. And you?"

"I'm here for pleasure. I needed to escape Boston for a while," I replied, glancing at Aiden.

"Aria's the President of Communications at Raine Publishing," Aiden offered.

Sienna looked toward Connor. "Raine Publishing, isn't that where you've—"

Aiden quickly interrupted, "I've been interning under her excellent leadership for the last couple of months."

A knowing look seeped into both Connor and Sienna's expressions. Nicholas, though, was the one who spoke. "Oh, so you're the Ms. Cason that Aiden has mentioned? He speaks very highly of you and the inner workings of Raine Publishing."

"Does he?" I asked, astounded. "He can be quite challenging

at times, so I'm rather surprised to hear that."

Nicholas was quite handsome—not as drop dead gorgeous as Aiden, but extremely excellent eye candy none-the-less. If the way his eyes were glued to my chest was any indication, he approved of me, also. He looked at his brother, who was throwing him a warning look.

"Yes, Aiden has always been the challenging one of the bunch," Sloan piped in with a smile. Again it was as though I was missing out on some private joke.

"Well, it was great meeting you all, but I really must go if I'm going to catch the ferry. I hope you enjoy your vacation. And sir, I hope the business end of your trip is productive."

"Yes, it was lovely meeting you, Aria," Sienna added, appraising my attire, and there it was—that conceited look that I knew I'd seen earlier. I returned her fake smile and turned to leave. Aiden followed me.

"That wasn't so bad, now was it? And what do you know, you still have enough time to run along and play with your new friends."

"Play with my new friends? What the f—"

"I need to see you later," he stated matter-of-factly.

"I'll call you when we return from our *play date*," I said.

"See that you do."

Not having time for his bullshit, I turned to leave. I felt his eyes on me as I walked away. A small part of me wanted to turn around to catch one last glance at his body, but I was not about to give him the satisfaction. His audacity was unbelievable. It was as though he was ordering me to meet him, as if *no* wasn't an option. What made him think he had the right to demand or expect anything from me? And why did he suddenly decide to join his family here? Yes, we certainly needed to talk later. There were a few things I needed answers on, and we definitely needed to iron out some shit if he expected me to go along with his little arrangement.

"Hey, what's wrong? You look upset. What happened?" April asked.

I was so lost in thought that I hadn't noticed where I was walking. I ended up heading toward the entrance of the main building and literally ran directly into April.

"Oh, it's nothing," I replied.

"Quite frankly I don't understand why you would be upset at anything at all. It's obvious he's really into you. And he's absolutely gorgeous. So what's the problem?" she asked in disbelief.

"Yes, April, you would say that," I replied, a little more harshly than I had intended. I thought I'd hurt her feelings and quickly apologized. "I'm sorry. You were right, I'm a little upset."

"Well, don't take it out on me. I'm just trying to be

supportive. Besides, I don't know all the details since you've failed to tell me what's really going on between the two of you," she accused. "But I can say this much — it's obvious that *something* is going on, regardless of whether or not you want to admit it."

"You're wrong. Nothing is going on. It's just a big bunch of missteps on my part. Missteps that I intend to straighten out once we get back from Lorient," I declared.

"Well, I'm here if you need to talk about it."

"I know, and I appreciate that. I really do." Sooner or later, I'd have to tell her everything, but not now.

"Okay." She reached out and pulled me into a hug. "I just wanted to put that out there."

"Where are the guys?" I asked.

"They grabbed a table for us. Come on, let's go have some fun!" she squealed, grabbing my hand and pulling me away from the complexities of Aiden Wyatt.

We hopped a bicycle taxi to the port in to order catch the ferry to the neighboring island. I was taking in the scenery and trying my best to concentrate on April, Kellan, and Blaine, but I found myself continuously thinking back to Aiden. The purpose of my trip was to get away from that man and the pressures that accompanied him, but, dammit, those pressures had just followed me to St. Barts.

The ferry was huge and somewhat more crowded than I'd expected. Obviously we were all of the same accord as we eyed the sleek boat docked near the ferry. Kellan and Blaine excused themselves to speak with someone near the quay. When they were a safe distance away, April let me have it.

"I said I'd be here for you as you sort this Aiden thing out, but I had no idea that you would be acting like this. What is going on with you?" she demanded.

"What are you talking about?"

"Oh please! You've been distracted ever since your run-in with that guy. You've missed nearly half the conversation this morning. I don't think the guys noticed much because I've been jumping in covering for your ass. But you need to snap out of this dazed funk you're in, or just make some excuse and go back to the villa. Either way you are not going to ruin my vacation!"

"Ouch!"

"I'm serious, Aria. I don't know what this guy has done to you, but he's definitely done something, because this behavior is so not you."

She was right, but I couldn't explain to her what I didn't understand myself.

I sighed. "I know. I'm sorry. You're right. His appearance has upset my day and that's not fair to you. We're here to have a great time and that's exactly what we'll do," I added, smiling.

"Yeah, whatever." She didn't sound completely convinced.

"I promise. I'll deal with that situation later. For now, it's about having a great afternoon with two hot guys and my best friend. Okay?"

"Okay, but if I see you sinking back into that stink mode, I'm pushing you off the boat." She tried to keep a straight face at the threat, but ended up grinning.

"Deal." I laughed as I tugged her back toward Kellan and Blaine.

The guys had chartered the sailing catamaran, which was a far better option than the crowded ride on the ferry. We boarded, and after a brief introduction to the crew and the amenities, the music began to flow. I watched the sails unfurl as we left the dock for our snorkeling site.

We started with a tour around the island. Everything was gorgeous! What could be more relaxing than sailing with your best friend, a handsome guy, and all the alcohol you wanted?

After an hour or so of snorkeling, we sailed along the coastline, admiring the stunning blue waters as we meandered through the islands. The white sand beaches and seaside cliffs were beautiful, as perfect as postcards. One of the crew members invited us to follow him to the bar, which was well-stocked and complete with a bartender. We ordered drinks and went back up to the deck to lie in the sun as we became better acquainted.

Sipping slowly on one of the island's exotic concoctions, I listened intently to Kellan. He was very intelligent and equally handsome. He was here for a bachelor party. One of his closest friends was tying the knot, and this trip was his last hoorah before the big day next week. He was a really awesome guy, and normally I would have fucked him, but after having been with Aiden, and knowing he was *here*, I couldn't imagine doing anything remotely intimate with Kellan. Just the thought of Aiden and the amazing effect he had on my body was enough to deter me from any other guy.

The trip back to the port was filled with more drinks and laughter. I had been able to keep thoughts of Aiden from my mind…mostly. But it did require a huge amount of effort. Every so often I would feel a small hammer in my stomach just knowing that he was waiting for me. I couldn't help wondering what he would say, what I would agree to, what he would do, what I would allow him to do.

I felt horrible for Kellan because I could tell that he was really into me, which was normally ideal because ultimately all I wanted was sex. And of course, being a guy, he was fine with that. But this was different; I had a different level of guilt because I was here with Kellan with my mind definitely on someone else.

Perhaps Kellan was someone who I could at least remain friends with.

April was really enjoying her time with Blaine. They appeared to really be hitting it off. The sexual chemistry was also equally apparent. But then again, with April there was always a sexual chemistry. That's just how she was. She was a petite sex-bomb — long brunette hair, a killer rack, and a butt that garnered a lot of well-deserved attention. I wondered if she would ever settle down. On occasion she had expressed a desire to get married and have kids, so I knew she really wanted a family of her own. Perhaps it was because her own family was so dysfunctional and she wanted a chance to get it right.

I loved April like a sister. I felt a pang of guilt about that because I have two biological sisters with whom I was once extremely close. I hadn't seen them in several years. An occasional text, email or Skype were all we'd shared since my first college graduation.

April and I met several years ago when we were in college. We connected in a Facebook group for a popular book series, got together one day for lunch, and the rest was history. She meant the world to me and she was the only person I had allowed to get close enough to where it would make a difference.

Watching her now with Blaine did my heart good. She looked so happy. I knew she was already wondering what could be between the two of them. She was so eager to connect with and be with someone in that capacity that it quickly overtook rational thinking. I constantly cautioned her to take her time and never assume she'd found Mr. Right. It was as if I were talking to an inanimate object because she continued to throw caution to the wind. Then there was me. There was no one…and there would be no one, period. I'd told myself that a long time ago. That was why the craziness with Aiden simply needed to stop before it ruined me.

But I knew it wouldn't be easy to let this go, whatever *this* was. I'd told myself that I would not allow him to affect me, yet I'd allowed him to do much more than that. My resolve, my willpower, everything I'd worked so hard to build and maintain, it was all being tested.

If it had been as simple as just sex with him, I think I could have handled that. But this seemed as if I were opening a book that I wasn't prepared to finish. He actually terrified me; what he *represented* terrified me. How could I make it clear that I could not go along with his suggestion? That what had occurred on the yacht the night before I left for St. Barts had to be my last intimate moment with him? How would I make him understand when I couldn't quite register it myself?

Upon reaching the port, I said that I was not feeling well and excused myself, but not before making breakfast plans with

Kellan to make up for the white lie. I explained to April that I needed some time alone to talk to Aiden, so she and Blaine made plans for an early dinner alone.

We walked back to the villa in silence. She knew I was struggling with this and allowed me time to gather my thoughts in peace. Once inside, she gave me a reassuring hug and then went to her room. Opening the door to my own room, I gasped. Aiden was there—sitting in a chair near the bed.

❧Chapter Nine❧

"What the fuck? What are you doing here? How did you know where I was staying and how did you get in here?" The questions flowed without pause.

"Which question would you like for me to answer first?" he asked as he stood and casually walked over to me. Or so I thought. He actually walked past me to close and lock the door. I turned to face him as I heard the lock click.

"What do you think you're doing?" I demanded. I was beyond pissed. "Surely you realize I could have you arrested! You can't simply enter anyplace you want. Unwelcomed and uninvited, I may add."

"Can't I?" he asked smugly, as if he actually could do whatever he damned well pleased. My anger did nothing to lessen his calm demeanor, which was very aggravating.

It no longer mattered at this point. This was the last straw. Everything regarding his fucked up proposal — which I had actually considered earlier today and was quite frankly still jumbled in my head — didn't matter. I wasn't going to sit by and allow him to do whatever he wanted, whenever he wanted!

"I don't know how you got in here, but you are leaving — now! Get out! If I have to say it again, I'm calling security."

He replied with an exasperated sigh, as if dealing with an unruly child.

"Aria, we agreed to speak after your excursion, did we not? I'm simply expediting our discussion."

"Are you serious? So you see nothing wrong with this picture?"

"Well, since you asked, I don't particularly care for your choice of attire. Not that I don't thoroughly enjoy seeing every bit of your body, but that's just the problem. It wasn't for me; it was for that ridiculous guy you were with earlier. I didn't like that."

What planet was this guy from?

"Aiden, there is so much spinning around in my brain right now that I literally don't know what to say." I walked past him to the bathroom. He followed me, of course. Why should that surprise me?

"How about I start?" he asked.

I looked in the mirror, and the reflection staring back at me was a hot mess. My hair was doing its own thing, and my makeup was pretty much non-existent. I'd planned to have time to prepare myself before seeing him, but now, with him here, everything that I'd planned eluded me. I was both nervous and upset that he had invaded my privacy; he had a shameless disregard for boundaries where I was concerned. After splashing some cold water on my face, I reached for the towel. Aiden grabbed it from the warmer and turned me to face him, drying my face. I didn't bother objecting.

We stood facing each other, staring intently, my anger quickly dissipating as the deep facets of his green eyes sought out and captured me. "You know I want you, and I'll admit my methods to make that happen have been less than ideal, but I don't think rationally when it comes to you. I'm not at all myself."

"Oh, so this breaking-and-entering thing isn't the norm for you? Hmm, never would have guessed, because you're quite proficient at it."

He laughed. I loved his laugh; it was sexy, just like everything else about him.

"I would say thank you, but I don't think it was meant as a compliment. Besides I don't wish to be complimented for breaking the law," he said.

"Then maybe you shouldn't break the law. Now there's a novel idea."

"I'm relieved to see you've recovered your sense of humor. I was worried earlier; you were quite agitated."

"Was I?" I asked sarcastically. *What? Did he expect me to run into his arms and ask what took him so long to get here?* Seriously. "Are you going to answer my questions, or do I have to force you to leave — which I should do anyway — because this is insane."

"I understand my being here caught you off guard. So how

about we start there?"

"No, we really don't need to start there. You explained you were here with your family. While I think there is more to it, I'm not going to focus on that right now. I need to know how you knew what villa I was in, how you got in, and how you knew this was my room."

He offered his hand to me. Mindlessly, I placed mine in his and followed him from the bathroom. He led us to the chair where he'd been sitting and pulled me into his lap.

He looked at me before tracing his finger down my cheek.

"First off, you ignored me when I emailed you. You should know I won't tolerate being ignored."

"Excuse me? If you think—"

He placed his hand over my mouth. "Do you have any idea how badly I want you?"

I pulled his hand away. "No, but I'm starting to think its bordering on obsessive."

"Funny you say that…" he started but trailed off, not bothering to finish his thought.

"What?"

"Nothing. I was thinking aloud."

There was a sudden knock at the door.

"Aria, I'm leaving to meet Blaine. Let me know how things go with tall, dark, and gorgeous."

I blushed, embarrassed and annoyed that Aiden now had the satisfaction of knowing that we'd been discussing him.

"Okay, have fun," I replied.

I sat staring at him, waiting for the sound of April leaving the villa. Every ounce of my resolve disappeared when I looked into his eyes. They imprisoned every part of my mind. As soon as we heard the door close, he pulled me toward him and softly kissed me. It wasn't the aggressive kiss I'd grown to expect from him. It was slow, soft, and deep. His tongue entered my mouth and softly dueled with mine, sensually exploring. His hands, initially cradling my face, moved gently down my neck to my shoulders and then to my back, forcing me closer. I didn't pull away. I sank deeper into him, tasting him. His kiss changed, morphing into the ravenous assault with which I had become familiar. He scooped me up as he stood, and laid me on the bed. He straddled me, kissing me as if he had a need that only I could sate. His hands moved down my thighs, reaching underneath, kneading my behind. When I moaned into his mouth, he broke our kiss, sitting up and looking down at me, and breathing as heavily as I was.

Every rejection I'd ever thought of feeding him was gone. I wanted him inside me. He traced his finger across my lips and breathed deeply, closing his eyes.

"Now, back to your questions," he said.

Wait, what? He had done it yet again! In a matter of minutes he'd managed to alter my emotions from shock, to anger, to lust, and finally exasperation. He was the puppeteer, and I reacted to whatever string he pulled. I was baffled as to how this was happening and why I couldn't seem to stop it. I detested this vulnerability, but it was apparently beyond my control.

"Aria."

"Yes?"

"Did you hear me?"

"Yes, I heard you. Get off me," I demanded.

He looked at me for a brief moment and slowly stood, returning to the chair.

Hoping to gain some semblance of self-containment—now that he was no longer touching me—I sat up and moved to the edge of the bed. "My questions. Okay. Well, how did you know where to find me?"

"I contacted the concierge," he stated.

I crossed my arms and his eyes flickered from my face to my chest then back to my eyes. "You asked him? And just like that, he told you the location of the villa?"

"Yes."

I tilted my head and narrowed my gaze as I considered his obvious lack of detail. "So, you're saying that if I were to call the concierge and ask for the location of your villa, he would just tell me?"

"I'm pretty sure he wouldn't." He started to smirk but stopped when he saw my temper easing from behind its wall.

"So what am I missing here?"

"I'm not sure what you mean."

"Oh, I think you are. Please stop with the games and tell me what I want to know. If you can't do that, I want you to leave."

He sighed. "When you met my family, my father mentioned that we were here on business. Well, his business is this property. He visits once a year and we all come. Something of a family vacation."

"So you're saying that your father has some type of property ownership here, sort of like a timeshare?"

"Yes, sort of."

"How did you get inside the villa?" I asked.

"The patio door," he replied. "It was open."

Did we rush out without locking it? I crossed my legs and thought back to this morning. That very well could have been true because I didn't recall locking it.

"So you saw that as an open invitation to come inside?" I asked.

"I didn't say that," he replied.

"You aren't saying much of anything," I said.

"I'm sorry you see it that way." He stood and walked over to the window.

I turned toward him. His back was to me. "How did you know this was my room?" I asked.

He turned around and his eyes rested on mine. "It smelled like you."

I knew it was insane, but hearing that he was familiar with my smell did crazy things to me.

"I want this to happen, Aria," he stated. He crossed the room and sat on the bed.

I fervently wanted to say no, but some part of me that I didn't recognize just wouldn't let me. I sighed and pulled my bottom lip into my mouth. "I want this too, but on my terms."

"Your terms?" he asked, grinning. "I don't think so, sweetheart."

"And why not?" And why was he so irresistible?

"My proposition is what it is. There will be no negotiations."

"I think you've seen enough of me to realize that this is asking a lot, possibly more than I can commit."

"Of course. I know it's a challenge for you because you're accustomed to being in control and having everyone do as you say. But so am I. That being the case, I'll tell you how this is going to play out. When it comes to us, doing this, I'm the one in control." I opened my mouth to object, and he reached over and pinched my lips together. "No, no, no, we aren't going to have any of that back talk."

"Back talk? Who are you supposed to be, my father?" I asked, removing my cover-up, leaving me in just my bikini.

He glanced at my chest and shifted his gaze to my face. "No, but if you'd like, you can call me daddy when I'm fucking you. Besides I wasn't finished. You need to make a decision—now."

I willed myself to break eye contact before I caved. Looking down at my feet, I lectured myself on all the possible downfalls to my agreeing.

Aiden stood and then kneeled in front of me. He looked up at me and smiled. "What are you thinking?" I turned away from his beautiful eyes, but he reached up and placed his finger on my chin, forcing my gaze to meet his.

"Aria?" His eyes sensually pleaded for my consent.

How did he go from demanding to enticing in the span of seconds—both tactics compelling me to acquiesce? I swallowed my refusal as I peered helplessly into his beseeching green gaze.

"Yes," I whispered.

He exhaled deeply and pulled me into his arms. "I promise you will not regret me, Aria."

How could I have possibly told him I already did?

❧Chapter Ten❧

The remainder of my trip was an anxious blur. Aiden had left my room with a promise that I wouldn't regret him, and I hadn't heard anything from him since. When April had returned to the villa, I filled her in on everything—or at the very least, I told her Aiden liked me and wanted to have a sexually monogamous relationship for the next four weeks. She was…well, she was April. She was excited, turned on, and insistent that this was an ideal agreement. I, on the other hand, knew differently. I skipped over the parts about the excessive masturbation that he'd inspired. I also somehow left out the incidents that had occurred in the elevator, in my office, and on the dinner cruise. I'd tell her all of that later, when the shock of my even considering this wore off.

Later that evening, April and I joined Kellan and Blaine at one of the local clubs, which in the end was not the remedy I had hoped. I barely paid attention to the conversations or to Kellan. I apologized for my rudeness and explained that I was worried about a work-related issue. Being a bit of a workaholic himself, he offered his understanding.

This trip was so unlike our previous getaways. April and I never entangled ourselves with guys to this degree. Well, at least I didn't. I blamed Aiden. He had thrown everything out of whack, not just by showing up, but by making me anxious about what was coming next.

The next morning we had breakfast, grabbed a shuttle to the welcome center, and checked out. April and I headed to the airport in silence. I was lost in thoughts of what awaited me in Boston. April, all goo-goo over Blaine, was in the midst of texting back and forth with him.

"I miss you already." April hugged me before we headed to our separate gates.

This was always the hated part of our trips. "I know. Me, too. You should move to Boston."

"Especially now, because you need my help with Aiden," she joked.

I couldn't have returned her smile if I'd tried. She noticed my reticence, and squeezed my arm in encouragement. "I know better than anyone why you have your walls up with him, or with any man for that matter. But it's going to be okay."

"Well, I guess I'll find out soon enough." I pulled my phone from my pocket to check the time.

"Enjoy it, Aria. And promise me you won't renege on your agreement with him."

"Okay." I wasn't sure if I could make that promise.

"I'm serious."

"Okay, okay. Geez."

"And let me know how it goes." She hugged me again. "I love you."

"I love you, too. Have a safe flight."

My return flight was uneventful, but long. I donned my headphones and loaded one of my favorite playlists to make the trip more bearable. I arrived at Boston Logan International Airport at three o'clock, grabbed a cab and headed to the condo. Odd how it didn't seem as though I'd escaped at all, since my problem had simply followed me to St. Barts. I was even more rattled now than when I'd left.

As I headed to the elevator, I was greeted by Silas, who walked around the front desk to hand a package to me. I didn't pay much attention to it as he secured my luggage and escorted me to my door. I thanked him and he headed back to his station.

Opening my door, I was immediately embraced by a lovely, sweet fragrance — the room was filled with Phal Sogo Rose orchids. Orchids were my favorite flowers and these arrangements were breathtakingly beautiful. Some of the flowers were in vases, others floating in water in glass cylinders. I walked over to the bar and retrieved the envelope sitting where I wouldn't miss it. There was nothing on the front. I opened it.

Welcome home, Aria. I recently learned these were your favorite. They are exquisite, but pale in comparison to you.

A.

I read the card again and looked around the room in disbelief at the dozens of deep red orchids. I closed my eyes, inhaling the wonderful fragrance. I found myself smiling and reluctantly thinking warmly of him. He had invaded every part of my life. Even if I wanted to forget all about him, he was obviously not going to allow it.

I called Silas and asked about the flowers. Apparently, they'd been delivered about an hour before I'd arrived home. I was relieved to know that Silas had opened the door to allow the delivery person in. I was sure that was the case, but after walking in on Aiden in my villa in St. Barts, I wanted to be certain.

I walked over to the iPod in-wall mount control and gently tapped on the multi-touch display, swiping through a range of applications to locate my music files. Once I'd selected a playlist, I headed to the bathroom to start a bath, and was surprised to find two more orchid bouquets on the bathroom counter, and another envelope lay beside the glass vase. I couldn't help but feel excited…nervous, even. I picked it up and was disturbed to see my fingers trembling. What had this man done to me?

Aria,

I'm sure you've noticed that orchids have been placed in every room of your home. Each time you see an orchid now, you'll think of me. I'm most assuredly thinking of you.

A.

Even in his absence, I felt his presence. I ran my fingers across the words on the note, smiling at his handwriting, pleased he'd taken the time to write the note himself. I didn't quite know what I expected from Aiden, but it wasn't to be wooed or courted. I'd never experienced that before. Not because there weren't many eager men, but because I never allowed anyone to get that close. This feeling was new to me, and, surprisingly, I actually liked it — but I recognized that part of me didn't want to. As exciting as this was, the piercing intensity of warning bells sounded in the background.

I admired the flowers while various Aiden-filled scenarios raced through my head, then returned the note to the counter before turning to start my bath. The sounds of Alec Blaac's, *I'm The Man*, filled the room. That song could be a tribute to Aiden Wyatt — he was undeniably a man who broke the mold. A man who exuded strength, a man who showed no signs of surrender or retreat.

I left the bathroom in search of a bottle of white wine. Entering the kitchen, I found more orchids in vases and glass cylinders, and yet another note. I opened it.

Aria,

Text me when you've read all four notes. I'm anxious to hear your reply.

A.

Four notes? What fourth note? I poured a glass of wine and walked to the bedroom. There were orchids on each nightstand, but no note. I checked the guest rooms and the guest baths and found more flowers, but I still didn't see a note. I walked downstairs—more flowers, but no note. I returned to the bedroom, passing my luggage and the package from Silas. I slowed my search and turned, focusing on the package Silas had given me downstairs.

Picking it up, I walked to the bathroom, where I sat at the bureau and opened the box to see another box with the Bergdorf Goodman logo. It was an order I'd placed before leaving for my trip. Since I couldn't find the fourth note, I decided to forego the search and take some time to unwind.

After a long soak and two glasses of wine, I was relaxed and tired when I finally emerged from the tub. I finished the last of the wine as the evening progressed and eventually fell asleep in bed while watching TV.

The next morning, I awoke surrounded by the sweet fragrance of orchids. I smiled and sighed happily, thinking about the person responsible for my concentrated olfactory impressions.

I'd planned to work from home today. I was glad I did, because I wasn't quite ready to face Aiden. The doorbell rang. I wondered who that would be at eight o'clock in the morning. I got out of bed, donned my robe, and headed to the door. I looked at the monitor and saw that it was a delivery man. My home deliveries were typically work or food related. I hadn't ordered any food so maybe it was something from the office.

"Package for Ms. Aria Cason," he said, when I opened the door.

"Yes. I'm Ms. Cason."

"Can you please sign here, ma'am?"

I signed, and he passed the package to me. I reached for my purse sitting on the table near the door to give him a tip.

"Thanks, Ms. Cason, but the sender has more than covered the tip. Have a great day, ma'am."

"Thank you…" I looked at the name tag on his shirt. "Henry."

"You're welcome." He nodded with a smile and turned to leave.

Rather perplexed, I closed the door and looked at the package. It was a box; I shook it and heard slight movement. I doubted this was from work. Taking a seat on the couch, I unwrapped it, and atop the white gift wrap tissue was a note. I opened it and immediately recognized the handwriting. It was from Aiden—the fourth note! I silently scolded myself for feeling this elation, but I smiled all the same.

Aria,

I'd initially thought we should enjoy a quiet dinner at my place, but I ultimately opted for something a little different. Please meet me outside your building promptly at 7:00 this evening. Your attire is enclosed. Looking forward to our evening.

A.

I placed the note on the sofa and removed the tissue from the box. The first item was a white short-sleeved sheer voile shirt. He had good taste. I placed the shirt on the sofa and quickly retracted my statement about his good taste when I held up a very short plaid skirt. In a rush, I reviewed the other contents: a pair of Chloe wedged sneakers, white knee high socks, a black ultra-sheer lace bra. Confident that it was the wrong size, I held it up: 36C. Damn, he even picked the right size. Should I be pleased that he knew my body so well? I wasn't. In a relatively short amount of time, he'd gotten to know me on a disturbingly intimate level.

The last thing in the box was a pair of matching lace boy shorts. I placed them beside the bra. They really were sexy. I ran my fingers over the soft material searching for the tags and was surprised to see that they were Kiki De Montparnasse. The only place I'd seen these was Barney's in New York. I analyzed the other items. Each piece had a designer name tag. What the fuck? Something didn't add up. I knew his salary didn't support routine shopping at Barney's.

I held up the skirt again. It was super short; if I were to bend over even in the slightest, my ass would be exposed. I was sure that was his intent. I felt a twinge in my lady parts. *Damn you, Virginia.* Must you always betray me when it comes to that man? I dropped the clothes in the box and headed to the kitchen to get a cup of tea.

Although I hated to admit it, I was extremely excited and curious. I couldn't imagine what he had planned or where he would be taking me that those clothes would be appropriate. On second thought, perhaps I should be less excited and a little bit worried. Where *would* he take me that these types of clothes would be appropriate?

Should I text him and get some details? Nah. He would frown on that. He was constantly telling me I was too uptight and overly cautious. I couldn't let him see how right he was by trying to wrangle information from him about tonight. Should I just go with it? Could I even do that? Maybe I should focus on my curiosity. If I would be wearing that scant outfit, I was definitely intrigued about his attire.

I decided to "go with the flow" as Aiden put it. I realized I had a goofy smile plastered on my face and tried to mask it by biting my lip. He really was quite amazing.

I went about drinking my tea. The aroma alone was enough to make me smile, and the taste was absolutely delicious. Just as I was about to go for a refill, my phone buzzed somewhere in the background. Damn, where had I left it? By the time I'd finally located it on my bathroom sink, I'd missed the call. I never remembered to change it from vibrate when I awoke or when I left the office. Glancing at the call log, I saw that I had missed two: one from April, and the most recent was from Aiden.

Ping. A text. It was Aiden.

I just called your cell; no answer. Checking to see if you received the gift.

I quickly replied. *Gift? Is that what it was? I thought it was delivered to the wrong address. Looks like it should have been delivered to a boarding school student. Judging from the length of the skirt, I would say a 5th grader?*

His reply was instant. *Is that a sense of humor? Didn't know you had one of those. Oh, I forgot, it was in the box, too. Glad to see that it fits.*

I laughed out loud. *Speaking of fitting…how did you know my bra size?*

He replied, *I'll tell you tonight.*

Tell me now.

No…tonight. I'll pick you up at 7:00.

I'm not sure about this.

Just go with it, Aria.

I looked up at my reflection in the mirror. Could I do this?

Ping. Another text from Aiden.

Don't analyze this, Aria.

Fuck it. I replied to his text: *I'll see you at 7:00, fully dressed in my grade-school attire.*

Good, that's just how I want you. See you soon.

I spent the better part of the day in teleconferences or sending and replying to email. Around three o'clock, I decided to call it quits for the day. I was still anxious about tonight. I felt giddy inside, almost like a child anticipating Christmas.

My phone rang as I headed to the kitchen for a bottle of water, and I reached for it as I opened the fridge door. "Hello."

"Finally! Where have you been?" It was April, and she was yelling. "Do you have any idea how many times I have called and texted you?"

"Sorry, April, I've had a lot going on." I grabbed a bottle of water and closed the fridge.

"What can you possibly have going on other than work? Don't answer that because I already know: nothing. When it comes to you, that's all it ever is, since you don't date or fuck unless it's out of town."

"Welllllll," I said, dragging out the "l".

"Oh my God! No!"

"Yes, I'm going on an actual in-town date, and believe me, I'm just as shocked as you are." I grabbed a glass of ice and opened the bottle.

"Why am I just hearing about him?"

"You kind of already know about him."

"Wait, is it Aiden?"

"Yes," I replied and took a long sip of water.

"So you didn't back out! I knew you wouldn't. I knew something was there. The sexual tension between the two of you was seriously hot."

"Really?" I checked the time and headed to the bathroom.

"Yes, really."

"Sorry, I haven't really given you many details because I was on the fence for a long time, especially since he gagged and fucked me in my office."

"You're fucking kidding me! Not you! Not Ms. Always Professional! Tell me everything!"

"I'll have to catch you up later, I need to get showered and shave my legs before he gets here. He has some sort of kinky surprise for me."

"Kinky surprise?"

"Yes, I received a delivery package today, and I opened it to find a note and really trashy, although sexy, outfit—complete with a three-inch prep school skirt and a pair of Chloe wedged sneakers!"

"I need details. Now!" She practically screamed.

"I will. I promise. Tomorrow. For now, I need to get a move on."

"Okay, tomorrow, first thing. But before you go, there's something I really need to talk to you about," April said.

"Can't it wait?"

"No, it can't."

I sighed, growing terribly impatient with her. "Okay, what's your emergency this time?"

She let out a deep breath. "Well, it's not so much as my emergency as it is yours."

"What? What are you talking about?"

"Remember our trip to Venezuela last summer?"

"Ugh! Yeah, how could I forget?" I said with disdain, as unwelcomed memories flooded my mind.

"Well, you weren't saying *ugh* when you were coming, now, were you?" she asked.

"No, I'm not referring to me and you. Well, not really. I'm thinking of that drunken regret better known as Dane."

"Well, actually, that's why I've been trying to reach you."

"Really? Why? That's definitely not anything I want to be reminded of. What happened in Venezuela stays in Venezuela. Isn't that our standing agreement for all trips?" I opted for a bath instead of the shower, thinking it would soothe my nerves. I sat on the side of the tub trying to decide which bubble bath I wanted.

"Well, yes it is, but something's happened," she said, her voice laced with worry.

I waited for her to finish. When she didn't say anything, I

asked. "What is it?"

"His wife called me."

"What? Wife? What are you talking about?"

"Fuck. Talk about timing. Hey, Blaine is on the other line and we're trying to plan a trip this weekend. I'll call you back in a few. Answer your phone!" She hung up.

What the hell? My stomach a tangle of anxiety and confusion. Dane, my vacation hookup, was married? And why did the wife call April? Oh hell, just what I need to add to my crap list.

There was nothing I could do but place the Dane thing on the back-burner until April called back. I was in hyper mode as it was and unable to focus on too much craziness at once. The apprehension about tonight had already taken its toll on me. I wanted to just go with it, but I was finding that awfully difficult. The insane outfit was more than enough to cause me to back out, but the part of me that was mesmerized by that man wouldn't let me.

After a long bath, I dried my hair and walked to the bedroom. I looked at the clothes lying on my bed. Butterflies fluttered like crazy in my stomach as I stared at the skimpy clothing. I took a few deep breaths, hoping to calm my nerves. I couldn't bring myself to put the clothes on just yet so I returned to the bathroom to finish my hair and makeup. I wasn't sure of the appropriate hairstyle for those clothes. I laughed at the thought of pigtails. If we weren't going out, I would have actually tried that. In the end, I opted to wear it straight, deducing that it would complete the "school-girl" look.

I glanced at the clock and saw that I had only thirty minutes before I would see Aiden. I tossed my towel on the bed and slipped on the boy shorts and bra, appreciating the feel of the soft lace on my skin. Sitting on the bed, I pulled on the knee socks, followed by the shirt, skirt and shoes. *I must look like such a floozy.* I walked into the closet to see my reflection in the full length mirror. Everything fit perfectly, I'll give it that much, but I looked like a slut. I turned to the side and bent over as though touching my ankle and just as I suspected, my ass was on full display.

I stood up and wondered what Aiden's first thought would be when he saw me. I realized that was a ridiculous question. He would immediately think sex. I did look hot; I would certainly do me. I went to my nightstand for my faux reading glasses and returned to the mirror. Perfect way to complete the look. The style of glasses was even more appealing, given my high cheek bones. I was actually turned on by the image staring back at me. Long, raven-black hair cascaded my shoulders, offering a contrast to my golden skin. My light hazel eyes, framed by long, curly lashes, were twinkling with excitement despite my extreme apprehension. The finishing touch was bright red Rogue Dior lipstick to accentuate my full lips. I smiled as I thought of him smearing it later.

It was a quarter to seven. Grabbing my phone, I took a few selfies to send to April. I could easily picture her face when she saw these. Her eyes would bulge and her mouth would be wide open. That's the exact same reaction I had when I looked in the mirror.

I couldn't go downstairs dressed like this. I grabbed a short, fitted coat with a concealed zip and slipped it on. It was short, but still considerably longer than my barely-there skirt. I grabbed my purse and headed downstairs.

I stepped out of the elevator and saw Aiden walking into the building. He was wearing an exquisitely cut charcoal gray suit. He was so fucking hot that it was impossible to look at him without reacting. He smiled at me, and I practically stopped breathing. Would he always have that effect on me?

Within a few strides, he was beside me. "Hello, gorgeous."

"Hello, Aiden." My stomach was doing flip-flops and my heart was racing. I was always in hyperdrive every single time he so much as glanced at me.

"I like the glasses."

"I'm glad you approve. But seriously, what was the thought behind the costume?"

His eyes narrowed slightly. "Are you referring to the clothing that had better be underneath that jacket?" he asked.

"And if they aren't?" I teased.

"Do I look worried?"

"Are you always so fucking arrogant?"

"Is your mouth always so foul?"

"What can I say? I guess some people bring out the worst in me."

"Oh, is that what it is?"

"Definitely."

He leaned in and kissed me softly on the cheek. I inhaled, savoring his unique smell, then he grabbed my hand and led me to the door.

"Good evening, Ms. Cason. Good evening, sir," Silas said as he held the door open.

"Hello, Silas," I replied. I took a deep breath and walked into a night I was certain I wouldn't soon forget.

৯Chapter Eleven৯

A limousine was parked in front of the building, complete with a chauffeur positioned near the rear door. I stood there, slightly bewildered, as another detail of the evening presented itself. Aiden placed his hand at the small of my back, leading me to the limo. I looked up at him, again questioning his intentions.

"What?" he asked.

"What are you...? What's going on?"

He motioned for the driver to open the door. "Aria, just get in please," Aiden said impatiently.

I glanced at the chauffeur and back at Aiden before I nervously slid in. Aiden said something to the driver that I couldn't quite hear before joining me.

"Relax," he breathed in my ear, his voice smoky.

My stomach was doing somersaults.

The car maneuvered into the flow of traffic and we were off.

Aiden found my hand and slowly traced his fingers lightly across the top—an attempt to place me at ease that had the opposite effect. I was more on edge. I didn't do well without details. I needed to know what was going on.

Gazing out the window, I made a useless effort to determine our destination. I was unable to ascertain much more than the obvious as we approached downtown Boston. Turning toward him, I found he was looking down at me. I was certain he saw the trepidation in my eyes; there was no way I could have hidden it even if I'd tried.

He smiled and my stomach fluttered. The prominent jawline, the full lips, the deep emerald eyes—he was a devastatingly handsome man!

"This is challenging for you," he said.

"Yes," I replied, my voice small.

"Trust me, Aria," he said, his eyes compelling me, but I looked away as he continued to stroke my hand.

Did I trust him? If I did, would my stomach be in knots like this? Was it a matter of trust or the lack of control that made me want to ask him to take me home? Or maybe it was the fact that underneath this jacket was a scantily dressed woman who could have easily passed for a stripper.

The car eventually slowed and stopped in front of a tall building. I couldn't quite see the name. When the driver opened the door, Aiden got out and offered his hand to assist me. Once on the sidewalk, I could read the tasteful script of the sign. *Seducente.* What had I gotten myself into?

Aiden continued to hold my hand as we walked towards the entrance. The last person whose hand I held in public was April. I *never* did this. It felt nice; I loved the warm feel of his hand over mine.

I didn't recognize the building or the name. It was a relatively new construction with a unique façade, which didn't follow a regular grid pattern. The windows resembled doors with shutters, alternating between opened and closed. On either side of the entrance, there were two doormen in expensive looking suits who seemed more like a security detail than doormen. What was this place, and why would Aiden want me dressed like this? What the fuck had happened to my sense of judgment since meeting this man?

"Good evening, Mr. Wyatt," they both said as we approached. Aiden nodded as one of them held the door open. We stepped into a lavish lounge complete with oversize chairs, large TV screens on every wall, and a bar on both sides of the room. At the center was a large desk with two seated attendants. The wall directly behind them boasted the *Seducente* logo in a silver cursive font.

We walked past the desk, behind the wall, to a discreet set of elevators. Aiden hit the call button and when the elevator arrived, guided me inside and pressed the button for the twentieth floor. He was still holding my hand, passing his thumb back and forth along the top, once more trying to reassure me—it was as though he knew whatever he'd planned was going to totally freak me out.

The elevator stopped at the twentieth floor, and the doors

opened to a scene that gave me more questions than answers. The room was dimly lit and there was music playing in the background. It seemed like a club, but more subdued — some people were dancing, some just relaxing, listening to the music and drinking cocktails. To the immediate right of the door was another attendant. She was an attractive brunette dressed in a formfitting black uniform. It was very sexy, yet tasteful, suiting the overall look of everything I'd seen so far. I was even more uncomfortable with my clothing after observing the elite atmosphere in this place and its clientele. There was no way I was taking off my fucking jacket. Why would Aiden do this? Upset, I pulled my hand from his as I looked around the room. He looked at me, questioning my reaction.

"Good evening, Mr. Wyatt," said the brunette. She was smiling, a bit too much for my taste, as she looked at Aiden. He whispered something to her and she passed him a card and then glanced at me.

"Aria." He turned, holding his hand out to me. I reluctantly grasped it, and he led me to a closed door that opened on a long corridor. At the far end of the hall was another door, and Aiden unlocked it with a slide of the card. He opened it and turned to me. "Ladies first."

I walked in and again was shocked, as it was not what I had anticipated. Honestly, I didn't know what to expect. In the far corner of the room was a table set for two, complete with candles, wine chilling in a bucket, and silver domes covering plates.

"See? Nothing to be anxious about," he said. "I hope you're hungry."

I was so nervous that my hunger had faded somewhere far into the background.

"Can I help you out of your jacket?" he asked.

"No, I'm fine."

He laughed. "Do you plan to wear it all night?"

"And what if I do?"

"Do you think I would even allow that?"

"It's not like you have any say."

"Surely you don't think I requested you dress a specific way only to have you keep it hidden from me?"

"I don't know what to think, quite honestly." I replied curtly.

"Fine, Aria, I'll humor you, at least until after we've eaten." He pulled out a chair for me, and I begrudgingly took a seat.

Once he'd poured a glass of wine for each of us, he removed the silver domes from the plates.

"It's dover sole with capers and bay shrimp," he said, eyeing me closely. "Are you going to eat, or will you refuse to do that also?"

I took a sip of wine. "I'll eat, but only because I want to. If I already had something in my stomach, nothing would give me more pleasure than to refuse, if for nothing else than to show you that you aren't in control."

"Oh, but I am, Ms. Cason," he replied, taking a bite of his food.

"So, it's back to *Ms. Cason* again?" I asked.

"It's whatever you want it to be."

He was right, he was in control. Despite my obvious resistance, the result was always the same—his words, his eyes, or his touch obliterated my resolve.

We finished our meal and stepped outside to the patio. I was still wearing my jacket. He stared intently at me. "You're beautiful," he said, leaning down and kissing me softly on my cheek. "What's it going to take to get you out of that jacket?" he asked, appraising me from head to toe.

"Lots of alcohol," I replied.

"Let's go inside." He grabbed my hand, led me back into the room and closed the door. I watched in nervous silence as he strolled over to a bar and poured two drinks, and then held one out to me.

"Drink this. It will help you relax."

I looked at him and then glanced at the crystal glass of cinnamon-colored liquor.

"Help me relax, or cause me to go along with whatever freaky escapade you have in mind?"

He chuckled and cocked his head in that sexy way that made me want to do whatever he asked — even without the liquor. "Sweetheart, you're going to do as I say regardless, or you wouldn't have come this far. But this will not work if you're not willing to part with your control issues."

What the fuck? *Hello kettle, I'm cat.* "*My* control —"

He placed his finger over my lips before I could finish. "Drink," he ordered.

I stared at the glass he'd proffered and finally took it from his hand. Looking directly into his eyes, I hesitantly placed the glass to my mouth.

"You can trust me," he said, his voice was low and husky. "I won't do anything to you that you won't enjoy, and if I do, you can stop me."

He studied me as the glass lingered at my lips. He'd been very reassuring up to this point, and he was right — why come this far if I were planning to back out? I did as he said and the soft burn of the liquor slid down my throat. It was strong, but it was really good. "What am I drinking?" I asked.

"Armagnac. It's a cognac."

"It's good, I like it."

"Drink. It. All," he said, seductively enunciating each word. And just like that, like some spellbound teenager, I did exactly as he said.

"See, you can be good with the proper incentive."

"Did I blink and miss something? What incentive?" I asked.

He took the glass from me and placed it on the bar.

"Oh, I think you know."

"Well, I don't think I do," I challenged.

He grabbed my waist and pulled me to his chest. "Let me taste." He placed his mouth on mine, slipped his tongue between my lips, and skillfully traced the inner edge of my mouth. "Mmm, it does taste good." Pulling me closer, his strong hands glided down my back, and lower still as he grabbed my behind and clutched it tightly. He licked into my mouth and I moaned, relishing his taste, his touch, and his hardness as I felt it slowly rise, pressing against my stomach. He slid one hand up, reaching the nape of my neck, and then he suddenly grabbed my hair and forcefully yanked my head back. His tongue snaked the side of my neck, and then I felt the gentle sting as he bit the hollow of my throat.

"Ahh," I moaned.

"Hmm, seems I've found a sensitive spot. That's good to know." He chuckled and slowly released me. "Take off the jacket, Aria." His eyes were hooded with lust as he stepped back, looking at me expectantly.

I didn't know if it was the music, the dark lighting of the room, or the liquor—probably the latter—but I had totally fallen prey to this man's will. I wanted him to do whatever he pleased. I was willing to do whatever he asked if it resulted in the erotic heat that was pulsing through every part of me. That was saying a lot for someone like me who rarely — no scratch that — who *never* released control of anything. Very slowly, I unzipped my jacket and shrugged it off. Aiden's gaze darkened as it traveled down my body. He was pleased.

"You like?" I asked.

"Indeed I do. Very much. Turn around."

I did as he asked and then looked over my shoulder to see him approaching.

"Bend over."

Knowing what he wanted to see, I slowly leaned down and grabbed my ankles.

He walked behind me and grabbed my ass. "Very, very nice, Ms. Cason," he said as he moved his hands across my cheeks. He reached between my legs and rubbed his fingers over the lace material that provided the thinnest of barriers to my sex.

"Come have a seat," he said.

I followed him, thinking we would sit on the leather couch in the center of the room, but he walked past it. He led me to another room that looked, inexplicably, like an office. He motioned for me to sit in the chair facing a desk, which he walked behind and took a seat.

"Ms. Cason, I understand that you were caught cheating on your final exam."

I stared at him—dumbfounded.

One dark brow arched, and then it dawned on me. He wanted me to role-play. That should be easy enough, especially with the number of fantasies I'd acted out with B.O.B. So why was I hesitating?

He continued. "As the college dean, it is my responsibility to act in accordance with the bylaws, which stipulate that your infraction is grounds for immediate expulsion. I'm somewhat hesitant to render such a harsh decision after reviewing your transcript. You've performed remarkably well, and you're in the top five percentile of your graduating class."

He was awfully good at this.

I glanced around the room and the choice of clothing for the evening finally made sense. The office was complete with all of the décor one would expect of a college dean's office. If I hadn't known where I actually was, I would have thought I was really on a college campus.

I looked at him, not knowing how to play this out, but the cognac must have been working its magic because this game had become exciting. Or maybe it was just him. He exuded his usual confident and sexy Mr. Fuck Me demeanor, which made my body respond even when I didn't want it to.

He continued with his script in this enticing game. "So, Ms. Cason, as I'm sure you can understand, I'm torn as to the most appropriate manner in which I should resolve this situation. Therefore, I'm awarding you an opportunity that I have never offered another student."

I looked at him, wide-eyed, like a hopeful, desperate undergraduate.

"Would you like to know what that is, Ms. Cason?"

"Um, yes I would," I replied.

"You don't appear to have much respect for those in positions of authority, Ms. Cason. I'll remember that when I decide your fate."

"I'm sorry, Dean Wyatt, sir. It's just that I'm extremely nervous and worried that I'll be kicked out of school. I really can't let that happen, and I'm willing to do anything to ensure that I continue my studies."

"We'll see if you really mean that, Ms. Cason," he said, his eyes smoldering as they dropped to my chest.

"I do, sir, I sincerely do."

"That said, I think it wise to review the rules with you to ensure that you don't violate them again. And then, of course, I'll need to render some type of punishment. I think that will really impress upon you the importance of adhering to our university's guidelines. Do you agree, Ms. Cason?"

"Yes, sir." I was so hot for him. I wanted to climb over that desk and straddle him, to show him just how much of an apologetic and needy student I was.

"Good, I'm pleased to hear we're on the same page. When I was a child, I occasionally got into trouble myself. My father would sit me down to make sure I fully understood what I'd done, so he would go on and on and on, talking until I wanted to run screaming from the room. Once, I actually stood up and walked away. Of course, he came after me and finished his speech, but I still wanted to run. Thinking back on that makes me wonder if you'll be tempted to change your mind and run from this room before we complete a very necessary conversation."

What was he getting at?

"No sir, I'm willing to sit this out." I sat back and crossed my legs.

"You'll have to excuse me for not taking you at your word, I mean after all, you *are* here due to your deceptive behavior—are you not?"

"I can certainly understand your position, Dean."

"I think it best that I perform certain steps to ensure you don't leave before we're done," he said as he reached into the top drawer and pulled out some rope. Rising from the chair, he continued with his reprimand and walked over toward me. "I would like to restrain you so that you aren't tempted to run, Ms.

Cason."

I looked at him and shook my head. "Dean, I really don't think that will be necessary. I'm quite capable of sitting here and giving you my undivided attention, sir."

He stopped directly in front of me. "I'm afraid I must insist. If you will stand, please."

I eyed the rope entwined in his long fingers. I swallowed the lump in my throat and slowly rose from my seat.

"Now, if you will turn to face the chair."

I did as he instructed — my heart rate accelerating as I did so.

"I want you to place your knees in the seat and reach over toward the floor."

I followed his directions, positioned myself so that I was facing the back of the chair, and then bent over it. My skirt was doing exactly what I knew it would do — exposing my ass. He walked around and grabbed my wrist and tied it to one of the legs. He repeated this with my other wrist. This was crazy as hell.

He then moved toward the back and placed a rope around my right knee and tied it to the right side of the chair's frame. He did the same with my left knee. *Fuck.* I couldn't move.

He turned the seat so that I was facing his desk. I could barely look at him because my arms were pulling me down and my torso was draped over the back of the chair. He returned to the desk and opened a drawer.

"You know, when I was in school, if we were caught cheating, we were sent to the principal's office. The principal explained why the behavior was wrong, then he spanked us and sent us on our way."

Spank! Did he say spank? I know he didn't think he was going to spank me? Surely this was only part of the game. Thinking he wouldn't actually go that far, I decided to act out the scene with him. I wanted to see how far he would take this charade.

"I think we should've maintained that type of system, don't you? I mean, I think it was quite effective." He reached into the drawer and pulled out a glass paddle. My eyes widened as I stared at it.

What the fuck is he planning to do with that?

He looked at the paddle, turning it over in his hand. Slowly raising his eyes from the glass, he looked at me. I was certain I looked like the nervous, desperate girl now, because I actually didn't know what to say or what to do in this situation. And I couldn't fucking move.

"I've explained why your behavior was wrong, so that means the next step is your spanking."

He walked behind me and lightly touched the cold glass to my exposed behind.

"I must say, Ms. Cason, you have such full, lovely cheeks. My dick gets hard just looking at that tight, round ass."

The paddle moved across my behind, already teasing me. Aiden slid the paddle between my cheeks, groaning as he moved it back and forth. It was such a fucking turn-on. My sex was getting wetter with each stroke. I'd almost forgotten my unease until he suddenly removed the paddle and without warning — smack! He slapped it against my right cheek.

"Ah!" Shit, that hurt. "Sir, I really think that I understand the ramifications of my actions, and I don't think a spanking is necessary." I yanked my arms, trying to loosen the ropes.

"Ms. Cason, I beg to differ. Besides, you've stated that you'll do whatever required to remain in school. Has that changed?" He rubbed his hand over my stinging cheek.

"No. I'm not saying—"

"Okay, then. Hush and let's get this over with. The sooner I get your ass spanked the sooner you can return to class."

The salacious threat clenched my insides, but only slightly—I think Virginia was as nervous as I was.

"But I think it best if we keep you quiet." He walked around and knelt before me and pulled a handkerchief from his pocket. "Open," he said.

I again went along with his directive and I opened my mouth. He inserted the handkerchief and then removed his tie and placed it over my lips. This guy seriously had a thing with gagging!

After removing his jacket, he resumed his position behind my chair. I felt his hand on my ass and then he pushed my skirt up. If this wasn't me releasing all control to him, I didn't know what the hell was. I was both terrified and wanting.

He moaned. "I could admire this sight all night," he said as he moved his hands over the soft lace that barely covered my behind. I was so hot for him at that point that all my initial inhibitions dissipated. His hand moved between my thighs, his fingers tracing over the heated area.

"You're so fucking sexy, Ms. Cason."

He pushed through the fabric, teasing my throbbing sex. Positioning his finger underneath the lace material, he moved it between my lower lips. I knew he would find me already soaked and anxious for him.

"Shh. So wet," he whispered. His hand slowly eased upward, accessing the top of my boy shorts, gently pulling them down, and then he was softly caressing me. I was being seduced by the seductive tenderness of his touch, and then abruptly, his hand was gone. Only to be replaced with a slap from the paddle to my left cheek. I jerked forward and he smacked it again, this time a little harder.

I cried out through the handkerchief. The sting was painful, almost unbearable. He rubbed his hand across my inflamed ass and then leaned in, gifting it with a soft kiss. He then struck my right cheek in the same manner — twice, but rubbing it afterward.

Biting the gag, I closed my eyes, absorbing the pain. He slapped the paddle on my ass again and again, my unremitting cries pointless, as he continued, his merciless punishment.

His breathing became harsh as he dropped the paddle and pulled at my panties, yanking them down as far as they could go, which wasn't very far with my legs spread apart. He became impatient and ripped them off. The next sound was that of his pants unzipping, and heightening my anticipation as he slid a finger inside me. "You're already so wet, Ms. Cason," he said. "I like that."

Pulling my cheeks apart, he eased a fraction of his massive hardness into me and pulled out slowly, teasing me — preparing me for the fullness. He was so hard, if I hadn't known better, I would've sworn it wasn't flesh. He placed his hands on either side of my ass, farther spreading me open.

"Your pussy is so perfect and so beautiful, just like you," he said gruffly.

I moaned as he gradually filled me and then slowly, he pulled out. With a fierce thrust, he slammed back into me again, so hard that he dug into my flesh to hold me in place. And then he pulled out again, slapping his hard cock on my ass before spreading me and slowly easing back inside the moist tightness. Once more, he slowly eased out of me, growling, and rushing to refill me, rapidly forcing his oversized manhood inside me. The pounding was a deep rhythm, his balls slapping the back of my thighs with each forceful thrust. The delicious pain — his roughness and the force with which he contacted my sore ass — was almost more than I could take. Grunting, he plowed into me over and over again; I was straddled the chair, forced to take it all. He slowed and swiveled his cock inside me before sliding in as deep as he could and remaining there. "Fuck, you feel so good," he groaned.

He leaned over and reached under me, grabbing at my shirt, pulling it apart to gain access to my aching breasts. He slowly peeled away my bra and grabbed my tits whole in his hands as he started moving in and out of me again. He rolled my nipples between his fingers and tugged; I let out another muffled scream, overwrought by the delightful torture. Releasing my breasts, he traced his way to my back, and clutched a handful of my hair, firmly pulling. "Is this what you expected as punishment, Ms. Cason?"

I only moaned in response.

He slapped my ass, hard. "Answer me," he demanded. I shook my head and he released my hair, his hands recapturing my backside, spreading me open. And then the tip of his finger moved over my ass, and I immediately tensed.

"Relax, Aria," he said, moving his finger back and forth over the tight hole. "Have you ever done this before?"

I quickly shook my head.

"Well, I want it," he said, his voice a seductive whisper.

Virginia clenched, freaking the fuck out.

His thrusts slowed, and I relished each one, anxious for the next.

"Will you let me have it?" he asked, massaging my sex with the thickness of his manhood. He felt so good inside me, and I wanted to please him. I wanted him to please me, but this?

"Say yes, Aria. Let me give this to you, baby," he said as he continued moving his finger around the opening.

My heart was racing and I couldn't think. There were too many emotions, too many pleasure points soaring through me.

"Sweetheart, give this to me. I promise to make it good," he coaxed.

As if there was only one possible reply, I nodded my consent.

"I want you to feel safe. I want to hear you so I can stop if I hurt you." He reached up and removed the tie.

Using my tongue, I pushed the handkerchief out of my mouth.

He spread my ass wider than he had before, spit on the taut tissue, and then slid the tip of his finger in.

I tensed again.

"Relax, baby," he whispered. "Focus on my cock and how it feels inside you."

My thoughts quickly zeroed in on his deep strokes.

"There you go. Don't think. Just feel," he said, pushing in deeper. The muscles of the puckered tissue tightened again. He removed his finger and leaned back toward the desk.

I felt something cold when he next rubbed his finger around and in my ass. After a few gentle prods, he was sliding in and out of me without much resistance.

"How's that?" he asked.

"Better," I whispered, as I tried to focus on him inside me, on his voice, on the sound of the wetness as he moved in and out of me, anything but the finger in a place that I knew would be spread much wider.

"Good girl."

He was moving back and forth, his finger sliding in and out of me as I started to lose myself—unable to absorb the foreign sensations before I felt the expansion of an additional finger.

"Oh shit," I moaned, clutching my lip with my teeth as I moved from the shallow water and traipsed deeper into an ocean of unfamiliar territory. I was at a place between awareness and ecstasy as he stroked inside me, prepping me for what he really wanted to give. As I started to relax, he pulled his dick out of me, and after a few more strokes in my ass, he removed his fingers.

"Don't think, Aria. Just feel me," he said. His voice was a sexy murmur, as he slowly inched inside the taut opening.

"Oh, fuck," I panted. He was so big. As he went deeper, my

breathing became harsher. I was overwhelmed.

"Breathe naturally, Aria," he whispered. "Relax."

I attempted to slow my breaths, but it was a difficult task because the pain of his entrance was demanding my attention.

"There you go, baby. Just focus on how good your pussy feels."

I took a deep breath as one of his fingers and then another eased into my sex. It hurt, but at the same time, it was indescribably satisfying. He was all the way in and I was feeling sensations that I couldn't comprehend.

He continued fingering my pussy as he moved in and out of my ass. I panted and moaned as he tortured both openings, my pussy clenching and greedy — my ass tight and overfull.

I screamed out at the delicious pain. Oh fuck, it hurt! But I didn't want to stop. He increased the brutal rhythm in and out of my ass as he slammed into me over and over, punishing the too-tight hole. My core ached, about to explode as he pushed me higher and higher, the pain and pleasure of his torture rippling through me.

"I'm going to come, Aiden," I panted as the expanding and contracting of my sex forced my juices out onto his fingers. The erotic sensations flowed through me like a shot of adrenaline. My body trembled as he removed his fingers and placed his hand on the other side of my ass and plowed into me.

"Shit, your ass is so tight," he grunted, forcing his cock deeper inside me then abruptly pulling out, spilling his hot seed all over me.

"Fuck," he growled as the spurts continued, dropping thickly on my ass. With the last drop, he rubbed the head of his cock along the opening, smearing his come there before rubbing it all over my cheeks.

He retrieved a towel and began wiping me clean before untying me. Once he freed me of the last restraint, he pulled me from the chair and turned me to face him.

"You were amazing, baby," he said, leaning down to kiss me softly on the lips. He leaned back and looked into my eyes. "Are you okay with everything that happened?"

"Yes," I replied. Probably too quickly, because I really wasn't sure.

"Good. Kiss me."

I lifted my face to his, and he sealed his mouth over mine, kissing me deeply.

❧Chapter Twelve❧

The drive to *Seducente* was vastly different from the drive there. The detectable apprehension had been replaced with incredulity, and instead of staring bug-eyed out the window, I was snuggled against Aiden's chest. He planted soft kisses on my head every so often as I reveled in what had just happened. I couldn't believe that I went along with all of that. The clothes, the unknown, the role-play, and anal? All in the span of a few hours. I couldn't help but wonder what he thought of me now.

"So now that you've obtained what you so diligently pursued, what's next?" I asked.

"Although you did present an immense challenge, Ms. Cason, I realize that the larger challenge is to keep you," he replied.

I didn't expect that, and I didn't know how to reply. *Keep me?* I thought this was only about sex. Had things changed?

"Spend the night with me," he said.

I froze; I'd never spent the night with a man before. It violated my Fuck Rules. "Aiden, I have work tomorrow, and I need time to rest and to process whatever it is that's going on with us, and I suspect I won't be able to do that when I'm near you."

"That's precisely why I don't want you out of my sight for the next several hours."

I looked up at him. Staring into his eyes, there was no way I could deny him anything, no matter how much I sensed I needed to.

"You have a tendency to over think things, Aria."

I looked away to regain my sanity.

"Fine, if you won't stay with me, I'm staying with you," he said.

"No," I replied.

"Okay, then." He pressed a button on the side panel. "We'll be going to the penthouse instead of Ms. Cason's."

"Yes, sir," the driver replied.

Aiden released the button, looking at me as if daring me to object, which I didn't.

This was bad. Really bad.

"Tonight was amazing," he said, looking down at me.

"For me, too. It was definitely not at all what I expected."

"Exactly what did you expect?" he asked.

"I honestly was clueless."

We both laughed, then I sighed.

"What is it?" he asked.

"If you insist on doing this your way, as you seem to do everything, I would much rather be in my own surroundings."

"Whatever you want, sweetheart," he replied and announced the change to the driver.

A short while later, the limo stopped in front of my building. Aiden looked down at me before the driver opened the door. "Are you sure about this? I don't want you to be uncomfortable."

"Since when?" I asked, incredulous. He'd made a habit of making me uncomfortable since the first day we met, and he fucking knew it.

"There's that sarcastic wit of yours. That's going to cause that sweet little ass of yours a lot of hurt one day," he warned.

"Oh, you mean more than what I experienced tonight. I hope not, because I don't think I could take much more."

He was suddenly serious. "Aria, did I hurt you tonight? You said you were okay."

"Of course it hurt, Aiden, but not in the sense you mean. I actually liked it more than I can express. I was only kidding."

He looked at me, a frown indicating his disapproval. "Don't kid about things like that," he reprimanded, grabbing my hand and pulling me from the car.

Geez, excuse me for having a sense of humor.

We entered the lobby of my building—it felt odd. Silas glanced at us and then quickly lowered his eyes. I'd lived here for almost three years, and never had a man accompanied me home. I was certain Silas was just as shocked as I was.

In the elevator to my floor, Aiden looked at me, and a smile graced his beautiful mouth. "Thank you," he said, gazing into my eyes before leaning down to plant a soft, chaste kiss on my lips. I'd decided when it came to kisses from him, they should never be quick. They should always be slow, long, and deep. But who was I kidding? Any closeness to him at all was mesmerizing.

"For?" I asked.

"Tonight. You did as I asked with everything, and I know that was especially difficult for you."

I laughed. "For me maybe, but not for Virginia," I replied, more so to myself than to him.

"Did I miss something?" he asked, confused.

"Nothing. Just a private joke," I replied. I quickly faced the elevator doors hoping he wouldn't ask anything further.

"Let me in on the joke."

"Well," I hesitated.

"Well, nothing. Tell me," he said.

The elevator doors opened, and I reached into my purse for my keys. "I was referring to my, uh, sex." I looked at him, waiting for him to question my sanity, but he laughed instead.

"So you've named that treasure?" he asked.

"Well, yeah. She's quite the character at times, and I didn't want to refer to her with vulgarity, so I gave her a name." I unlocked my door, and we stepped inside the condo.

"Is that right?"

"Yes. Don't tell me you don't have some type of reference or name for your equipment." I removed my jacket, tossed it on the sofa, and turned to face him.

"Equipment?" He glanced down at the bulge in his pants, and I followed his gaze. "Why such a mechanical name for something so rare and pleasurable?" he asked.

I tore my gaze away from his crotch and met his green eyes. "Is that what you think it is?"

"I know *you* do."

Hell yes, I did. I didn't understand how the hell he was still single. If I were not a commitment-phobe, I would never let this man out of my sight.

"Have a seat." I sat and motioned for him to sit beside me. "You have no idea of my thoughts on that, Mr. Wyatt."

He walked over to the sofa and reached for my hand, motioning for me to stand. He then took a seat and pulled me into his lap. "I have a pretty good idea, but I would prefer you tell me."

"Tell you what?"

"Your thoughts on my 'equipment,' as you call it."

"What? Do you want me to inflate your ego even more than it already is? I don't think the world could handle much more of that, Aiden."

"My powers of deduction lead me to believe that you're very impressed with it." He reached up and placed a loose strand of hair behind my ear.

"I didn't say that."

"You didn't have to. Your body does. Virginia especially does. She's extremely responsive."

"Is she?"

"You know it."

"Ugh!" His hubris knew no end.

"What?" he asked laughing.

His eyes were bright and playful—I really did get lost every time I looked into them. He sifted his fingers through my hair and held onto a lock of it. "So if you had to give it a name, what would it be?" he asked.

I watched as he twisted the ends of my hair. I was easily recalling the feel of his long fingers inside me earlier. "Hmm. Let me think. You've described it as rare and pleasurable. Any other descriptors?"

"Sovereign, majestic, supreme—you know, all of the standard terms," he added, smiling.

"Just stop. It sounds as if you already have a name in mind, King Aiden."

He grinned. "Is that what you're going to call me the next time I'm fucking you?"

"Do you want me to?"

"Do *you* want to?" he countered.

I looked at him, and he tilted his head and presented that sexy lopsided smile—the way he was looking at me literally made me weak. He was an incredibly seductive man and it enveloped every fiber of his being.

"Back to your question," I said. "I have a name. But before I tell you what it is, I need you to know that it's based on what *you* think, not me."

"Okay, so what is it?" he asked.

"Kingston."

He grinned even more broadly. "I like it."

"I figured you would. It fits everything *you've* described."

"It fits everything you know it to be, sweetheart."

He was so arrogant.

"'I'm going to let you in on a little secret." He leaned over and kissed my earlobe as he whispered. "If recent events are any indicator, Kingston and Virginia are going to be very, very close friends." He pulled me into a kiss. This time it was the slow, deep, long caress I preferred.

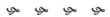

I awoke for the second time the next morning, the only difference being that I was in bed alone this time. As I reached toward the bedside table to silence the alarm on my phone, I spotted a note.

Good morning, Princess,

Although I would have preferred waking up with you, I needed to get home to change for work. I would have never thought it possible to enjoy lying beside you as much as being inside you. To my surprise it was. I'm crazy about you.

I'll see you soon.

A.

Swoon. This man was just too much. I smiled, stretching and moaning at the soreness that reminded me of last night. He had expanded and pleasured almost every opening of my body, and the mere thought of him made me ache for more.

Last night was incredible. After we'd settled in, Aiden suggested I pretend he wasn't there — as if that was even remotely possible — and do what I would normally do. That part was easy — a long relaxing bath. After having selected a bottle of wine, I grabbed two glasses and walked to the bathroom. Aiden insisted on sitting in "quiet observance," as he called it, while I bathed. That *quiet observance* lasted for about two minutes. Within seconds of his watching me move the sea foam sponge over my breasts, he'd undressed and joined me in the tub.

That was the first time I'd actually seen the full glory of his body, and I was salivating, to say the least. Of course, I tried to appear nonchalant, but it was terribly difficult to mask my admiration. He was perfect. Well, maybe not, because perfection didn't exist, but if it did, it would only apply to this rare specimen. He watched me as I watched him. His manhood hung heavily in a neatly manscaped area I couldn't tear my eyes from. His cock was beautiful, just like every part of him. His thighs were lean and muscular and his upper torso — which I'd had the pleasure of ogling in St. Barts — could certainly be classified as a work of art.

He smiled slowly as he walked over to the tub and bent over to kiss me. He motioned for me to slide forward, which I did, allowing him to settle in behind me. He reached for me, guiding me to recline on his contoured chest. We were both silent for a while. I listened to his calm heartbeat, its steady rhythm soothing my racing thoughts, enabling me to soak in the tranquil moment. I never imagined him wanting this type of connection with me. It was surprisingly comforting, but did I really want to be this comfortable? I wanted the sex — we'd both agreed on that much, but we didn't specify anything further. This closeness was blurring the lines, and I needed to clear that up as quickly as possible.

We sat like that for long quiet moments until he asked about my interests outside work, my family, and friends. I didn't really have many interests other than music and traveling. I told him that my family was something I didn't really care to discuss, and the only person I considered a real friend was April.

I learned that he, too, was an avid lover of music and the arts. He was musical, playing the piano and guitar. I told him that I would love to play an instrument. He asked which—I told him piano, and he made an offer to teach me, which I graciously accepted. I asked him what it was like to have grown up so quickly—he'd graduated high school at the age of thirteen. He'd never had a girlfriend until he was twenty-one because it was always awkward—given that he was surrounded by girls who only saw him as a younger brother. When he was in college, he did meet a few girls, but his parents never approved. They'd introduced him to someone in whom he had a fleeting interest, and even though it felt forced, he'd continued to date her in an effort to please his parents. I sensed then that he had issues with doing what they expected of him. I didn't say anything to that effect, of course.

We talked until we were both wrinkled and the water was nearly cold. "We need to get you to bed, Ms. Cason. It's late and you need to be on your *P*s and *Q*s tomorrow if you're going to keep your intern on his toes."

"Oh, yes. My intern. He's turned out to be quite the interesting handful."

"Oh, he has, has he?" he asked, laughing. We both washed, helping each other with our backs and stopping occasionally to share a tender kiss or a sensual touch. He stepped out of the tub and grabbed a towel to wrap around his waist and another he opened for me to step into. I reached up to kiss him softly on his lips. "Thank you," I said.

"For what?" he asked, staring down at me.

"For tonight. For everything," I replied.

"Are you mocking me?"

"No, why would you ask that?"

"Because I said the same thing to you earlier."

"Well, can't we both be thankful? Besides, I'm thanking you for something different."

"Okay. What?" he asked.

"For encouraging me to let my hair down. For being everything I didn't expect."

His brows furrowed, but before he could ask anything further, I pulled from his embrace and walked to the bedroom, realizing I shouldn't have said that. I could think it, but I couldn't—shouldn't—say it aloud. He was breaking down my defenses, and as badly as I wanted to keep them up and keep him at arm's length, I couldn't. Not anymore. But that didn't mean I needed to tell him.

I slipped on a nightie, and he slid into bed beside me—naked. Virginia, who'd been questionably quiet during the bath, was wide awake and wanting.

He pulled me close, laying my head on his chest, and let out a content sigh. He kissed the top of my head.

"Good night, Aria."

"Good night." Virginia was disappointed and so was I. I was exhausted, though. So maybe sleep was best. I yawned and drifted off in mere seconds.

ᕍ   ᕍ   ᕍ   ᕍ

I moaned softly, awaking to the stimulation of a hot tongue between my thighs. Aiden licked the sensitive flesh with a deliberate slowness so intense that I couldn't help the explicit words escaping my lips. He slid his tongue between the slick folds, pushing into me, spreading me open. His tongue circled the silken tissues, my hips rotating as my core tightened. The focused tip of his tongue flicked delicately over my clit. He growled and closed his lips over the responsive bud and sucked gently. I reacted to his touch as though for the first time, amazed at the giftedness of his tongue. My hands were in his hair, gripping as he began thrusting his tongue deeper and deeper into me. I started to move my hips to his rhythm, grinding forcefully on his tongue. My climax was building; he slid two fingers between the wet slit as he licked and sucked my swollen clit, and that was my undoing. I came hard as I breathed his name, relishing in the pulsing of my sex as he removed his fingers and began lapping my juices. I floated back down from my erotic high as he softly planted sweet kisses along my inner thighs.

He sat up, leaning back on his knees. "Get on your knees for me, sweetheart."

I turned over and positioned myself on all fours, and he moved closer behind me. I could feel his erection against my behind as he moved his hands over my curves, letting his fingers trace a titillating path from the nape of my neck to my lower back and then down between my cheeks. I closed my eyes, breathing heavily, anxious to feel him inside me.

The waiting was torture, which he only heightened by teasing me as he rubbed his cock over my ass.

"Aiden, please."

"Please what, baby? What is it you want?" he whispered.

"I want you to fuck me," I said.

"How badly do you want me to fuck you?" he asked, goading me.

"Please. Don't make me beg," I replied.

"I want you to beg. I want to know how badly you want this dick."

"Please, Aiden," I begged, inching back toward him, moving my ass against his hardness. "I want so badly for you to slide your cock in me and fuck me. Please, baby," I said, desperate for him.

He groaned as he eased inside me, stretching me as he slid

deeper. I cried out, the luscious pain increasing with each inch forward.

As he slowly filled me, my sex pulsed and clenched with a desperate need for more. With both of his hands grasping my ass, he plunged into me. Hard. I cried out again, the delectable fullness overwhelming me. He forced his big cock deeper into me with each ferocious thrust, bolting me forward. The sound of him slapping hard against my ass as his man jewels grazed the back of my thighs was normally stimulation enough to take me over the edge, but not now. I wanted more. I just didn't know how much more I could take—I was still sore from our schoolgirl fuck. He yanked my hips back to meet his punishing thrusts, grunting as he rapidly immersed himself into my aching sex.

"Oh, shit, I'm going to come," I breathed.

"No, you aren't, sweetheart," he said hoarsely, quickly pulling out of me. He grabbed my waist, turning me, and positioned me on my back. He then lay on his side, his feet in the direction of my head.

He reached for my ankle and lifted my leg, sliding between my thighs until his hard rod was at the entrance of my sex. Pulling me down toward him, his cock opened and penetrated me, not wasting any time resuming his rapid forceful pace—not that I was complaining. I loved the feeling of the fullness when he forced himself inside me, driving me, pushing me higher. With his hand on my thigh, he pulled me downward, making me feel all of him. Trembling, I cried out his name, begging him not to stop as I came gloriously around his hard length.

"Fuck!" He growled, erupting violently inside me. He eased out of my clenching sex and reached for me, pulling me out of bed. He sealed his lips over mine, prodding with his tongue, demanding entrance. He hungrily licked inside my mouth, sliding his hands down my back and gripping my ass. He moaned inside my mouth as he tasted and toyed with my tongue. And once he began kissing my neck, I sank into him. He turned me, grabbing my breasts, massaging, groping and pinching my nipples. It hurt, but the pain was mixed with the sensuality of his kisses and the gentle sucks on my neck. Reaching between my thighs, he rubbed my clit as he guided my body forward.

"Place your leg on the bed," he said gruffly. I followed his instruction, and he fell to his knees, licking and sucking my pussy with avid ferocity. I shivered and moaned, swiveling my cunt over his lips, coating his mouth with his seed and my essence. His hands were on my ass, pulling me closer to his mouth, feeding his desire, as if he were famished. I felt another orgasm building as his tongue moved back and forth over my sex. I panted and moaned uncontrollably, savoring the expertise with which he pleasured me. He lightly circled his tongue inside of me and within seconds, ripples of ecstasy were again flooding through me.

He stood quickly and pushed his dick inside me. How the hell could he keep going like this? I screamed his name as he slammed his iron hard length into my soaking depths. His hand was on my back, pressing me down so that my chest was level with the bed, and then he fucked me, hard. He grunted as he pounded into me, and I cried out with every plunge. He growled and cursed as his cock jerked inside me, prompting yet another orgasm, my core shattering as my sex clenched, milking him. I climaxed, shuddering as the rapture whipped through me, depleting me.

Aiden slid his hands up my body until he was lying flat against my back. I could feel his heartbeat. It was rapid—as was his breathing, which matched mine.

A few moments passed before Aiden pulled himself out of me, and sensing I was too exhausted to move, he helped me into bed.

"I'm sorry for waking you," he whispered.

"I don't think you are, Mr. Wyatt."

He leaned in to kiss me lightly on the lips. "You're right. I'm not, Ms. Cason. And neither are you."

Pulling me closer, he placed my head on his chest. And again, I was asleep in a matter of minutes.

I wondered what time he'd left and why I hadn't heard him. I was surprised that finding him gone upset me. This was a first for me, so I didn't know what I expected to feel, but it wasn't this overwhelming sense of loneliness. Maybe this was normal, especially after the emotional and physical closeness we'd shared last night.

The sex was…well, it was beyond anything I'd ever experienced with any other man. I stretched again and squirmed as I realized I was sore in places I didn't think possible. I needed to get out of bed and loosen my muscles. Slowly sitting up, I cursed at the twinge of pain in my abdomen. I then turned and flopped my feet over the side of the bed and willed myself to stand. *Oh my God!* Everything hurt! I had a sudden urge to pee and started to make my way to the bathroom, but had to slow my steps. I was sore, everywhere. After some very short careful movements, I finally made it to the bathroom and reached the toilet. Sitting down was a task, and peeing was an even larger one. What had he done to me? I rose from the toilet and walked over to the sink, and my reflection nearly made me fall back.

There were marks on my shoulders from where he'd grabbed me and pulled me back toward his cock. That had catapulted me to my third, maybe fourth orgasm. My breasts revealed evidence of his playground also. The memory of his grabbing, sucking, and biting them sent a jolt of passion directly to the spot that was already sore. My thighs had minor marks, too. Those must have been from the pressure of being tied to the chair at *Seducente*. I turned to look at my backside and found bruises and hand prints on my ass. There were also small marks toward the top of my back from his pulling me to meet his hard thrusts. Ms. Virginia was too depleted to do much more than wink at the salacious memory.

I took a hot bath, thinking it would soothe my aches and pains. It did help, but I knew I would be moving with carefully measured steps the remainder of the day. I slowly dressed for work, popped two aspirin, and headed out to start my day.

The drive to work seemed different somehow. I typically kept my focus on the road and on what I hoped to accomplish at work. But this morning I was smiling at everything. Maybe it was the sun shining brightly, spilling rays of happy energy. Or maybe it was the beautiful canvas in the sky; it was a sea of ribbons this morning — all different shades of brilliant blue. I was also perplexed as to why the normal nerve-wracking flow of traffic with the honking horns, the abrupt starts and stops, the Bostonians walking illegally across the streets — even the jerk that cut me off at the intersection — didn't faze my mood. Then it occurred to me, I was genuinely happy. And it was because of *him.* And that scared the hell out of me.

I made my way to the parking garage and then to the elevators, which I shared with a few ladies from legal and accounting. They looked at me as if I were an alien when I made casual small talk with them. I couldn't help but laugh as we went our separate ways, sure that I would be the topic of conversation over the break room table.

Approaching my office, I saw Raina working busily at her desk. I reached her before she saw me. "Good morning, Raina."

She looked up from the file on her desk with a smile already in place.

"Good morning, Ms.—"

"What is it, Raina?" I asked when she broke off her usual greeting.

"Umm, nothing. I, well, you look…unlike yourself."

"How so?" I asked.

"Well, you're smiling for one, and your eyes, they seem different somehow."

"I must normally be a real Debbie Downer, then?"

"No, you're just very focused on what you do, and your personality never really seems to come out. You hide it."

"It's just the after-effects of time away from the office," I explained. It wouldn't be wise to let the staff know I'd been fucked into oblivion by my intern for several of the last twenty-four hours.

"Speaking of which, how was your vacation?" she asked.

"It was great." *Full of surprises*, I thought.

"It would appear so. Good to have you back. Don't forget you have a lunch meeting with the distributor from L.A.," she said as I opened my office door.

I turned at the sound of laughter and saw Jennifer and Aiden talking near the elevators. I took note of the proximity of her body to his, and jealousy, a very new emotion for me, was immediate. I didn't like the feeling; it was very unsettling. She placed her hand on his forearm as she laughed. He stepped back slightly, moving away from her touch. That small gesture made me feel much better. He looked gorgeous as usual, refreshed from the previous night's exertions. You would have never known he'd been fucking all night.

Do I look as refreshed as he? I wondered as I stepped toward my desk. I couldn't possibly, because I was dog tired! Not just physically, but emotionally as well. I had broken so many rules and opened myself to so many new things that I had not yet processed. Aiden was right to have demanded to be with me last night, because I was sure I would have found a way to ease out of this arrangement. And quite frankly, I didn't even know what the arrangement was now.

My phone rang, and when I answered, I was surprised to

hear April's voice — she never called me on my office phone, so of course I was instantly on guard.

"Damn it, Aria, why is it so difficult to get in contact with you lately?" she demanded.

"Well, hello to you, too, April." *What had crawled up her ass?*

I looked up to see Aiden standing in my doorway. He looked as delicious in a suit as he did naked — always so appetizing. He closed the door behind him. I slowly shook my head, signaling him to not do that, but of course he didn't heed my request.

Instead, he sauntered over to my desk and stood there, staring at me.

"April, hold on for just a second okay?" I placed the call on hold.

"Good morning, Aiden," I said.

"Good morning, princess."

Princess. That was twice now. Was that his new name for me?

"I really need some privacy to speak with April. I have a ten o'clock meeting with you, Raina, and Josh. Until then, I have a very busy morning and I don't have time to play with you."

"Play with me? Is that why you think I'm here?" There was a mischievous glint in his eyes as he looked at me.

"Well, you addressed me as *princess,* and, correct me if I'm wrong, but I don't think that's a greeting from someone who came to my office for business," I said.

"Touché," he said with that same gleam. "Let's have lunch today."

"I can't. I already have a lunch date."

His face froze and the green dance of his eyes halted. "Date? Male or female?"

"Does it matter?" I asked, agitated.

"Aria, don't—"

"It's a business lunch with one of our distributors, Aiden."

He visibly relaxed.

My phone beeped, reminding me of April on hold.

"Finish your conversation with April, and I'll see you at the meeting." He took a few steps backwards and then turned to leave.

I bit my lip as I watched him casually stroll out of my office. I couldn't help but think of the body beneath that suit. I shook off the heady effects and returned my attention to my best friend.

"Sorry about that, April. I'm sure you're calling about the Dane situation. What's going on?"

April went on to explain that when we'd met in Venezuela, Dane had been there for business, which I knew because he'd told me. But he never mentioned a marriage. When Dane returned home, his very suspicious wife checked his phone and saw a text that Dane sent to April asking about me. To sum it all up, Dane's wife contacted April, saying she knew about everything and wanted to speak with me. She'd filed for a divorce and wanted me to testify in the court proceedings.

I was stunned into silence; various images and outcomes ran wildly through my mind. "Fuck! I can't do that." The whole purpose of an out-of-state romp was to remain discreet. Something like this could be very bad for me. "What did you tell her?"

"I followed our mantra of 'deny, deny, deny,' but when I realized that she was planning to go public with the information, I told her I would get in contact with you."

"Go public? That means she really *does* know who I am, and how this information would look for me if it's exposed."

"Yes, I think so."

I sighed, rubbing my already throbbing forehead. "So after making contact with me, what did she want you to do?"

"She wants you to call her. She's given me her contact information. That's if you want it."

What the hell *did* I want to do? What *could* I do? The ramifications of this disclosure flooded my brain.

"Aria, are you still there?"

"Yes," I whispered, so low I barely heard it myself.

"What are you going to do?"

"I really don't know. I need some time to sort this all out before I do anything." I stared blankly at the monitor and saw the crazed reflection looking back at me. Why was this happening?

"I hate to pour on the pressure, but this lady was quite anxious to speak to you, and if you don't call her back, at least to appease her and buy some time to figure out your next step, there's no telling what she's liable to do."

"Yes, I know. Will you do something for me?" I asked.

"Sure, if I can," she replied.

"Can you call her back and tell her you've spoken with me, and tell her she can contact me this weekend? That will give me the remainder of the week to sort through all of this and figure the best way of handling it. I think I should contact my attorney to see if I can threaten her with some type of slander or libel suit if she discloses any information about me."

"That's a good idea. I'll call her back as soon as you and I hang up."

"Okay. Thanks, April."

"Of course. I'm always here if you need me. You know that."

"Yep, for as long as I can remember it's been you and me against the world. You're like a sister to me, and I'm so glad you're still in my life. I already have so much going on right now, things you would not believe. Now I have to deal with this bullshit."

"Well, I'm happy you've allowed an entrance for Aiden. And the pictures of your outfit you sent last night were hot! You need to let me know what that was all about."

"I'm still trying to process what type of entrance I've given him," I said dryly.

"Oh, no. Not the 'processing' again. Stop it and enjoy things, Aria. I have to go, but I'll call you after speaking to the wife."

"Okay, talk to you then. I love you."

"I love you, too."

I hung up the phone and glared at it, wanting to toss it across the room. How could this be happening? What a great way to start my fucking day!

❧Chapter Thirteen❧

My meeting with Aiden, Raina, and Josh was odd, albeit productive; one of the largest obstacles in our project was overcoming issues with the most recent campaign details. The primary stumbling block was Blake and his far-fetched ideas. And then there was Aiden, who vehemently disagreed with most of Blake's suggestions. Aiden's demeanor and opinions had actually become rather common place and we tended to lean toward his stance on several key decisions, which typically meant I would later have to go head-to-head with Blake in a sidebar.

I didn't quite know how to behave in a room with Aiden after all that had transpired over the last few days. I felt as if everyone knew. I tried my best to conduct myself as I normally would. However, I no longer knew what normal was for me.

It was very difficult to be near Aiden without my thoughts drifting into areas inappropriate for the work place. He and I exchanged a few heated glances during the course of the discussions, making it that much more difficult. I was hoping that Josh and Raina weren't aware of our exchanges. The tone of our meetings had already been altered since Aiden had joined our team, so maybe they would attribute it to that dynamic of having a new player.

At the conclusion of the meeting, Aiden remained in my office, which really wasn't a shock to me at all.

"Who's the lunch date?" he asked as soon as the others were out of hearing range.

"I told you earlier. Even if I hadn't, what makes you think it's your place to ask?"

"If it's not my place to ask, then whose is it?" he countered.

"Aiden, we cannot do this here."

He looked at me, scowling. "Where then? I think we need to revisit the St. Barts conversation. I'm sure you must recognize that the situation has already complicated itself."

"I have. And I don't know where we can talk about it, but it will not be here." As I saw it, *he* complicated the situation. It hadn't complicated itself.

"My place after work," he suggested.

"Sure."

"I'll text you the address," he replied, turning to leave.

By the end of the day, I was running on fumes. I needed rest, and I was still sore from the night before. As badly as I needed to see Aiden, I planned to cancel. I knew he wouldn't like it, but I also needed my senses in working order when I was with him. It was damned near impossible to refuse him anything when I was on full alert, so there was no way I'd be a match for him in this state.

It was nearly five o'clock when I sent him a text.

I will not be able to make it tonight. Tomorrow night?

I waited nervously for his reply. To my surprise, I didn't receive one. I breathed a sigh of relief as I busied myself with closing files and shutting down my computer. As I left my office, I saw Raina was about to head out also.

"Have a good evening, Raina."

"You too, Ms. Cason," she replied as we both strolled toward the elevator.

"Any plans this evening?" she asked.

"Nothing beyond ordering dinner and diving into bed directly afterwards. I'm beat. What about you?"

"I have to attend an after-school event with the hubby and kids, then we're going to grab a late dinner afterwards."

"That sounds nice." I really envied her. She'd given her family the life I'd deeply longed for as a child.

There was a ping just as the doors opened and, low and behold, there was Aiden. Raina may not have noticed, but I zeroed in on his irritation as soon as I saw him. And I was almost certain his frustration was due to my text. But I was tired, so at that point, I could care less about him not having his way. What did he expect from me? 24/7 access? Deciding to ignore him, I stood near the front of the elevator, needing to avoid whatever he had brewing.

"Hello, Aiden. Looks as if we're all headed for the exit," Raina said.

"That it does, Raina," he replied.

"Ms. Cason and I were just discussing our plans for the evening. Do you have anything special planned tonight?"

"As a matter of fact, I do. I have a date."

What the fuck? A date? Is that why he didn't reply to my text? A sinking feeling eased into my stomach. Disappointment? Hurt? Both?

"Well, who's the lucky lady? Someone special?" Raina asked.

"Yes, she is. She's very special," he replied.

I had the sudden urge to throw up.

"You know, a lot of women at work will be very disappointed to know that," she said.

He chuckled at Raina's reply.

The doors opened for the first floor, and although my car was in the garage, I wanted out of there. I stepped to leave, but Aiden grabbed me subtly at my waist.

"Isn't your car in the garage, Ms. Cason? I parked beside you after lunch."

"Oh. That's right. What was I thinking?" I shrugged his hand off, still facing the elevator doors.

"Good thing you have me here," he said.

"Yes, it would seem so." *Lucky me.* "See you in the morning,

Raina," I said as she stepped off the elevator.

"Good-bye, Ms. Cason," she said.

The elevator doors closed. I didn't say anything and neither did Aiden. When the doors opened for the garage, Aiden and I both stepped out. I headed to my car with him following close behind me. After pressing the button on the key fob to unlock my door, I reached for the handle, but Aiden had placed his hand at the top of the window, keeping the door closed.

"I thought we had plans tonight," he said.

I spun around to face him. I wasn't in the mood for his shit. "Obviously you had plans with someone other than me, so you should be good, right?"

"What?" he asked.

"You know. The 'special someone.'" I turned back to the door; his hand was still pressed against the top, so I couldn't open it.

"Move your hand," I demanded. He stepped closer, his body slightly touching mine.

Removing his hand from the door, he grasped my shoulders and turned me to face him. "The special someone I was referring to was you, Aria, and you know it."

"Do I?"

"Are you fucking kidding me? Are we here again?" he asked, his brows furrowed as he searched my eyes.

I glanced around, hoping no one saw our exchange. "Aiden, I'm tired, and I need to get home and get some rest. Please let me do that."

He took another step closer, and I quickly moved in reverse, my back nearly pressed against the car. "How about you come home with me? You can sleep at my place while I prepare dinner. I'll wake you after a couple of hours and we can talk while we eat."

"Oh, so you cook, too?" I asked, with a hint of sarcasm. "Why am I not surprised?"

"Why do you say cook like it's a dirty word? Yes, I can cook. There's a story behind that though."

"Sorry. It's just that sometimes you seem too good to be true, and I wonder why someone hasn't taken you off the market."

"Maybe the right person hasn't come along."

I looked at him, wondering if there was more to the story, but I was sure I would never know.

"Follow me home," he said.

Looking past him, I tried to figure a way to make him understand this was all moving too fast—that I needed time to think. I reluctantly met his gaze, prepared to refuse his offer, but the moment our eyes connected, I somehow lost the capacity to say no.

I let out a sigh. "Okay."

Aiden kissed the hollow of my neck, tingles traveling through me as his lips graced my skin. He planted two subsequent kisses along my collarbone, and then his tongue was at the base of my neck, tracing back and forth. He was driving me insane.

"Dinner's ready," he said.

I never made it to his bed. It was a little nippy, so as soon as we entered his lavish penthouse, he'd started a fire. I sat on the couch watching him and was asleep in no time.

Cradling my face, he stared into my eyes. I could only imagine what he saw. I'm sure I looked a tired groggy mess — that's exactly how I felt.

"I asked you here so that we could talk and attempt to make some sense of what's happening between us."

"Yes," I replied. What happened to "not placing a label on this"? I sat up and he grasped my hand and led me to kitchen. Dinner was arranged on the table, complete with wine and salad. It smelled wonderful. He pulled back a chair, offering me a seat.

"Did you really cook this?" I asked, taking a spoonful of soup.

"Yes, it's my mother's recipe. It's one of the few meals she could actually make without our having to pull out a fire extinguisher," he said, smiling.

"It's delicious. What is it?" I asked.

"Chicken and avocado lime soup," he replied. "I'm glad you like it."

After dinner we cleared the dishes and moved to the living area. I noticed how richly designed his home was. My attention was immediately drawn to the grand piano near the window and the guitar on the stand beside it. "Do you play often?" I asked.

"No. And when I do, it's only for entertainment purposes around a campfire," he replied, keeping the relaxed mood going.

I continued looking at it, thinking of my attempt to play as a child.

"I know you wanted to learn to play the piano, but what about the guitar? Can you play?" he asked.

"I tried. It didn't work out. I would love to learn though."

"I can teach you that, too, if you'd like. I wouldn't have guessed you to be musical."

"That's because I'm not." I smiled sheepishly. "I started lessons as a child, and I learned one extremely simple song. Well, it's more of a melody than a song."

Aiden walked over to the guitar and removed it from the stand.

"Play it for me."

For a moment I just looked at him, trying to decide whether I should or not. Eventually, I grabbed the instrument and began to strum a few chords. He stared, wide-eyed and smiling.

"What?" I asked. "Why are you looking at me like that?"

"I'm surprised you did as I asked so easily. I didn't think you could do that."

"I wonder if my reluctance to do as you ask has anything to do with the fact that it usually involves my going along with whatever kinky sex idea you've worked up."

He chuckled. "So does that mean you regret last night?"

"How about I let you know the answer to that question when I'm firing on all cylinders?" I passed the guitar back to him, and he propped it against the sofa.

"I'll do that." He sat beside me. "I guess we should begin with a not so difficult elephant in the room. I imagine you're wondering how I can afford such a place on an intern's salary."

I raised my eyebrows and shook my head. "No, I wasn't really." Then I admitted, "Well, yes the thought did cross my mind."

"I guess we can begin there. You know part of my history, the educational part at least. Remember when I told you my father was a successful business man?"

I nodded as he continued.

"Some things I own are a result of his success. I'm stubborn and have refused some luxuries he offers because they come at a price. Then there are certain aspects of my relationship with him that I tolerate for my mother's sake. That's an entirely different story, which I hope to share with you one day. I've also done exceptionally well with investments, which has allowed me to start a business of my own. It's nothing like what my father does, but I'm passionate about it. I'm sure you have questions, but I promise we'll get to those at a later date. For now, I want to talk about us." He propped his elbows on his knees and looked at me.

"What's happened between us has been like Alice falling down a rabbit hole," I said hesitantly. "It's foreign to me, all of it. I can't help but wonder if it's all been a dreadful mistake. Yet, I can't seem to stop myself from wandering deeper."

He smiled at me as he reached to place a strand of hair behind my ear. "Good. I don't want you to stop it," he replied, obviously ignoring the part about it all being a mistake. I froze as his finger lightly skimmed my cheek. He removed his hand and I continued.

"I know this may sound silly, but when I've thought of the effect you have on me, I pictured myself as a cartoon character."

He shook his head in confusion. "What?"

"I remember as a child seeing Tom lure Jerry into a trap with a huge piece of cheese. The delicious aroma would drift out and the innocent victim would float through the air, unable to stop, as the delectable smell drew him right into the villain's trap." My eyes glazed over as I thought back to those days in front of the TV. "Well, that's me. I know I should stop, but I simply can't help myself."

"Firstly, I'm no villain. And I mean no offense, but I would hardly describe you as the innocent victim."

"Oh really?" I asked.

"Really. Our recent trysts more than destroy the image of your innocence. Secondly, you were very willing, so if you were the victim, you were an extremely pleased victim."

"You smug bastard."

"Wait. I'm not being pretentious. I'm simply stating facts. You're a woman that appreciates factual data, are you not?"

I stared at him as he continued.

"Ms. Cason...well, first off, I think we're beyond the Ms. Cason stage, don't you?"

"That is yet to be determined," I replied.

"Very well. *Ms. Cason*, we're both extremely attractive people who are extremely attracted to each other. We acted on that. Should we stop? I say no. I can't. And thinking back, I don't know that I can say that I ever thought one time would be enough. The first time in your office, as soon as I came and pulled out of you, I immediately wanted more."

I didn't know what to say. Despite my many reservations, I felt the same way.

"You say you're drawn to me," he went on. "Well, it's the same for me. I can't stop thinking about you, and not just in a sexual sense. In everything. I want to know you intimately, in every possible way. I've told you countless times I want you."

His deep green eyes penetrated mine. We sat and stared at each other for long, heated seconds, and before I knew it, I was on my back, his firm body pressed against mine as he kissed me slowly, deeply, his tongue exploring my mouth. I felt his manhood harden against my stomach and my hunger for him took over. He reached under my shirt, kneading my breast and then pulling down the cup of my bra, touching my bare skin. I moaned as he pinched my nipple…and then I heard his doorbell. He abruptly stopped and looked down at me.

"Fuck, who would be at my door at this hour?" He stood and straightened himself. I sat up and my eyes went directly to his bulge. He smiled at me and leaned over to pull my bottom lip from the clutches of my teeth. "See what you do to me? I'm always so hard for you. The night I came to your house with dinner, I was so hard that I thought I'd suffer blue balls. That's why I left so abruptly."

There was a knock at the door.

I raised my brows. "You'd better get that. It could be your special someone. You know, like a girlfriend."

His face fell into a frown. "Don't do that. I don't have a girlfriend. It may be hard to believe, seeing how things happened between the two of us, but I don't sleep around. And I don't invite anyone here, ever. Actually, I'm somewhat wounded that you would think that of me." His frown deepened, and he walked off to answer the door.

Damn, I really did offend him. It wasn't my fault he was so fucking hot that I assumed he got his fair share of ass, and then some. I was actually surprised he didn't have an extremely active sex life. Still, I must remember to apologize for that.

I was lost in my musings about his carnalities when I heard voices. I strained, but couldn't make out anything, but the voices were getting closer. I double checked to make sure I didn't look as though I'd been manhandled on the couch by that delicious man. I didn't have a mirror, so the best I could do was ensure my hair wasn't mussed up as I sat up straight, crossing my legs and looking at the fire.

"I knew it! I just knew you had a girl in here. I knew that was why you were behaving so weirdly."

I turned to see Aiden entering the room with a beautiful petite brunette whose hand he was holding. Aiden followed my glance to his entwined fingers, held up their hands, and placed them on his heart.

I suddenly felt sick.

❧Chapter Fourteen❧

My heartbeat quickened as I considered my escape. Rising from the sofa, I plastered a forced smile on my lips, looking at the strange woman and then back at Aiden.

"Forgive me for my lack of manners. Aria, I would like for you to meet Allison, my sister."

Sister? She *did* look familiar, but she wasn't with them in St Barts. I thought back to our first day working together, when Aiden had discussed his education and background. I didn't recall our discussing the number of siblings. I normally bypass such small talk, primarily because I preferred not to discuss my own family.

I suddenly remembered why she seemed familiar; she was the girl who'd held my cab outside of RPH after the elevator incident. I sighed inwardly, my tension evaporating as quickly as it had occurred, now that I knew this woman's connection to Aiden.

"It's nice to meet you, Aria. What a beautiful name," Allison said, smiling at me and then looking back at her brother.

"Thank you. It's nice to meet you as well," I replied, feeling like a complete fool. Allison seemed very excited to meet me. She wore a fitted white dress with a brown braided belt, her brunette hair back in a loose ponytail. She was a very pretty girl with a peaches and cream complexion, high cheekbones, and full lips like her brother. Her silver-green eyes were bright and cheery.

"Allie, can you give us a moment? Why don't you go select a bottle of wine for us?" Aiden asked. Allison looked at her brother and frowned like she would argue. "Allison, go," he ordered.

"Fine, but Aria doesn't leave until I get back."

"Allison!" he warned.

"Okay, I'm going, geez." She turned and headed toward the kitchen, her dark pony tail swinging along her shoulders.

Aiden turned toward me. "You didn't think Allison was my—"

"Uh, yeah, I did, and you would have, also, in the same situation."

"I apologize for not introducing you as soon as we came in. This is not a common thing for me," he said.

"What? Having someone meet a member of your family, or juggling two women at once?" I asked.

"You're doing it again. I'm not partial to your idea of me as a fucking womanizer," he said, his irritation with me apparent.

"I apologize. For that, and for my earlier comment," I said, embarrassed.

"Thank you. What I was attempting to say before I was insulted, was that I was taken aback, given what was going on when we were interrupted. Quite frankly, I didn't know the proper way to introduce you."

"Oh," I said, wondering what the appropriate introduction would be at this point in this contorted relationship.

"My sister is in town for a week or so, and I forgot she was stopping by tonight," he said.

I looked over to where Allison disappeared. Aiden gently touched my chin, turning me to face him. "Don't worry about Allison. I don't want you to leave."

I stared up into his beautiful eyes, not wanting to leave, either, but feeling the need to.

Aiden grasped my shoulders, sliding his hands along my arms to hold my hands, giving them a reassuring squeeze.

"I'll stay," I said.

A smile played at the corner of his perfect lips. "Now that we've settled that, let's locate my sister," he said as he released one of my hands and turned, pulling me behind him.

My first instinct was to retract my hand, not wanting to elicit any further assumptions from Allison, but I liked the way my fingers felt entwined with his. Leading me to the kitchen, Aiden pressed a button on the wall near the refrigerator. The back wall moved, revealing a huge pantry. We stepped inside, and to the immediate left was a modest wine cellar. Allison wasn't there.

"Allison?" he called, walking behind the first row of wine and finding her sitting on the floor engrossed in a telephone call. She motioned that she needed privacy. He looked at her for a moment longer before she waved him off again. "I hope it's not our mother," he said, shaking his head in exasperation, once out of the pantry.

"Is everything okay with your mother? She's not ill is she?" I asked.

"It's nothing like that. It's just that she can be quite intense at times, is all," he said. Aiden was less relaxed than he was a moment ago—I wondered what that was all about. He walked over and opened the wine climate cabinet and found it empty. "I thought there was at least one bottle in here," he uttered. "Since we've been banned from the wine pantry, how about I show you around while we wait on Allison?"

"Sure," I replied, as he closed the door and led me out of the kitchen. I was rather curious about the other areas of the penthouse. I was sure they were as amazing as the kitchen, which was one any chef would appreciate. There were two stone work-tops, one with a programmable backsplash that would be great for displaying recipes. The other island contained a glass stovetop, warming drawers, and a bar area. Beyond the island was an espresso bar, directly under a shelf of porcelain coffee cups and saucers. There was a control panel in the center of the island for the audio and visual components for the entire penthouse.

A spacious conversation area sat adjacent to the kitchen—it held a stainless steel fireplace and clerestory windows. Its décor was in line with what I'd seen of the other rooms so far, which were done in modern contemporary.

Aiden continued to hold my hand as we toured the other rooms in the penthouse. The color palate was primarily white and brown; the masculinity was obvious, but not so overt as to offend. Very tasteful. The last room was his bedroom. As I walked over the threshold and gazed around the room, I started to feel a slight unease, and attempted to pull my hand away from his. He responded by tightening his fingers around mine and turning to face me.

"Is something wrong?" he asked.

"No," I lied.

"Are you sure?" he pursued, with a teasing smile.

"Yes. What could possibly be wrong?"

"I'm not sure. I've been holding your hand for the last ten minutes, and as soon as we enter my bedroom, you pull your hand away. If I didn't know better, I would think you were nervous."

"What would I possibly have to be nervous about, Aiden?"

"I can't think of anything. But that doesn't change the fact that you seem that way," he said, taking a few steps closer to me.

I was affected by him, as always, and he knew it. How could I not be? Memories of him inside me, of doing things with him I'd never done with another man, flashed through my head. I was out of my element with this guy. He'd given me more orgasms in a few days than I'd had in the last two years, excluding the self-induced, ones of course.

Aiden lowered his head, his lips grazing my ear, his breath warm and seductive against my skin. "Am I making you nervous, Aria?" he asked, planting a barely-there kiss below my earlobe.

I swallowed hard and maintained my faux calm as he planted another kiss on my cheek and then pulled back to look at me.

"Can we finish the tour, or do you plan to seduce me in the doorway with your sister only a couple of rooms away?"

He chuckled and pulled me toward the double doors across the room. He opened them, revealing a breathtaking view of Boston. It wasn't quite dark yet; a gentle breeze floated across my face. We stood in silence, taking in the evening scene. The skyline was one worthy of canvas; the sun, almost set, cast an orange-colored streak across the horizon. I sighed happily.

"Beautiful," he whispered.

Indeed, it was a beautiful sight.

I looked up to see his eyes on me. "You're exquisite," he whispered.

I continued to look at him as he stood against the background of the purple dusk. He was unbelievably beautiful. I knew some men wouldn't care to be described with that word, so I didn't dare say it aloud. His dark hair was cropped on the sides, with the slightest of sideburns. Thick, dark brows sat above those insanely beautiful emerald green eyes. His nose was straight and refined, and his full lips were as seductive as an aphrodisiac. I longed to feel them on mine. The thought of his lips — knowing they had been on mine, his tongue in my mouth — nearly caused me to forget Allison was close by. I continued to study him. His chin was distinguished fitting the elitist air, he sometimes gave off, and his jawline…holy hell…it could chisel granite. It was as though each part of him was carved to create the perfect male specimen. How could you not stare? How could you not be instantly and uncontrollably drawn to this Adonis?

He cupped my face, his eyes searching mine before he slowly lowered his head to my mouth. The initial contact was warm and soft. His tongue skimmed along my bottom lip before seeking entry into my mouth. Skillfully, his lips moved across mine as he pulled me closer, searching for my tongue, which I willingly relinquished. I sank into him as he deepened our kiss, our tongues moving to the rhythm of our accelerated heartbeats. I was lost. My senses had been taken over by this man. I only felt what he made me feel. He moaned into my mouth, sucking my tongue, slowly pulling it deeper into his.

"There you are."

We immediately severed our connection at the sound of Allison's voice.

How long had she been standing there? She walked toward us with a quick glance at me before she focused her attention on Aiden. What she must think of me? Was she accustomed to seeing her brother tongue-lash wanton women?

"Are you finally available to continue your visit with your favorite brother?" Aiden asked.

"Who says you're my favorite?"

"Let's see, there's our mother, our brother, our sister, your girlfriends, oh, and you!"

"Well, that was *then*. I think I'll need to reevaluate what constitutes favorite."

"Is that so?" he asked.

She laughed. "Yeah, it is so."

He smiled at her, and she jumped toward him for a hug. "It's so good to be with you. I nearly forgot how much fun you can be sometimes."

A few pangs of sadness touched me as I watched their exchange. It was obvious they were close and adored each other. I had that with April somewhat, but I'd be lying if I said I didn't want that type of relationship with my sisters. I quickly banished that thought as Allison announced she had assembled a fruit and cheese snack to go along with the wine. Aiden reached for my hand, and I willingly obliged. Why bother to hide our hand-holding at this point? His sister saw us practically about to rip each other's clothes off.

Aiden and I followed Allison back to the kitchen, where the wine was breathing. Walking behind the bar, she grabbed three wineglasses. Aiden picked up the bottle and glanced at the label before pouring for each of us. When Allison took a seat at the bar, I followed her lead, and just as Aiden was about to sit beside me, his phone rang. He slipped his hand into his pocket and a frown marred his perfect face when he glimpsed the phone's display.

"Excuse me, I have to take this," he said as he left the kitchen. My eyes followed him as he walked away, admiring his taut backside and recognizing the desire that was always quietly sitting there, waiting for him to flick the switch that transitioned me into a mindless ball of lust.

"He's gorgeous, isn't he?" Allison said, observing my appreciative survey of her brother.

I blushed and turned to face her with an embarrassed smile. Well, slightly embarrassed. I mean, really, it was what it was. And that man was every woman's fantasy.

"There's certainly no denying that," I replied.

"How long have you been dating?"

"We're not," I replied. I took a sip of the wine.

"Really?" Allison asked, puzzled.

Why was she confused? It was true, we weren't dating.

"Then my brother must really be into you," she said. She grabbed a few grapes from the tray and leaned on the counter.

"Why would you say that?" I asked.

"The way he looks at you, the hand-holding, the, umm, heated kiss I interrupted earlier. Aiden is not one to do that. He's very contained, to the point that it's infuriating. He's playful with me, but that's because I've worn him down and he tolerates me."

I took another sip of wine considering what Allison revealed. *Contained*? He had actually accused me of the same.

"So how did you meet?" she asked.

"We work together."

"I'm sure that makes for interesting days at work," she said.

If you only knew. It's teetering on the brink of insanity.

"Let's just say it's never boring," I replied.

Aiden returned, looking stressed. Allison asked if he was okay but he basically blew her off. He reached for his wine and walked over to the cheese and crackers. I watched as he placed one in his mouth, curious as to the swift change in his mood.

"I hope you haven't been grilling Aria, or filling her head with any of your stories," he said, petulance tainting his voice

"Oh, Aiden, are you afraid I may tell her something that would scare her off?" she teased.

"Possibly," he replied. He smirked, but I could see a hint of truth in his response as he and Allison exchanged glances.

"Was that Daddy on the phone?" she asked.

"Why would you think that?"

"Your mood. He's the only one that changes it so abruptly."

He tossed her a warning look, and she changed the subject. We talked the remainder of the evening. Actually, I mostly listened, which was ideal for me. I knew right off that I liked Allison; she was very animated. Her eyes, already bright and lively, lit up even more when she filled us in on her new romance. I also caught another weird exchange between them when she voiced how thrilled she was to be away from her parents. I sensed Aiden felt the same. Allison and her brother were very playful with each other, affording me a tiny glimpse into the parts of him I didn't usually see. My interactions with him were always so intense. Sure, we had some relaxed conversations, but those were few and far between.

Near the end of the evening, Allison left to meet some friends for a nightcap. She reminded Aiden of her upcoming ballet performance and gave him two tickets. She gave me a hug good-bye and said she hoped to see me soon. Aiden closed the door and immediately pulled me into an embrace.

"I hope tonight wasn't too weird for you."

"No, I rather enjoyed it. I like your sister. She doesn't seem as standoffish as your other family members."

He laughed. "In all fairness, you only met my family for what, five minutes. As I recall you were unable to actually spend any real time with them because of your date, remember?"

"It wasn't a date, and besides, it doesn't take a tremendous amount of time to pick up a distant air from someone."

"If you felt they were distant, it was more than likely due to the shock of my introducing you to them. That doesn't really happen much. Or ever."

"Do you typically hide your girlfriends from your family?"

"I don't typically *have* girlfriends, and when I do, my family usually knows the person before I do, so introductions aren't actually necessary."

"Oh." That was odd. But then again, at least he'd had girlfriends; I'd never had a boyfriend. I never wanted one.

He walked me over to the couch. "I know we didn't have much time to talk, and it's getting late."

"Yes. I really should be getting home."

"I would like to at least establish my expectations."

"Okay, shoot."

"I asked you earlier if you had any idea how badly I wanted you. You didn't reply. I wanted to clarify my intent. I was not referring to wanting you in only a sexual context. I want all of you."

Despite his attempt to explain, I was clueless as to what that meant. I purposely avoided interactions that would ever lead to conversations such as this.

"Aiden, I didn't reply because I honestly don't know what to say to something like that. I'm not ready to hear anyone tell me that, let alone you. We agreed to one thing in St. Barts, and not even a week later, you're changing the terms, which makes me think that my consent was a mistake. I should go."

I stood, but Aiden grabbed my hand.

"Why is running your go-to response?" he asked.

"I'm not running, Aiden. I'm living my life as I see fit — doing what's in my best interest. I won't allow myself to get caught up in whatever it is you have planned. I'll only end up losing myself in the midst of it all."

"It's apparent that your work is your life. You aren't letting yourself experience anything more than that. So in that sense, you've lost yourself already."

I wanted to slap him. "I don't need to hear this shit from you," I said angrily, because whether he knew it or not, he'd struck a nerve.

He continued. "I know you want more than this. You're afraid, Aria, and it would seem that you can't trust...or is it that you *won't* trust? Have I given you any indication that I would hurt you? You say I don't know you, but I've seen you. I've seen the person you want to hide from the world. She's a strong, courageous, beautiful woman. Not this controlled, safe person that you've convinced yourself that you have to be."

I sank back into the couch. Was that how the world perceived me? How he perceived me? If so, he saw things in me that I didn't see in myself. Things I would love to own, but I simply didn't see myself in that light.

I stared into his shining eyes, feeling ashamed and exposed. A single tear rolled down my cheek. He reached and wiped it away.

"Just let me in."

This man had the capacity to break me. I wouldn't let him. I closed my eyes, needing to shut the door he had somehow opened.

Things were so clear and orderly before he came along. I was certain of my thoughts, my dreams, and my decisions. But since he'd entered my world, I found that I was questioning myself. I didn't like it. I was vulnerable, and I hated being vulnerable to anyone or anything. I needed to get away from him, but I knew I couldn't.

"You agreed to this, and I'm not letting you back out," he said.

"You can't stop me."

"I don't think I have much to worry about. You want it. You wouldn't be here otherwise."

"I'm still in the decision-making process, so don't get too

cocky, Mr. Wyatt."

Smirking, he reached over and grasped my hands. He looked into my eyes and sighed. "What can I do to get you fully over to my side?" he asked, his eyes darkening.

I bit the corner of my lip. I knew what it would take, but would he go along with it? "In St. Barts, we made an agreement and you said 'no negotiations' and I foolishly went along with that. I need *you* to agree to modify."

"That would depend on the nature of the modification. What do you want, Aria?"

"You want to be in control of my orgasms. Well, I want to be in control of yours," I said looking at him, gauging his reaction. "I recall an offer that you made some time ago, and I need you to make good on it."

"What offer?" he asked, confused.

"To dominate you."

❧Chapter Fifteen❧

Aiden's lips parted slightly. I stared at his handsome, expressionless face, awaiting his reaction. Cocking his head, he squinted, assessing me. Finally, a slow smile appeared. He released my hands, resting his elbows on his knees.

"Is that what you want, to dominate me? Is that what it will take for you to stop running?"

"What if it is?" Quite honestly, I didn't know, but I knew it was a step toward my comfort zone, and therefore it was a necessity.

He walked to the kitchen and returned with the bottle of wine. "What's your description of domination?" he asked.

"What, are you afraid?" I teased.

"Should I be?" he asked, and we both laughed.

"You're extreme, Aria, and I think most men find it intimidating."

"But not you?"

He refilled both of our glasses. "No, I find it intriguing…and challenging."

"So this is all about the challenge for you?" I asked, taking a sip of the wine.

"I didn't say that." He sat back and crossed his leg, his ankle propped on his knee as he rested his arm on the back of the sofa.

"What are you saying?"

"Do I like a challenge? Yes. But there is so much more to you than just that aspect. If it was just the challenge, I would have fucked you in your office and kept it strictly business from that point forward, sweetheart."

"Well, damn," I said.

"I'm just being honest," he said.

"To clarify, I'm not referring to any of that extreme dominatrix stuff, so no, you shouldn't be worried. I just want to be the one in control of your orgasms from time to time," I said.

He looked intrigued. I could see the wheels turning, but he had yet to reply.

"You said you like challenges so I'm presenting you with one. Are you going to accept it?" I asked.

As his eyes darkened, that slow smile I adored touched his lips. "Game on, baby," he said and pulled me into a deep kiss.

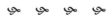

The next couple of days were filled with an abundance of work and play. I thoroughly enjoyed both, as they both involved Aiden. We discussed scheduling a standing "business lunch" twice a week. This was more of a way to ease the sexual tension, as he couldn't seem to keep his hands off of me, not that I minded at all. I'd never had so much sex with anyone, and each time was as incredible as the last. He made sure of it.

I'd started planning my domination exploit with Aiden and had most of the details worked out. I wanted his experience to be as memorable as mine had been. I couldn't wait to show him how I exerted my control. Although we'd discussed the possibility of it being a two-time encounter, I'd decided, unbeknownst to him, that I wanted this routinely. It wasn't my norm, but it restored the balance between us and I needed that.

It was Friday, almost three o'clock. The days typically flew by so quickly that I had to be reminded that it was time to go. Today was different. Every day had been different since Aiden, and tonight was especially exciting.

I was replying to an email from the editing department when my phone pinged.

Reaching in my drawer, I glimpsed the display and saw it was a text from Aiden. I smiled as I read it.

Can you get a message to Virginia for me? If you'll let her know that Kingston has been thinking about her all day, I would appreciate it.

I most certainly will. I'll let you know what she says.

Thank you. I eagerly await her response, so tell her not to keep me waiting.

I understand. She is usually very quick to respond.

Yes, I've noticed that. It's one of the things Kingston loves about her.

I told her what you said, and she said that she thinks Kingston may have the required assets to maintain permanent employment. But she would need a few more interviews with him before she could properly assess the situation.

Kingston was resting, but when I told him of Virginia's reply, his head immediately rose. And FYI, tell her that Kingston is always "interview ready."

I would love to continue delivering messages from Virginia, but I need to finish up some work before I leave. I've a date with a really hot guy, and I think I'm going to get fucked tonight.

What a coincidence, I have a date tonight, also. It's with a really hot babe, and I know she's going to get fucked tonight.

I squeezed my thighs as Virginia tightened, excited by the notion of an impending reunion with Kingston. Banishing my Kingston thoughts and forcing myself to focus, I continued with my emails and phone calls until it was nearly five o'clock. As I was shutting my computer down, Raina stepped in to inform me of her departure. This was the weekend, she and the family planned to visit Salem Willows Park, so she was anxious to get home and get on the road. I wished her a great weekend, and since I couldn't exactly tell her about Aiden, I tried to rein in the excitement of my own plans. Grabbing my phone and purse, I followed her out.

Aiden had invited me to attend Allison's dance performance,

and I was looking forward to a night out on his arm. It was our first real date. Yes, we'd had lunch and dinner together in the past, but it was in the privacy of our homes. This would be our first time going out. Well, if you didn't count the schoolgirl role-play, which was more of a fuck than a date.

I had selected a Juan Carlos Obando alice blue silk satin deep V-neck gown. It had a wide waist tie and a crisscross strap at the back. I chose this as a method of torture for Aiden. The V in the dress was as low as my navel, with a very generous view of my boobs.

I expected Aiden at my door shortly after seven o'clock, but I wanted to meet him downstairs to gage his reaction in a more public place. I sent him a quick text and told him I would meet him at the entrance of the building.

Just as I was closing my door, I received a text from Aiden, stating that he'd pulled up to my building. I tapped a quick reply that I was on my way down.

Entering the lobby, I saw Silas seated at the concierge desk. He raised his head to greet me, and his eyes fell to my chest. "Good evening, Ms. Cason," he said, lifting his gaze, his reddened cheeks giving him away.

"Hello, Silas," I replied as I sauntered across the room, toward the doorman who held the door as I exited the building. As I stepped outside, the door to a limousine opened and Aiden emerged. He was dressed in a black suit, and he looked as if he belonged on the cover of *GQ*. I had to catch my breath and remind myself that I wanted to take note of his response to me instead of getting caught up in my own reaction to his appearance. I watched as his eyes toured my body, his appraisal pausing momentarily as he took in the curves of my breasts.

"Wow. You're gorgeous," he exclaimed.

"Thank you. You don't look so bad yourself, handsome."

"I'm pretty sure all eyes will be on you, princess."

I loved when he called me that. Tonight I especially felt as though I looked like a princess going out with her dashing prince.

I looked at the awaiting car, reminded of the last time I'd had a limo ride with him. Although only a few days ago, it seemed longer than that.

Aiden followed my gaze toward the limo. "This was not my doing, it was Allison's. Well, it's more the ballet company. They arranged transport for the family members."

"What? I didn't say anything," I offered, smiling, as was he.

"You didn't have to. I know what you were thinking."

"Oh, so you're a mind reader, too? So many talents."

"I am when it comes to *your* mind," he said, taking my hand and escorting me to the car as he motioned to the driver that he would take care of the door.

Once inside, Aiden poured drinks for the two of us.

"I didn't say I wanted a drink."

"Oh, but you didn't need to." He tapped the side of his forehead with his index finger. "Mind reader, remember?"

We both laughed.

If I hadn't already fallen for this man, there was no chance I'd be able to keep from doing so. I'd seen so many facets of his personality, and each one made me crave more.

He was complicated, just as I was. There were parts of us that we both kept hidden from the world. I understood why I did. But why did he? I needed to know, but I hoped that whatever I found wouldn't cause me to pull away. At this point, I couldn't imagine anything doing that, though.

"Do you have any idea how stunning you look this evening?" he asked, leaning in to kiss my earlobe. He placed his hand on my thigh, sliding it up to my stomach and up further still to cup my breast. With his free hand, he pressed a button to raise the privacy window and began planting a trail of soft kisses down my neck.

I moaned, leaning into him as he moved his hand beneath the fabric for direct contact with my breast. I reluctantly stopped his progression, and pulled his hand away.

"You can look, Mr. Wyatt, but you can't touch." I felt his smile on my neck before he lifted his head.

"Is that a rule? I think we both know I don't do well with your rules."

"Well, unless you want the tape holding this dress in place to come off, the rule is necessary, at least until we leave the ballet."

"So I was right?" he asked.

"About?"

"You wore this to drive me crazy, didn't you?"

A hint of a smile played on my lips. "Now, why would I go and do a thing like that to someone who has never once done a thing to drive *me* crazy?" I asked.

He grabbed my hand and slid it over his crotch. He was hard. I looked up at him as Virginia responded to his gesture.

"See what you've done?"

I smiled, pleased that I had this type of effect on him.

"You're going to need to do something to help me out, Aria. Either cover up or..."

"Or what?" I asked.

"Make me come," he said.

"What do you mean?"

"I would imagine since you went to such extremes to tease me all night that you also devised a plan to handle the fruit of your labor? You're such a detailed person, I'm confident you've something in mind. So let's hear it."

"I don't actually have a plan, but I'm certainly open to suggestions."

"That's all I needed to hear." He kissed my cheek and gulped the remainder of his drink, then turned and stared out the window.

What just happened? Is the conversation over?

He didn't say anything the remainder of the drive to the ballet, nor did I. I took a few sips of my drink and followed his lead, staring out the window.

The limo slowed and we turned into a line of cars. Easing toward the entrance, I finished my drink and placed the glass on the bar. I glanced at Aiden, and he was still looking in the opposite direction. He hadn't so much as touched me.

The car stopped beside a fountain near the entrance of the building, and the driver was at Aiden's door moments later.

Aiden stepped out of the limo, and then turned to assist me. His gaze was cast downward, fixed on the reason for our tiny discord. I noticed his temples flexing just before he leaned in and kissed my cheek. "You're beautiful."

I didn't reply. I just stared at him, wondering what the hell was going through his head.

"Shall we?" he asked, as he turned toward the building.

I was bothered that he didn't continue holding my hand as I'd expected. *He is spoiling the date before it even has a chance to start,* I thought as we entered the double doors of the Boston Ballet Company.

Aiden reached into his jacket to secure the tickets and passed them to the attendant who greeted us at the door. After reviewing the stubs, he returned them and provided directions to our seats. Aiden placed his hand at the small of my back and ushered me into the lobby, where he requested a number for our drinks to avoid the wait at intermission.

There were a few couples in front of us heading towards their seats, and the lights dimmed as a chime sounded, alerting us that the performance would begin shortly. The usher passed two programs to Aiden and then led us to our seats.

Once we were settled, I opened the program to read the synopsis. I was surprised to see Aiden Wyatt on the list of financial contributors. Surprised by my discovery, I glanced at him.

"Everything okay?" he asked, looking at me.

"Yes, everything's great," I replied, smiling.

The lights dimmed, and the orchestra conductor arrived. A few moments of applause and some instrument flourishes later, a melody floated from the orchestra pit and the curtains opened, revealing the opening scene of *A Midsummer's Night Dream.*

It was an incredible performance, and Allison was a very talented dancer. Then again, that anyone could spin or leap around in circles without topping over into the orchestra pit was amazing in itself to me. I glimpsed at her brother, who was beaming with pride as he watched Allison in the pas de deux. We applauded as the curtains closed and the house lights came up for intermission.

I went to the powder room as Aiden waited outside the door for me. He said that we'd get our drinks afterwards. The line for the restrooms was extremely long. I only needed to check my makeup and make sure my tape was firmly in place, which it was. I exited the rest room, and Aiden was nowhere to be found. I looked toward the cocktails bar and didn't see him there either. Maybe he'd went to the restroom himself. So I stood and waited.

My phone pinged and I opened my clutch to check my text. It was from Aiden.

Make a right near the restroom and go down the hall to the third door on the left. We can have our drinks here in private.

He is so odd at times, I thought as I followed his directions to the room. I looked behind me before reaching for the doorknob. The hallway was empty. Opening the door, I stepped inside to see Aiden standing near a desk in the center of the room with his phone in hand.

"Lock the door," he said.

As I followed his instruction, there was another ping of my phone.

"Check your text, Aria."

I looked at him, questioning his demand.

"Do it."

I opened my purse and pulled out my phone.

You said you were open to suggestions. I have only one. Suck me off.

Afraid to meet his eyes, I concentrated on slipping the phone back into my purse. Although we'd engaged in several sexual encounters, I had yet to give him a blowjob. I felt as though my heart was thumping against my breast bone when I lifted my gaze to his. To see him standing there, staring at me, looking every inch the hot alpha male that he was, it was quite intimidating. There was always that something about him that made me nervous. He was so skilled in bed and his talents didn't stop with his cock, his tongue was the orgasm sexual fantasies were made of. I wanted to give him at least a portion of what he'd given me. And that was the thought that drove me. The thought that pulled me to him — that pulled me to that place — the one that made me forget everything else. My thoughts were only of us, of him, of giving him what he'd demanded.

Anxious to please him, I stepped closer and, without breaking eye contact, I dropped to my knees, my attention fixed on the erection that was trapped within the confines of his suit. Reaching for his zipper, I quickly lowered it, releasing his manhood from the constricting material. Being so close to him — to his cock — it somehow seemed even larger than it had in the past, which made this challenge all the more alluring. I breathed him in, moaning as his unique scent took control of me.

The plush head was already glistening, anxious for the mouth it had yet to touch.

My thumb skimmed the tip, spreading the clear moisture over the thick crown, and unable to resist, I leaned in for a kiss, fluttering my tongue around and in the opening. He inhaled a sharp intake of breath and then his hand was cradling my head.

My tongue moved along the length of his hardness, tracing the protrusion of veins through his skin, and then slowly, I took him into my mouth, easing toward the root as my mouth expanded to accommodate his girth. I hollowed my cheeks and quickened my pace, sucking harder, knowing we only had a few moments and wanting him to have what he aimed for—a release. A low growl reverberated in his chest and his hands moved to the back of my head, prodding me to suck faster.

"Oh fuck. Don't stop," he murmured. I reached for his balls, gently massaging them as I continued to move him in and out of my mouth. "Suck it harder," he ordered, and I eagerly complied, tightening the suction as I pulled him into my mouth. "Ah…shh. Just like that," he said, his voice raspy. When I moaned around his length, his pelvis started to move, meeting my mouth with solid thrusts, urging the tip to the back of my throat, and then his cock was pulsing, signaling that he was about to explode. I prepared myself as he hardened more. Thick, hot come erupted, filling my mouth. I swallowed, nearly choking as a second helping burst forth. Not swallowing quickly enough, some of his thick cream slipped from the corner of my mouth. I reared back, moving him out of my mouth and then tracing the edge of my lips with my tongue, capturing the sweetness that had escaped. I looked up at him as I licked the other side of my mouth. His gaze was heated, dark, a clear indication that he wanted to fuck me into oblivion.

"Stand up," he said gruffly.

He positioned me in front of the desk and turned me around. "Bend over."

Once I was level with the desk, he lifted my dress.

"Damn. I love your ass, baby. Do you know that?" he asked, as his hand moved between my thighs. "Shit. You're so fucking wet."

The next sound was that of my panties ripping, followed by his dick slapping hard against my ass.

He filled me with the first thrust, and he was just as I'd expected, deep and rough.

When I cried out, his hand covered my mouth, as he pounded into me, over and over again.

"You feel so good, Aria. So tight."

I was about to come, and he obviously felt it. "Wait for me," he grunted.

Fuck, fuck, fuck. Wait for him? How the fuck was I going to do that with him fucking me like this? I tried not to come, but it just felt too fucking good. I was almost there.

I shook my head, signifying he needed to move his hand.

"I'm about to come, Aiden."

"I'm right there with you. Come for me, baby."

With that, my pussy quaked, and I bit my lip, muffling my screams of pleasure. Aiden growled as he filled me with yet another hot release of his seed, grunting as he pulled out of me.

Not wanting to mess my gown, I held it in place as I turned to face him. He reached in his jacket and passed me a handkerchief, which I used to clean myself as much as possible. I would need to go to the ladies' room though. How can anyone come as often and in such copious amounts as this man?

He was watching me as he also put himself back together. Damn, he wore the 'I just fucked you look' so well.

"You were amazing, baby."

"Really? You liked it?"

"Hell yes. I want it again…like now."

I shook my head at him, secretly pleased that he'd enjoyed it as much as I had. I was sure we'd be going for round two pretty soon. For now we needed to get back to our seats, but I was missing something. I glanced at the desk and then on the floor beside me.

"What are you looking for?" he asked.

"My panties," I replied.

"Oh," he said, looking almost apologetic as he turned to help me find them. "Sorry," he said, as he passed them to me.

I examined my torn undergarment and looked up at his dancing eyes. "Why do I not believe you?"

"Here, drink this," he said as he passed the alcohol to me, which I sipped. He, on the other hand, gulped his.

"We need to get back," he said.

"I know, but I really need to get to the ladies' room."

"There's one over here." He pointed to a door in the corner.

After a speedy clean up, I re-touched my makeup and replaced the falling strands of hair with a bobby pin from my clutch. Satisfied with my appearance, I turned off the light and walked out to find Aiden standing near the door waiting for me—a smile forming on his handsome face.

"What?"

"You look amazing. You would never know you were just fucked."

"I could say the same of you, man-whore."

He burst into laughter, as did I. We walked out of the room, down the hall and hurried back to our seats.

We barely made it. Intermission was ending. The lights briefly dimmed again as the warning chime sounded. We were the last ones in our row to return to our seats. As we passed by the others, I smiled to myself, wondering if we smelled of sex. What would they think of us if they knew why we were late returning?

After we were seated, I saw Aiden touch his nose and smile a few times. What the hell was that about?

"Am I missing something? What are you doing?" I whispered.

"Smelling your pussy."

My mouth gaped open, but I quickly closed it, biting my lip. I was then, of course, both distracted and turned on by his pronouncement.

"How does it smell?" I asked.

"Delicious," he replied, staring down at me.

Oh fuck, that's hot! The way he looked at me when he said shit like that should be bottled and sold. I could literally come just from eye-fucking this man. Virginia was at full alert, anxious to give him more than just a whiff. I pictured his head between my thighs, licking and sucking my pussy until I exploded in his mouth.

With a wink, I turned away, looking straight ahead, hoping to focus on the performance. That proved to be a futile endeavor, especially when he placed his hand on my thigh. As I continued to ignore him though, his spell eventually wore off and my attention was again captured by the beautiful scene unfolding on the stage.

What an incredible performance it was. We continued

applauding long after the curtain closed. During the curtain call when Allison appeared, Aiden whistled, and I looked up at him and smiled. I loved seeing how much he adored his sister. I thought of my sisters and how I should be there supporting them just as Aiden was for his.

Once the house lights came up, we gathered our programs. "I want to go backstage to congratulate Allison," Aiden said as we walked out into the crowd.

While we were backstage awaiting Allison's emergence from the dressing room, an older couple approached us.

"Hello, Aiden. How are you?" the silver-haired man asked.

Aiden reached to shake his hand. "Allen. I'm well, thank you."

It's so good to see you, Aiden," said the woman. She tossed a suspicious look my way when she moved in to hug Aiden.

"Did you enjoy the ballet?" she asked.

"Yes, I did. Immensely. Allison never ceases to amaze me. She's a remarkable dancer," Aiden replied. "I would like you to meet Aria Cason. Aria these are Allen and Michelle Lane."

"It's nice to meet you, Aria," Allen said, his eyes focused on my cleavage.

"Yes, it's nice to meet you," Michelle replied with a tart smile.

This couple reminded me of Aiden's parents. Prudish.

Fortunately, Allison's dressing room door opened then, and her face lit up as soon as she spotted her brother. She then noticed me and her smile widened.

"Aria, you came!" she exclaimed as she rushed over to hug me. Her excitement took me by surprise, as it obviously did Aiden, judging by his shocked expression.

"Excuse me for a moment," Aiden said and walked toward one of the backstage attendants. Allison turned to greet Allen and Michelle.

"Did your parents fly in for the ballet?" Michelle asked Allison, while still eyeing me suspiciously.

"We sure did, and she was magnificent," answered a voice from behind us. Allison and I turned to see that her parents had joined us.

❧Chapter Sixteen❧

"Mommy, you actually came? And you were able to drag Daddy from behind his desk! My night could not be more perfect," Allison exclaimed, embracing them both.

"Allison is performing next week at the New York Lincoln Center and we won't be able to attend, so we thought we'd surprise her tonight," Sienna explained to the Lanes.

"Well, this is unexpected," Aiden said, returning to the group with a beautiful bouquet of peach roses, golden yellow calla lilies, and orange oriental lilies. "These are for our graceful and talented ballerina."

"Thank you, Aiden. They're absolutely beautiful," Allison said, hugging her brother.

"Don't you have a hug for your mother, Aiden?" Sienna asked.

"Of course, Mother. Don't be dramatic." Aiden embraced his mother. He leaned in for her to kiss his cheek and I could see from her brief appraisal of her son that she adored him.

Aiden's mother gifted me a forced smile as she assessed my appearance. I saw the judgment in her eyes and the appreciation in his father's as they glimpsed the top of my gown. I sensed neither of them approved of me as Aiden's date, and I easily discerned that Aiden was aware of their opinions.

"Mother, Father, you remember Aria Cason," Aiden offered.

"Why, yes. How lovely to see you again, dear," his mother said, as she glanced from me to Michelle, sending a mental message that the other woman apparently understood because she walked over and asked Sienna to speak with her privately.

Connor, Aiden's father, said, "Of course, Ms. Cason. With Raine Publishing, right?"

"Yes," I replied. "Are you familiar with the company?"

"One could say that. It's definitely on my radar." Connor reached out to shake my hand as he tossed a warning glance at Aiden. What was it with this family and the mental messages? It wasn't as if others couldn't tell something was going on.

Aiden sighed, exasperated. "So what prompted this very unexpected visit?" he asked, visibly annoyed.

Sienna glanced toward me as she and Michelle joined us, and answered her son's question. "We weren't sure we'd be able to attend due to various commitments, but we moved some things around. It's a good thing we did," his mother replied.

Still seeming annoyed, Aiden turned and softly murmured, "I didn't expect my parents would be here. If I had, I wouldn't have asked you to accompany me."

Well, that hurt. Was I not worthy to be in the presence of his stuck-up parents?

"Aria, forgive me. That didn't come out right," he said.

"You think?" I asked.

"Excuse us," Aiden said, and led me away from the group. "I told you, I've never had to deal with situations like this, and it's uncomfortable for all of us."

"But why? We're on a date. What's the big deal?"

"It's complicated. We can talk about it later," he replied.

I looked over at them and saw Michelle and Sienna looking as though they had swallowed two canaries each.

"What do you say we all go back to the penthouse for a nightcap?" Sienna suggested.

Ugh. I did not want to be around these people any longer than the time we spent backstage, which at this point was already too fucking much.

"Aria and I had plans, but by all means, the penthouse is all yours — literally," Aiden said.

"Can't you both join us, Aiden? I would like to get better acquainted with Aria."

"And why is that, Mother?" Aiden snapped.

"Aiden, don't be rude to your mother," Connor reprimanded.

"Actually, I'd promised Aiden and Aria they could attend the small celebration with the other dancers," Allison lied. "I was really looking forward to that, Mommy," she added, attempting to eradicate the awkwardness. And it really *was* awkward. What was up with these people?

"We're only here until tomorrow afternoon, Allie. Your mother and I would like to spend some time with our wayward children," Connor said jokingly.

Allison looked apologetically at Aiden.

"It's fine, Aiden. I can catch a cab. You should spend time with your family," I whispered to him.

"No," he replied angrily. "We'll join everyone for one drink and go to the party directly afterwards," Aiden added, looking at Allison for corroboration.

"That sounds perfect. Excuse me for just a moment. I need to say good-bye to some people," Allison said as she wandered off.

Aiden quickly assessed my demeanor and grabbed my hand. We waited in silence as his parents and their friends engrossed themselves in conversation. I would have preferred to end this night right here and go home, but I knew it would be difficult to get Aiden to agree. He stared straight ahead, irritated. I pulled my hand, attempting to free it from his, but he only held it tighter. What the hell was going on?

Allison returned within a few minutes, and we headed toward the exit. Outside, the driver stood near the limo. Connor suggested we all ride together, a suggestion to which Aiden vehemently rejected. Allison agreed to go with her parents, affording us some time alone.

Once in the limo, Aiden poured a drink for himself, which he quickly drank, and then poured a second. He placed the empty glass on the bar and looked at me, heat radiating from his fluid green eyes. He cradled my face, gently trailing his thumbs along my cheeks before pulling me into a kiss. He forced his tongue into my mouth, probing as he pulled me closer. He tasted of alcohol, just that right amount to make me want to suck his tongue. The smell of the alcohol combined with his cologne and his own delicious scent was overpowering. Moving his hands from my face, he traced his fingertips from my neck, along my shoulders, and slowly down my arms, evoking a current that made my sex clench. He placed my hand on his lengthening shaft. I rubbed my hands over him, recalling the joy of him in my mouth earlier, growing hungry for him again.

"Did you actually think I was going to allow you to end our night with you catching a cab home? There's no way I'm missing the opportunity to help you out of this dress, princess." And with those few words, the tension of the last few minutes no longer mattered.

When we arrived at Aiden's place, he told the driver we'd be down in less than an hour. We silently rode the elevator to the penthouse. Aiden opened the door to find his parents, their friends, and Allison seated in the area around the bar. I unwillingly followed him inside. He promised we would only stay for about thirty minutes, which in my opinion was too long.

Another first for me — time with parents of the guy I'm fucking. *Fantastic*, I thought. Although we hadn't actually had the opportunity to get to know each other, his parents obviously didn't like me, and the feeling was mutual. I had witnessed enough to determine I didn't want to know them, and I hated the way Aiden changed in their presence.

We retreated to the conversation area with our drinks.

"We were surprised to see that Aiden had a date, Aria," Sienna said as she took a seat beside Connor.

I smiled, not sure how or even if I should reply to that.

"Did you enjoy the ballet?" she asked.

"It was excellent," I said.

"We're so proud of our little dancer," she said, beaming at Allison.

I glanced at Allison, who was smiling at me. I think her smile was meant as encouragement, or maybe it was an apology for her parents.

"So tell us a little about yourself. It's so rare that we meet a friend of Aiden's," Sienna said.

I wonder why that is, bitch. "There's not very much to tell, I'm afraid," I replied. I crossed my legs and presented her with a smile that I reserved especially for trolls like her.

"Are you from Boston? Do you have family here?" she

probed.

"No, I moved here several years ago to attend Boston State. Once I graduated, I decided to make Boston my home."

"And your field of study?" she asked.

I quickly glanced at the others and saw that everyone was fixated on me. *What was this?* "Marketing and communications," I replied. I placed the drink to my lips and swallowed a mouthful of liquor.

"When we met in St. Barts, you said the two of you worked together. Is that how you met?"

Sienna was asking too many questions—it felt more like an interview than a conversation, and it was starting to piss me off. "It is," I replied. *Damn what else did she want to know? My bra size? Ask Aiden, he knows.*

"How long have you been dating?" she asked.

I didn't reply; I looked at Aiden. Why was he sitting there letting her grill me like this? I needed to get out of here before I said something I'd regret.

"Or perhaps I'm mistaken?" Sienna asked, noticing our exchange. "Is this just two friends who have a love for the ballet, who decided to attend together to avoid going alone?"

"Mother, please stop with the inquisition," Aiden said.

"But Aiden, I was simply—"

"Enough, Mother. Either you stop or we're leaving," Aiden

spit out.

His mother recoiled as though she had been inappropriately scolded. Her practiced smile immediately resurfaced as she exchanged glances with Michelle.

This was just as I'd expected it to be. Horrible!

"How long will you be in Boston, Aiden?" Allen asked.

"That's undetermined at this point. I'm not sure where things will go after I finish up at Raine Publishing."

"Finish up? Connor said you were there to—"

"I'd prefer we not talk about work," Aiden interrupted, shoving a hand through his hair. I'd never seen him like this.

"You should stop by one night for dinner," Michelle said. "I know Nadia would love to see you."

Aiden didn't reply. He stood, and I watched him walk to the bar and fix another drink.

"Mommy, Daddy, when did you arrive in Boston?" Allison asked.

"Only an hour before your ballet," Connor replied, standing to join Aiden at the bar.

"Since you three are attending a party tonight, perhaps we can all meet for breakfast tomorrow? You haven't been home in months, Allison," Sienna said, frowning.

"Mom, I know. When this season's over, I promise to come for a visit."

I watched Aiden and his father. Aiden was very upset and his father…well, I couldn't really read him, but it appeared as though he was, too. Was this because of me? It couldn't be. I was missing something. Something that Aiden wasn't planning on sharing with me.

Aiden turned and saw me watching him. He smiled, but it wasn't the smile I knew. I turned back to the conversation to see Sienna eyeing me. *Yes, I was certain I didn't like this bitch.* Thankfully Aiden and his father rejoined us before she had a chance to say anything else to me.

"We should be going. Allison, are you ready?" Aiden asked her, though he was looking at me.

Allison glanced at her father, then at Aiden, her lips pressed into a thin line. We said our good-byes and left the penthouse. Though we gave the pretense that the three of us were attending the party, I was relieved when Aiden told Allison to go on without us. The disappointed expression on her face nearly caused me to ask Aiden if we could go, but the part of me that craved some alone time won out. A large part of the night had not played out as I'd anticipated; I wanted the last few hours to resemble the date I'd imagined.

Aiden insisted Allison allow the limo driver take her to and from the party safely. He gave her a kiss on the cheek, and she then turned to me and gave me a hug. "I'm glad you came tonight. Sorry about my parents," she added.

"I had a wonderful evening, and you're an exquisite dancer," I said.

"We should have lunch before I leave town," she suggested, grabbing my hand.

"Of course. I would like that. Aiden has my number."

"Yes, I can see that he does," she said, smiling playfully at her brother.

"Good night, Allie," Aiden said, rushing her off.

"Good night, brother." She gave me another quick hug and then turned to hug Aiden. With that, she was off.

I figured Aiden would hail a cab, but we walked toward the parking garage.

"So, who is Nadia?" I asked.

Aiden smiled. "You caught that, did you?" He grabbed my hand as we happily strolled into the garage. The Aiden I recognized and liked had reappeared.

"How could I not?" I said, raising a brow.

"She's no one important," he replied, looking straight ahead.

I sensed that he wasn't planning on saying much more than that, so I didn't ask any further questions. For now.

Aiden pulled a key from his pocket and pressed a button to unlock one of the cars. He'd never driven me before. I was the teensiest bit giddy because this was more in line with a real date, the guy driving me home afterwards. As unbelievable as it sounded, this was another first for me.

He grabbed my hand, turning me to face him. "I know this evening did not pan out the way we would have wanted, but I hope I can remedy that. I want to take you someplace."

"Well, tonight was not exactly what I had in mind. I can't complain too much because I've had the chance to spend time with a pretty awesome guy." I smiled and he leaned down to kiss me quickly on the lips.

"So where are we going?" I asked.

"It's a surprise," he said, as we resumed walking toward the car. We walked up to the passenger side of a sleek black sports car. I wasn't well-versed in cars, but I knew enough to guess that it was expensive. He opened the door and after I slid in, he closed it and walked around to the driver's side and settled in. He buckled his seat belt and started the ignition. The powerful vibration of the engine startled me. I turned to look at him and he was grinning at me like a child who was holding onto his favorite toy.

Exiting the garage, we entered the almost non-existent traffic of Stuart Street. I wondered where he was taking me. The anticipation gradually erased the unpleasantness of the penthouse nightcap. I stole a quick glance at him. He looked so confident and in control. And as though his sex appeal wasn't already through the roof, watching him behind the wheel of this magnificent car did crazy things to my libido. He made a left onto Charles Street as I continued to study him.

A slow smile graced his perfect lips. "Why are you staring at me?"

"I'm not."

"Really? Then what are you doing?"

I let out a sigh and bit my lip, wondering if I should tell him what I was really thinking. "I was actually wondering how you would respond to my leaning over, unzipping your pants and having a little talk with Kingston."

He lifted one dark brow. "Oh really?" he asked.

"Yes," I replied.

"And just what did you plan on discussing with him?"

"I was interested in his views on an encore."

"Kingston and I are very close, and he shares pretty much everything with me. It's almost as if we're actually one being, and I have it on good authority that he's been thinking about your earlier conversation with him all evening. And I can go as far as to say he'd give you his full attention whenever you wanted."

"So are you saying he would be fully alert?"

"He already is." He reached over and grabbed my hand and placed it on the bulge in his pants. I rubbed my hand back and forth along the restricted swelling, feeling it grow in hardness and length.

"Mmm. Can you do me a favor?" I asked.

"Sure," he replied.

"Tell him that I really, really like him, and I think we need to have a face-to-face conversation, like now."

"Why don't you tell him yourself?" Aiden suggested as he turned onto David G. Mugar Way and parked on the side of the street. He unzipped his pants and allowed my new favorite toy to emerge.

I wasn't as practiced in the art of fellatio, and quite honestly, I was fine with that fact. Until now. I'd simulated before with a banana as April offered her critiques. She had suggested I try it on B.O.B., but there were only so many ways you could practice on a dildo. I'd only had the nerve to do it with Dane during our vacation fling, and even then, I had to be tipsy.

I was pleased Aiden had enjoyed our ballet hall encounter, and my mouth watered at the anticipation of his hardness exploding for me again. Mmm...and the taste. It wasn't at all what I'd expected. He tasted of sweet pineapple. My experience with Dane had been an alcohol induced dare from April. The liquor had provided me the nerve to do it, but even then, I never swallowed. With Aiden, however, I was definitely in the mood to get my fill of his pineapple-flavored treat.

He reclined his seat as I leaned over and kissed the vast head of his cock. I licked softly across the tip and gently sucked. He moaned as he placed his hand on the back of my head, urging me to take him fully into my mouth. I wanted to please him; I wanted him to know how much I wanted all of him. I slowly eased down the length of his shaft, moaning as I did so, seduced by the feral sounds that surrounded us. I filled my mouth with as much of him as I could. He pushed my head down further, and when I gagged, he released my head and allowed me to lead. I moved up the length of his dick as my tongue caressed the side, stroking him until I reached the tip.

"Fuck, I want to taste you," I said, my gaze fixated on his cock as I stroked him, eager for his release.

"Then make me come, baby. Suck me."

A spurt of pre-come surfaced. I licked my lips as I coaxed him, hoping for more. Unable to resist, I lightly licked the clear liquid. I leaned back, looking at the string of sticky sweetness that followed. The string broke, and I went back for more, licking around the hole on the tip. I placed the tiniest amount of pressure on the small opening with my tongue, reveling in his reaction when he hissed and fisted my hair. Aiden guided me down the length of his hardness, and I opened wider to take him in, moving up and down, urging his release.

"Oh fuck, don't stop," he said.

He eased my head down again, attempting to completely

submerge himself into my mouth. His prompting caused me to suck deeper and faster. "Shit, Aria. I'm going to come," he breathed. I prepared myself for a creamy delight as his cock began to pulse. A bolt of hot come filled my mouth; I swallowed as I continued sucking him, eager for every ounce he offered. I suctioned my cheeks and tightly enveloped his thickness, feeling the throb of his dick as another burst shot into my mouth. I swallowed again. He released my hair and let out a deep, content sigh. I slowly licked the head and finished with a soft kiss.

"Why do you taste so sweet?" I asked, kissing the tip of his cock once more before sitting back in my seat.

"I didn't know I did," he said, smiling.

"Well, you do. So you know what that means, right?" I asked.

"That you're going to have dessert as often as you like?"

"Exactly." We laughed as he adjusted himself and zipped his pants.

"You know I owe you. Twice tonight. I can't have you trying to outshine me, princess."

"I don't think anyone can do that," I said, confident that it was a fact.

"Stay put," he said as he opened the car door. He got something from the trunk, quickly closed it, and walked around to open my door. He took my hand, assisting me from the car. In his free hand was a guitar. I looked up at him with a confused smile on my face.

"It's part of my surprise. Come." Holding onto my hand, we walked toward the Hatch Shell.

The Esplanade was actually one of my favorite places in the city. I'd been here several times for charity concerts, but never when it was vacant. It was a beautiful night, and being with him like this, I didn't want it to end. Once we reached the platform he located two chairs, placed them in the middle of the stage, and asked me to have a seat. He sat across from me and positioned the guitar in his lap.

Looking at me, he started to strum his fingers across the guitar strings. He was a different person, not at all the man I saw when he was with his parents. I immediately recognized the tune. It was Sam Smith's *I've Told You Now*. Upon hearing the seductive timbre escape his lips, I nearly melted. His voice was amazing. The lyrics were so beautiful and more meaningful to me than I think he realized.

I was in awe at the ease with which he sang and played. Although I knew I shouldn't, I couldn't help but hope he chose that song as a way to convey his feelings. While I didn't know him as well as I'd like, I did know he wasn't always the person he wanted to be. After seeing him with his parents, I'd deduced that he was living the life he was expected to, a life he had to live — which sounded quite similar to my own reality. Were we both pretending? Protecting ourselves from the world and only lowering the guise for each other? And even then, did we lower it enough to truly see the person behind the camouflage?

As the last notes faded into the quietness of the night, I sat gazing at him, letting my amazement show in my expression.

He broke the silence. "You told me how much of a fan you were of Sam Smith, so I listened to some of his music." He smiled warmly when I didn't reply. "This song reminded me of you, of the diverse parts of our relationship."

"I loved it. You have a beautiful voice, Aiden," I said, as two sad tears rolled down my cheek.

"I'm glad you liked it, but why the tears?" he asked.

"I don't know. I just don't know. You. This. I never thought of this as a relationship," I said.

"Well, it is. It may not have started in the most traditional of ways, but it resulted in one all the same. Initially it was an inexplicable attraction. I had to have you. I wasn't prepared to take no for an answer. Even after having been inside you, it wasn't enough. I found myself wanting more of you. As incredible as sex is with you, it's become more. I feel a connection with you that increases exponentially each time I'm with you. At first I didn't understand it. I still don't, but I've decided to stop trying to figure it out. I've chosen to do what I've always told you to do—just go with it."

His words shocked me. I knew things had changed between us, but I never dared to think about what those changes could mean, because I knew I would bolt.

"You need to help me out here. I've never really had anything with a man other than an arrangement. Just Sex. No love. No romance. I know that sounds rather callous, but I just never felt them worthy of anything beyond that. So you really need to fill me in on what you mean by *relationship*."

"I want us to be exclusive."

"You've already told me that. Wait. Allow me to rephrase, you *demanded* that of me in St Barts, remember? So I fail to see the difference."

"I want to date you. I want to woo you. I want you to think of nothing else but me. I want you to be mine."

The passionate gaze that accompanied his words quickened my heartbeat. Part of me wanted to run. The part of me that lacked all self-control around this man wanted to tell him that he already had all of that, and I wanted it, too, but I was afraid.

"Say something, princess," he urged, his eyes tender.

"When we're together, I feel like I'm a totally different person. I never know what I'm doing when I'm with you. I'm feeling things I don't understand, and the things that I *do* understand, I wish I could force them into a container and close the lid."

His face softened, and he placed the guitar on the stage. He walked over and reached for me, and I stood as he searched my face.

I quickly lowered my gaze, unwilling to meet his eyes. "I don't want your pity," I whispered.

"Pity? Why the hell would I pity you, Aria?"

"I know I come across as this confident, together person — some may even say I'm a bit of an overconfident bitch — but each day you unravel yet another one of the threads I've knitted around myself. You see how broken I really am. I've buried so many of those shattered pieces, and I don't want to deal with them, Aiden. I don't want to be this way, but I don't know any other way to be."

"Let me show you. I can help you. Just let me in."

I looked up at him, but I had nothing to say. No one had ever made me want to let them in before.

"I want to but I'm terrified. Of us. Of you."

He kissed my forehead and lifted my chin, forcing me to look into his gorgeous green eyes. "First off, you aren't broken. You have a past, same as everyone else. It's how you choose to look at that past that defines you. Secondly, you need to let me in, even though you're scared, even though it hurts. Don't hide the broken parts that I need to see. Aria, in order for this to work, you have to let go of the fear and trust me."

"I do. I do trust you—which frightens me even more. You're capturing something I vowed to never give to a man. And that means you're capable of destroying me."

"I would never do that." He stroked my cheek as he stared into my eyes. "You don't understand what's happening between us. And that's okay. But don't be afraid of us, Aria. Let this happen."

He softly clasped my face, his thumbs wiping away my newly escaped tears. He leaned in and placed his lips on mine. I closed my eyes, relishing the softness of his kiss. He moved his lips back and forth across mine, caressing them before sliding his tongue inside my mouth. All of the fear and worry evaporated as I melted into him. He moved one hand to my neck, the other sliding down to the small of my back, drawing me closer to him. It was a sensual kiss that made me feel adored and wanted. He moaned as he severed our kiss and hugged me tightly. We stood quietly for several moments. He eventually released me and stepped away, looking at me.

"It's getting late. Let's get you home." He turned to retrieve his guitar. "Are you hungry?" he asked.

"Now that you mention it, yes I am."

"So am I. Anything at your place we can scramble together?"

"I have some fruit, and I think I have enough ingredients for an omelet. Not much more than that."

"Sounds good to me," he said, as we walked across the stage.

"You know, you lied."

"About what?" he asked.

"About not being able to play the guitar."

He laughed. "I didn't lie. I think I said something like I could play for entertainment purposes. You were entertained, were you not?"

"You're such an ass," I replied, smiling.

He reached out to grab my hand as we reached the sidewalk. I loved the feel of my hand in his. I was content and happier than I thought possible, in spite of baring my soul ten minutes ago...or maybe because of it. Aiden had a way of somehow making me feel like everything would be okay. And amazingly enough, just then it did feel as though everything *was* okay. Maybe it was the night's tranquility — the sound of the water nearby and the perfect night sky. It all aided my peaceful state of mind, which I welcomed.

I sighed as I looked up at the darkness. It was a black piece of velvet sprinkled with shimmering gems. The moon hung majestically, overseeing the smaller facets of twinkling jewels. The night was perfect.

"What are you thinking about?" he asked.

"Nothing. Just enjoying the serenity of the night." I didn't want to think about anything. I only wanted to relish the feeling of closeness with Aiden.

"What are you thinking about?" I asked.

"Fucking you."

ꙮChapter Seventeenꙮ

Aiden's phone rang several times before going to voicemail. A few seconds later, another call, and then another—eventually awaking us from a well-earned rest. He'd kept me 'occupied' until the wee hours. For most of the night, he'd either been buried inside me or his head was between my thighs, more than making up for what he'd promised. And after hours and hours of endless sex, I had little to no energy at all, so I'd been looking forward to sleeping in.

Groaning, Aiden reached for his phone. He frowned upon seeing the name of the caller, and switched it off.

"Who was that?" I asked.

"Someone who shouldn't be calling so early. Good morning, princess."

"Good morning, my king," I replied in a throaty voice.

"Finally, the acknowledgment I so richly deserve," he replied as he pulled me on top of him, laughing—the rich, guttural sound rolling over me. I laughed, too, as I looked down at him, captivated by the shimmering green of his eyes, sparkling like two beautiful gems. After the endless night of mind-blowing sex, I was certain we both looked a mess, but he was a gorgeous mess, still alluring and still sexy as hell.

"What?" he asked.

"Nothing," I replied.

"One day when I ask why you stare at me like that, you will tell me. Understand?"

"Yes, my king," I replied jokingly.

My phone rang, and I leaned toward the bedside table to answer it. It was an unfamiliar number.

"Hello."

"Good morning." I immediately recognized the voice on the other end of the phone. "May I please speak with Aiden?"

I passed the phone to him. He gave me a strange look as he pulled it from my hand.

"Hello." A scowl clouded his face upon hearing the voice. "Why did you call her phone?" Another pause. "That's no excuse, and very inappropriate, Mother," he scolded. "You should tell her, not me."

He listened a moment longer and then sat up in bed, looking at me. "I don't think we'll make it. I have plans with Aria."

He pulled at the sheets, exposing my breasts. A devilish grin replaced his frown as he reached for my nipple.

"Fine. You would have to ask her," he said. He mouthed *I'm sorry* as he passed the phone back to me.

"Hello," I said, hoping I sounded cheery because I was anything but.

"Aria, I apologize for my call, but I was really hoping to spend some time with Aiden before we left this afternoon. I so seldom see him," she said, wistfully.

"I understand. It's okay," I lied. I squirmed as Aiden twisted my nipple, and I eventually pushed him away to avoid moaning in his mother's ear.

"We would love it if the two of you would join us for breakfast this morning. I have a suspicion that he'll not come without you. Could you persuade him? I would be so grateful."

My face froze. I definitely didn't want a repeat of last night. I looked at Aiden. He was staring, worried.

"I'll try, but he can be pretty stubborn, as I'm sure you know. But I'm certain he's just as anxious to spend time with all of you."

"Thank you, dear," she replied.

Ugh! I hated when I was referred to as *dear*. "You're welcome. Good-bye." I pressed the end button on the phone and looked up at Aiden.

"I'm sorry about that," he said. He pulled the sheets away and positioned his naked body over mine.

"It's not your fault. You should go spend time with your family," I said. *Damn, I love the way his body feels on mine.*

"Only if you will come with," he replied. He kissed my cheek and then traced his way to my neck.

I closed my eyes, savoring the feel of his lips on my skin. "I don't think so."

He lifted his head and looked at me. "I'm not going if you aren't."

"That's just great. Give your family yet another reason to dislike me, why don't you?" I pushed him away, and he rolled to the opposite side of the bed.

"What do you mean by that?"

"Aiden, don't insult my intelligence. We both know your parents aren't particularly pleased with your choice of female companion."

"Female companion? Is that what you think you are to me?"

"I don't know."

"Aria, I'm crazy about you. I thought last night made my feelings pretty clear."

Thinking back to his song under the stars — it had been like a scene from a movie. "I adored last night," I said.

"I adore *you*." He lifted my hand and placed my palm flat against his chiseled cheek.

"Well, if you keep doing things like serenading me in public, I may just start to believe you."

He looked at me, the persuasive power of his eyes exerting its version of mind control. "You'd better believe me regardless," he said vehemently.

I actually *did* believe him. I could see it when he looked at me, when he touched me.

"So, breakfast with my folks?" he asked.

I sighed. "Fine, but you'll owe me one."

"For something of this magnitude, I'll actually owe you more than one, and I can't wait to repay you," he said, smacking me on the ass as I walked toward the bathroom. I was falling deeper and deeper for this man. I knew it was dangerous, but I couldn't help myself.

Aiden joined me in the shower, stepping close and wrapping his arms around me. I leaned back into him, delighting in the feel of his wet skin against mine. His hands rested on my stomach as he gently kissed my shoulder. Easing his palms upward, his touch proved to be as sensuous as his kiss, sending heated bolts of lust throughout my body. He captured my breasts, groping and tugging as he planted soft, wet kisses along my neck. I moaned, the heat of my sex already stirring me. Releasing my breasts, he turned me to face him. I looked up, staring into the two forest pools of lustrous green that held and enchanted me. His gaze lowered as he seductively stroked his finger across my lip. Bowing his head, he unhurriedly placed his mouth on mine, biting my bottom lip before pulling it into his mouth, slowly sucking.

Reaching up, I placed my hands on his shoulders, pulling him to me, sliding my hands down his back, seduced by the feel of the hard muscles flexing as he hungrily caressed my body. His manhood grew, poking me as he slid his tongue into my mouth. When I reached down to touch him, he moaned as his hands slid down my back, cupping my ass, his kiss transitioning into an orgasm-induced assault on my mind and my body. I pulled him closer still, hungrily stroking his back, my sex tightening as his intense licks into my mouth melted my core. Aching with need for him, I raked my nails over his back, digging into his skin, shuddering as the ecstasy of his touch flowed through me.

He backed away slightly, looking down at me. His eyes glinted with a hint of mischievousness. I looked at him, nearly embarrassed by my unexpected climax.

"What are you *doing* to me?" I asked.

He brushed my hair back from my face. "What have you *done* to me?"

He didn't answer my question.

Neither could I answer his.

We finished showering, and I blow dried my hair as Aiden went to grab his bag from the foyer. My hair wasn't cooperating; I gave up and decided on a loose French braid on one side, which I pulled into a low ponytail.

Walking out of the bedroom, I found Aiden already dressed.

He was wearing jeans and a black shirt that accentuated his toned physique. He looked at me, but said nothing, not even a smile playing about his lips. I'd been pondering the question I'd asked him before our shower. I was sure he was thinking along the same lines. I walked past him to the closet.

I didn't know what to wear. I usually dressed however I wanted, so why not today? I stood looking at one piece of clothing after another trying to decide on something that Aiden's parents would approve. Ugh! This was definitely another first, and one that I didn't particularly care for. I ultimately decided on a beige crotchet sun dress with a halter neckline. It had a scalloped hem that fell three inches above my knees. It did accentuate my curves, but so did most of my clothes, so Mrs. Prude would just have to deal with it. A pair of beige crotchet linen sandals completed the look. I grabbed my purse and stepped out of the closet.

Aiden was sitting on the couch in the living room, looking up as I entered. I watched as his gaze glided over my body. He was pleased, that was all that mattered.

"Are you ready?" he asked.

"As I'll ever be."

He stood as I walked past him. "Everything okay?" he asked as we closed the door.

"Yes, fine," I replied, digging into my purse for my phone. It had pinged earlier, but I'd forgotten to check it. It was a text from

April.

Have you fallen off the face of the earth?

I felt guilty. I'd been so caught up with Aiden, that I hadn't been in touch after receiving her voicemail a few days ago. I quickly replied.

Lol. No silly. I've just been really busy. I'm sorry.

We need to talk. I've so much to tell you. Can I call?

I wondered if this was about Dane. I certainly couldn't talk about him now.

I'll call you this afternoon. I'm about to have breakfast with Aiden and his parents.

WTF??!!!!

IKR!!

Call me as soon as you can!

I will. I love you.

I love you, too.

Breakfast with the family wasn't as uncomfortable as I'd expected. Aiden's parents extended a very warm greeting. Allison was a joy, as always. The conversation primarily centered on Sienna's latest charity commitments and her attempts to rein Aiden in as a guest speaker for a new medical facility. They discussed Allison's upcoming performance in New York and surprised her with the news that her siblings Sloan and Nicholas had plans to attend. Connor asked about my family. I didn't reveal much, only that I had a mother and twin sisters in Ohio. He asked about my father, which was a natural question but a very uncomfortable topic. Thankfully Aiden redirected the conversation.

He placed his hand over mine, tracing his thumb back and forth, comforting me, a gesture that his mother didn't miss. I could see she was making an effort, and I appreciated that, so I did the same, asking her about her favorite charities and pastimes. She loved to garden if time allowed, but her charity work kept her pretty busy.

After breakfast on the terrace, we moved to the conversation area. Sienna left the room and returned with a thin wrapped box, which she presented to Aiden.

"I have something for you," she said passing it to him.

He took the box, slowly unwrapping it. After removing the lid, he smiled, then looked up at Sienna. "Thank you, Mother."

He lifted some papers from the box. It was sheet music.

"You're welcome. I know how much you love to play."

He turned to me. "When I was younger, my mother would gift me with original sheet music on my birthday or Christmas, and I would play for the family."

"It's been a while since you've done that," Allison said,

nostalgia lacing her tone.

"That sounds like a wonderful way to spend Christmas morning. I wish I could play," I said.

"You agreed to let me teach you," Aiden said, looking at me for confirmation.

"Careful, Aria. He taught me to play, and he was a great teacher, but really mean."

"Allison, you were such a slacker I had to be mean in order for you to commit."

"Why don't you play for us, Aiden?" Sienna asked.

Connor cleared his throat and looked at Sienna disapprovingly. Aiden noticed their exchange and sighed, but he stood and walked across the room towards the piano. We gathered around as he sat on the bench. Within moments of placing his long, slender fingers on the ivory keys, the room filled with the sounds of Chopin's *Ballade No. 1 in G minor*. I remembered this piece from a college music appreciation course; it was one of my favorites. I watched in awe as his fingers skillfully danced over the keys. As the melody encompassed us, Aiden transformed—he was no longer the Aiden who tolerated his family, nor was he the astute business man who commanded attention with his legal-speak. He wasn't the Aiden who unintentionally affected me, just by being. He was in his own world, with just the piano and Chopin.

The melody became discordant as it transcended into a loud, fierce conversation, Aiden's hands pressing the keys with precision and purpose. The intricate moves were as graceful and as natural as breathing for him. The sounds went from powerful and bold to gentle and light, sounding sweet like a twinkle. In the final seconds of the song, he came back to reality.

I was speechless.

"Absolutely magnificent, Aiden," Sienna beamed, kissing him on the cheek.

"Thank you, Mother," he replied, glancing toward Connor. "And you, Dad, did you enjoy it?"

"I've always enjoyed classical music, son, you know that," he said, sternly.

Aiden shook his head. "Thank you for the music, Mother. I haven't played like that in quite a while."

"You never taught me to play like that, brother," Allison accused.

He laughed. "I was barely able to teach you to play *Twinkle, Twinkle. Little Star.*"

"I know. It was torture," she replied, laughing.

"What did you think, Aria?" Aiden asked.

"I agree with your mother. It was perfect! I had no idea you were so talented."

"Thank you. Now, are you going to let me teach you?" he

asked.

I smiled, eager to learn something I'd so long wanted. "Absolutely. When can we start?" I asked.

"How about now? Come."

I never pursued lessons as an adult, but my passion for music remained immense. April, on the other hand, was extremely talented, playing several instruments, and had offered to teach me, but I never took her up on it.

I walked around the piano and sat beside Aiden. "How much do you already know?" he asked.

"Absolutely nothing."

"Place your fingers like this," he demonstrated, smiling. I did as he instructed and he explained finger placement on the keys. A few moments later, I actually created a simple melody. It only involved four keys, but I was excited all the same.

His father walked over and requested to speak privately with Aiden in the study. Aiden excused himself, leaving me with Allison and Sienna. Thirty minutes later, Aiden and Connor emerged, and Aiden seemed agitated as he walked over to his mother.

"Dad said that you're leaving within the hour."

"Yes, the doorman is on his way up to retrieve our bags," she replied.

"Thank you for breakfast, and for the music. Aria and I are

going to head out," he said as he hugged and kissed her on the cheek.

She looked at Aiden, confused by his abruptness, and then scowled at Connor. "Is everything okay?" she asked.

"Everything's fine. Dad was just reminding me of some projects he wanted me to work on." To his sister he said, "I'll see you before you leave tomorrow, Allie." Then he turned to shake his father's hand. "I'll be in touch, Dad. Have a safe flight."

"Good-bye, son."

"Good-bye, everyone, and thanks for such a lovely breakfast," I said as Aiden grabbed my hand, pulling me towards the door. *Damn…is he ever anxious to get out of here.* Not that I minded, but why the sudden rush? Once in the elevator, I asked, "What was that all about? Your father obviously upset you."

"It's just business. We don't tend to agree on things."

"What kind of things?"

"Aria, I don't want to talk about it."

I pulled my hand away from his, and he sighed, but I didn't back down. "Each time I ask you about some part of your life involving your family, you get this way. I don't like it. You want me to open up with you, yet you get to remain silent with me? That doesn't work for me, Aiden."

"I'm sorry. I just don't like talking about it. But you're right. I promise one day soon we can talk about any and everything you want, but not right now. Can you give me that?"

The pleading in his eyes made me relent. I knew better than most how difficult it was to discuss family stuff.

"Fine, Aiden, but soon."

"I promise, and thank you," he said, reaching for my hand again, kissing it softly and pulling me toward him for a hug.

"Thanks for the piano mini-lesson," I said.

"It was a pleasure. Are you serious about my teaching you?"

"Definitely."

"If you really want to learn, I'll be happy to teach you, but you need to know I expect you to make a commitment, which means routine lessons and practice."

"Is this what Allison meant by torture?" I asked, giggling.

"Possibly. Who knows with her? Her mind has always been on dance. She felt that anything else was a huge waste of her time."

"Then why did she start?"

He smiled. "I suppose one could say that I coerced her."

"How?"

"She needed a body for some of her dance practices. I told her I would help, but only if she would agree to let me teach her how to play the piano."

"You dance extremely well," I told him. I remembered watching and dancing with him on the dinner cruise.

"So you liked that?" he asked.

"Very much," I said.

"Well, that is a by-product of Allison," he said.

"I'll have to remember to thank her for that. Watching you is such a devilish treat."

"Devilish?" he asked. "I can show you devilish," he said, reaching under my dress to grab my ass.

"You promise?" I asked.

"Yes, but be sure to have plenty of cash, because I'll need to be well-compensated," he said.

"Oh, so you're going to dance for me? Dirty dance?" I asked.

"If that's what you want," he said.

"Oh baby, I would love that."

After stepping out of the elevator, we headed to the parking garage.

"When do you want to start your lessons?" he asked.

"Whenever you can squeeze me in. I give you my word that I'll commit to it. It will be difficult to practice, since I don't have a piano. I may need to look into purchasing one. Perhaps you can help me select it. That has also been a to-do on my list, once I learned to play."

"Sure, I can help you, but in the meantime, you're welcome to practice at my place as often as you'd like."

We were at the black sports car. He opened the door for me,

and I don't know how I missed the Porsche insignia before.

"What kind of car is this?" I asked once he was seated.

"It's a Porsche 918 Spyder," he replied cautiously. "It was a gift."

"I don't know much about cars, but I know Porsches aren't exactly inexpensive, so who would lavish someone with a gift like this?"

"My father," Aiden replied. His temples flexed as he gauged my response.

"I know you said you didn't want to talk about it, but is there something going on with your dad that's upsetting you?"

"When isn't there?" he asked, running his fingers through his hair.

"You can talk to me. I want to know you. Not just the part you choose to share—I want to know all of you. You've asked the same of me."

He reached over, stroking my cheek. I could see that he'd made his decision.

"You already know so much more than you realize."

"I don't understand."

"Later, Aria. We'll discuss it later. I promised, remember?"

"I know, but you just seem so torn up about it and—"

"Damn it, Aria, will you let this go?" I recoiled from the harshness of his tone. He'd never spoken to me that way before.

"Do not fucking talk to me like that, Aiden." I wasn't going to stand for his crap. "You know what? Take me home."

"Aria, I—"

"Take me home. Now!" He sat, staring at me, and didn't move. "Fine, I'll catch a cab." I replied, reaching for the door.

He reached over, grabbing my wrist. "I'll take you."

My hand stayed on the handle.

"Let go of the latch, Aria. I said I would take you, and I will."

I released the handle and sat back in the seat, looking straight ahead. He sighed and started the car.

"Can I come up?" he asked when we'd reached my building.

I desperately wanted to say yes, but I didn't. "No. I want to be alone," I lied as I opened the door and got out. I heard his car pull away as I neared the entrance to my building. I was somewhat hurt that he'd left. He rarely—no, *never*—took no for an answer. At least not from me.

"Good afternoon, Ms. Cason."

"Hi, Silas," I replied as he held the door open.

It was probably good that I did have some time away from him today. I was long overdue for some time to myself—time I needed to gather my thoughts. I was literally unable to do that when he was near me. I opened the door and went for the couch, where I flopped down and flipped on the TV.

A few hours later, I called April. She filled me in on her love life and I caught her up on mine. She was just as shocked as I was that I'd allowed Aiden to get so close. I told her about our small spat, and she assured me that everything would be okay. She hadn't heard anything more from Dane's wife, so we both hoped she and Dane had reconciled.

When nine o'clock came around and I hadn't heard from Aiden, I figured I wouldn't, so I went to bed early. I didn't want to sit and wait for something that wasn't going to happen.

❧Chapter Eighteen❧

I hadn't heard anything from Aiden since Saturday afternoon. On Monday morning, I anxiously wondered if there would be any awkwardness at work, since our last communication wasn't very pleasant.

My phone rang just as I was about to leave for work. It was Aiden, saying that he wouldn't be at work today; he was needed at home. He didn't tell me more than that, as he was at the gate to catch his flight. I wondered if his trip had anything to do with the discussion he'd had with his father after breakfast on Saturday. He texted a few hours later to let me know he'd landed safely and that he'd be in touch soon.

After lunch, I worked with the e-publishing division, and Aiden's absence was resounding. He typically offered many of the missing details that weren't apparent to anyone but him. After the meeting, I checked the time; it was one-thirty. I expected to have heard from him by now, but there hadn't been a word.

As the day dragged on, I was increasingly distracted and saddened by the fact that Aiden hadn't contacted me. I had no idea why he'd left so abruptly, beyond his informing me that he was needed at home. From the small glimpses I'd witnessed of his relationship with his family, that could mean any number of things. I was acutely aware of the change in him after he'd spoken with his father in private. He'd morphed into the Aiden who'd walked into the RPH executive conference room the first day I'd laid eyes upon him—cool, controlled, and untouchable. He wasn't the Aiden I'd allowed access to the essence of my being.

I hadn't realized until now how much I had bought into his declaration of feelings for me. I'd come to trust that he meant it when he said it wasn't just about the sex or the challenge of taming me. I truly felt he wanted me for me. It certainly didn't feel that way now. Could my initial impressions of him have been accurate? Was I just one of the distractions he needed at the time? Now that he'd gotten me to submit to his whims, was he done with me?

No, I couldn't have misread all of the signs. All of the emotionally connected moments we'd shared couldn't have meant nothing to him. I missed him.

I picked up my phone, lacking the strong will I possessed prior to Aiden. Should I initiate contact and call him? No. Maybe a text? Sighing, I decided against both. I'd give him another day, and if he didn't have the decency to contact me, I'd take it to mean that he didn't plan to.

What if that really was the case? How would I feel about that? A sinking feeling in the pit of my stomach was my answer.

Thoughts of everything being okay to acceptance that it was

over, were going back and forth in my head when a knock at my door revealed Blake and Adam wearing extremely anxious expressions. Of course, I hastily jumped to the conclusion they'd discovered my relationship with Aiden.

"May we come in, Aria?" Blake asked.

"Of course," I replied as Adam closed the door behind them. They each took a seat in the chairs facing my desk.

"You both look very worried. What's going on?" I asked.

Blake's revelation, while daunting, was not what I'd expected. After hearing everything, I determined it was actually best that Aiden wasn't here, because RPH would be dealing with a crisis that required my full attention.

Raine Publishing House was a subsidiary of Raine Industries, a multi-national conglomerate owned by multi-billionaire, Wesley Raine, who'd just suffered a severe heart attack. Rumors were already rapidly circulating that the company's future was in question. R.I. was an extremely successful privately owned family business—its stature was the envy of business tycoons around the world. Mr. Raine consistently assured his employees that his company began as a family business and would remain that way. However, with no one in place to steer the ship, attempts to infiltrate the company were likely. Someone like Wesley Raine wouldn't be as successful as he was without having safeguards in place to avoid such a thing, but the current state of affairs was still dreadfully unsettling.

Everyone knew that Raine was rearing one of his children to assume leadership of the company, but there hadn't been any official details as of yet, just that new leadership would be announced relatively quickly, given the circumstances. Needless to say, the RPH executives, and all the other Raine Industry officials, were in a state of panic since the news of Raine's medical issues.

Our meeting concluded with more questions than answers, and I was frustrated with myself that I was too distracted to truly focus. This was the reason I needed to stay far away from romantic relationships. They had a way of tearing you down to the core of your being, exposing your every emotion and weakness, and sometimes altering you into someone you'd never want to be.

Just as I grabbed my purse to leave for the day, I had a call. The display revealed it was Lorraine from Human Resources. Curious as to why she'd be calling me for any reason, I answered. "Hello, Lorraine."

"Hi, Aria. I'm glad I caught you before you left for the day. I wanted to speak to you directly about this, as opposed to sending an email."

"Sure. What is it?" I asked.

"I've received communication from Aiden that he will not be

returning to complete his internship."

I sank back into my chair, feeling even sicker than I had earlier. I didn't know what to say.

"Aria, are you there?"

"Uh, yes. Sorry, I was distracted by an email," I lied.

"I meant to contact you earlier, so my apologies."

"No problem," I said.

She went on to explain she'd received an email from him shortly after lunch, and then asked if I wanted her to forward a copy to me. I hesitantly replied in the affirmative, suspecting it may very well be my last communication from Aiden Wyatt.

After hanging up the call, I reached for my mouse to awaken my computer and opened the email. It was addressed *To Whom It May Concern*. What the fuck? I'll tell you who it concerned asshole! It concerned the company that allowed you inside its doors. It concerned your work associates. It concerned *me*.

I went on to read the email. It was very brief.

Please accept this as my formal notification that I'm unable to continue my internship with Raine Publishing House due to unforeseen circumstances. I appreciate the professional development and growth RPH has allowed me, and I'm confident you'll continue with the success that is synonymous with Raine Publishing House.

Regards,
Aiden Wyatt

I wanted to break, but I didn't…I wouldn't.

ഏ ഏ ഏ ഏ

I went home that day on cruise control. I had no idea how I got to my condo. I was consumed with thoughts of everything I'd shared with Aiden — every beguiling word, every provocative gesture. His promises, that *this* was meaningful, that it wasn't just a chase and conquest. I never wanted to believe him. Never. I fought it with everything in me, but ultimately I surrendered every doubt and every principle that had guided me for years, and I gave in to him.

He had me. I was his and he'd known it. I'd gotten lost in his words, words that I now felt were lies. All the time I'd given him that I would never get back. I felt like an idiot, a broken and shattered idiot. I literally felt ill.

I rushed to the bathroom as the contents of my lunch came rushing up like a broken dam in the midst of a flood. I was there on the bathroom floor, on my knees, expelling every piece of my day, gripping the sides of the toilet as if it were grounding me. Another dam broke, and a seemingly endless flow of tears began sliding down my cheeks.

※ ※ ※ ※

I was scheduled to appear at a fundraiser for the Boston Symphony Orchestra that evening. Although my patronage of music was a passion, I didn't feel much up to attending the benefit. I knew I needed to go—I needed the distraction. I frequently attended the symphony, most often alone, as I never dated anyone within the borders of Boston, or the borders of Massachusetts for that matter.

I ultimately decided to attend, but wanted to work out first in the hopes of relieving some of today's stress. Reaching the gym, I looked around at the equipment and opted for a run on the treadmill. I was too impatient to stretch, so I located a playlist on my phone and started running. I childishly imagined running away from this horrible sick feeling. It was futile. Every song somehow reminded me of Aiden. I couldn't banish my thoughts of him. Was he thinking of me, too? Did he miss me as I was missing him? Obviously not, or I would've heard from him by now. I felt like such a fool. A tear fled my eye, and I angrily wiped it away. Why was I responding this way? It wasn't as though he had been in my life in any capacity that would warrant this type of bullshit reaction from me.

After my workout, I tramped back upstairs to take a shower—not my usual thought-invoking bath. I didn't want to think. I didn't want to feel. I wanted to forget. I quickly dressed and headed to the Taj Boston Hotel.

I had actually planned to attend this charity dinner with Aiden. He hadn't known, of course. It would've been a surprise for him — the event and the invitation — since he was usually the one who planned everything. He loved music, and I thought this would be a heart-warming event for him as all the proceeds would benefit the musical aspirations of disadvantaged youth.

My phone pinged and my heart raced at the possibility that Aiden had texted me. I unlocked my phone and tapped the screen, but was disappointed. It was not him — it was my mother. What could she possibly want? I opened the text and saw that it was rather lengthy, which only indicated trouble. I tossed the phone in my bag, deciding to deal with it later.

I was sure it was about money. Although I hadn't returned home, I did send money regularly. She was a single parent, and I knew she needed the help. I suppose the money was a way of compensating for my absence, possibly buying some type of understanding from Mom. But deep down — well, actually not even deep down, it was right there on the surface, always staring me in the eye — I knew sending her money was a way to ease my guilt.

She had guilt of her own — for checking out on us when Dad left. I still didn't know why he'd abandoned us. From what I could determine as a child, Matteo and Melena Costanzo were very happily married. But one day, out of nowhere, Dad disappeared — leaving Mom with three kids. We hadn't heard from him since.

I was thirteen when he left. My twin sisters, Lia and Bianca, were four. Basically I had grown up with an absentee father and a shell of a mother. I had many wonderful memories of him, of our family.

Dad had been amazing to us, and he'd desperately loved Mom, which is why I found it hard to believe that he could have left us, left her, and never looked back. I'd always suspected that he maintained contact with her, but if that were true, why would she keep it a secret? And better still, why hadn't he come back to us?

❧   ❧   ❧   ❧

Arriving at the Taj Boston, I turned into the drive and stopped beneath the awning. I placed the car in park, and the valet opened my door, assisting me from my car as he passed a ticket to me. I entered the lobby of the hotel where two attendants stood greeting the guests and directing them to the grand ballroom.

The room was packed with one of the most distinguished audiences Boston had to offer. It had been transformed to accommodate tonight's festivities, into something like a musical theater. The orchestra was positioned in the balcony, instead of where they would normally be in an orchestra pit. There were enormous weaving ribbons of colored metal mesh sweeping across the length of the balcony. The rear walls were fitted with acoustic curtains to better suit the evening's performance. Despite my broken state, I felt privileged to be a part of tonight's event, and was quite anxious to hear the orchestral performances.

"What an excellent start to my evening," a nearby voice exclaimed.

It was a voice I recognized, but couldn't quite associate a name. I turned around and it took me a moment to place him, because it had been ages since I last saw him. He walked toward me and then I suddenly remembered that his name was Eric. *What the fuck was he doing here?*

"Not to worry, Aria. This just happens to be a pleasant coincidence." He smiled. "How are you? It's been a while."

It took a moment to regain my composure. "Hello, Eric."

I didn't like this. Something seemed off about him being here. The last time a one-night stand popped into my real life, I had to alert the security at both my home and work.

"May I get a picture, Ms. Cason?" asked an approaching photographer. Before I could object, Eric had positioned himself beside me, a hand at my waist drawing me close.

"We'd be happy to," he replied. I smiled for the camera,

noticing the photographer was from The Boston Globe. Typically the same photographers stalked these events, but I didn't recognize this guy. I would contact them tomorrow and get the picture before it circulated the media outlets. I didn't need any additional crazed wives popping up. I eased from Eric's embrace immediately after the camera's flash.

"So what brings you to Boston?" I asked.

"Business. I was meeting with the head of Boston International, who invited me to attend tonight's event."

"What line of business are you in, Eric?" I asked.

"Oh, that's right. We never really discussed many personal details, did we?"

"No, we didn't." *And this was precisely why – to avoid situations such as this.*

"I'm in commercial shipping."

"Hmm."

"Being that Boston is the oldest continuously active port in the country, I'm in Boston at least twice a year."

"I see. It was nice running into you, Eric. I see someone from work, and I need to say hello," I lied as I tried for an escape.

"Aria, wait. Any chance we can meet for drinks later? We had an amazing time last year. It would be nice to get reacquainted."

"I don't think that's a good idea. It's best we keep the past in the past. Enjoy your evening."

I walked away, grabbing a glass of champagne from the tray of the nearest waiter. I did the normal things one does at such events: shaking hands, smiling, making inconsequential small talk. The orchestra was playing softly in the background. It was beautiful. Aiden would have appreciated it, I was sure. I caught a few unwelcomed glances from Eric, but managed to avoid him the remainder of the evening.

The dinner and the speeches were also very standard; however, my anticipation soared as we neared the part of the evening in which we could thoroughly enjoy the talents of the Boston Symphony. One piece was so beautiful and emotionally evocative that I bit my lip to suppress the well of tears that threatened to escape. The last selection signified that the evening was coming to a close—I felt I'd hidden in the shadows of this event long enough. I said a few good-byes, and I made my way to the exit.

✼Chapter Nineteen✼

Arriving home after the charity dinner, I tossed on some PJs and grabbed a bottle of wine in preparation of reading my mother's text, knowing that the wine would allow me to swallow her words a lot easier. After the second glass, I grabbed my phone.

Hello Aria,

I hope you're doing well. I would have preferred to call but I know you're always extremely busy and don't typically answer my calls. You've been in my thoughts so often these last few weeks. I know we aren't as close as we once were, due to my issues, but I hope to change that. I have made some significant, long-overdue changes in my life that I wish to share with you. I'm hoping these changes will open the door to our being a real family again. Your sisters and I miss you terribly and hope to see you soon. Please call me. I love you. Mom.

This was not what I'd expected. I didn't know how to interpret this. Over the years since I'd graduated from college, my mother made an annual attempt to reach out to me, to either make me more inclined to come home or to put my mind at ease regarding her mental state. Or maybe it was to redeem herself. Whatever the case, I never bought into it. I think she thought that if I lost my negative perceptions of her, I'd reintegrate myself into the family. Of course, it didn't happen. I typically reached out to her in some fashion, however, by calling one of my sisters just to check that everything was okay, or sending a mass text to them all as a hello and update on how I was doing. In return, they'd tell me everything was great, and that was the end of that.

This time it was different. My mother acknowledged that there had *actually* been a problem, whereas in the past, she only made useless attempts to placate the situation. Had something truly happened to alter her view of reality? Was she finally coming back to us? I didn't dare hope, afraid of the disappointment that would follow if I was wrong. It was a big conclusion to draw from just a few words. Maybe I was reading too much into this because I needed something to hold onto before I crumbled.

I thought back to the unbearable days of my childhood. Every day began with heart-wrenching pain, and it ended the same. Every day I watched Mom transform, sinking deeper into despair. Her grief and insurmountable depression took its toll on all of us. It hardened my heart. It also resulted in my resentment of her.

I'd longed for the laughing, happy mother who departed shortly after Dad left, but there was nothing. The only time I saw any life in her at all was one day after I checked the mail. She became anxious and upset, and I couldn't understand why. She explained that she'd been submitting letters to publishers and preferred that only she check the mail. The letters very well could have been from publishing houses, but I strongly suspected that her rigid mail-checking had more to do with Dad. If that were the case, she would've never mentioned it to us, especially me.

I longed for the laughing, happy mother that left when Dad did, but when I realized neither she, nor Dad, were coming back, I ran wild. Skipping school, hanging out and drinking with a rough crowd. I don't know where I would have ended up if my friend Vicky hadn't died.

I had gone astray when I finally accepted that my father wasn't coming back. I began skipping school, hanging with other rebels, and basically giving mom a very difficult time. She didn't have a clue as to how to deal with me other than forcing me to meet with a school counselor twice a week, which yielded less than desirable outcomes. The only thing that reached me and began my cycle of redemption was the loss of my friend, Vicky. She and the other group of kids that I'd befriended were all from broken homes. Vicky had it worse than any of us; she was being severely abused and she felt she had no way out. I never thought she would end her life. When she did, it had been a wakeup call for me.

After Vicky's death, I met with the school counselor and tried to pull my life together. I was able to recover from the grief and deal with the reality of living in absence of my father and to a lesser degree, my mother. It also afforded me the strength to be there for my sisters in a way that my mother couldn't. I think a part of me hated her, at least the person she'd become because of a man. She was the source of the conviction I carried with me from then until now — that men were only good for one thing. I vowed to never give my trust or love to a man. I'd never place myself in a position to allow life to take chances with me. I'd create and follow my own path, not one that was dictated by the actions of others, like Mom or Vicky had done.

My pain had been a powerful motivator. I'd refused to let love alter my view of reality because, as I saw it, love had only two outcomes: empty and pathetic like Mom, or dead like Vicky. Therefore, I focused all of my energy on me; I became a focused, determined, controlled being and nothing had ever caused me to falter my stance…until now.

I couldn't understand how Aiden's presence could affect me so distinctly, but it had. Would he be the one to destroy me? Was this karma for cutting my family out of my life? For my contemptuous view of my mother?

Without further thought, I tapped the phone icon to dial Mom. She answered on the third ring.

"Aria?" The question in her voice was understandable, as this was my first attempt to call her in years. "Is that you, sweetheart?"

"Hi, Mom. Yes, it's me."

There was silence for a long moment.

"It's so good to hear your voice, Aria. How are you?"

I'm fucked up. I did the one thing I said I'd never do.

"I'm great, Mom," I lied. "So, I read your text and wanted to call and see how you were doing."

"I'm fine, Aria. Actually, I'm better than fine."

"Really? Well, that's great! You sound, uh, different."

She laughed. "I feel different, Aria."

I couldn't clearly recall the last time I'd heard Mom laugh. The sound was nostalgic.

"I'm not sure I understand," I said.

"The short version is….well, I guess I would say I've awakened from my deep, depressing sleep."

I plopped down on the sofa. "Well, yes, that's a short recap," I added, smiling to myself. "But what happened? I mean, I'm so happy for you, but I'm also curious as to what prompted it?"

"Seeing life, Aria. My eyes were closed to it for so many years. I woke up and got out of bed, most days anyway, but I was empty inside. I stepped out on life, on my children. For that, I'll never be able to forgive myself."

"Mom, if you're really okay, there's nothing to forgive, and no need to blame yourself. This is not your fault. It's Dad's."

"Aria, I'm responsible for myself. Not your father, not my children—me."

Yeah, but Dad started this, it was his fault. "You still haven't said—what happened?"

"Well, it actually all began one day in the park. The girls had urged me to get out of the house, and I didn't have any idea of where I could go and still be alone. The first place I thought of was the pond where I used to take you girls. You remember the ducks? I was sitting there, not really thinking of anything, just focused on feeding the ducks like we did when you were little."

She continued. "Then I heard a child laugh, and I looked over and saw, well, I guess you can say I saw happiness. There was a family: a mother, father, and three adorable little girls. I couldn't stop watching them. As I looked at them, I noticed the tender glances between the man and the woman. I noticed how they looked at their kids, and they were all smiling and laughing. I must have stared at them for a half hour or so, and then something in my heart broke.

I began to sob, and someone sat down beside me and asked if I were okay. I pulled myself together and talked to this total stranger, revealing the depths of my soul. He opened his wallet and pulled out a business card and told me to use it. It was the name of a therapist. He said he'd seen her many years ago after losing his family, and that she was someone who had brought him out of the same pit where I'd been dwelling. It took a while, but finally, one day I worked up the nerve to call and scheduled an appointment, and I've been on the path back to me ever since."

"Wow, Mom. I don't know what to say. I'm stunned."

She continued. "It wasn't easy. There were days where I wanted to crawl back into my shell, but the therapist would call and check on me, or the man I'd met in the park would send me an inspirational text, and I forced myself to continue with the therapy. I'm now finally able to face what I had put you girls through. And I'm so sorry, Aria. I know I'm the reason you never come home. I'm the reason you're out there alone—without a family—and I want to change that."

Tears had begun streaming down my cheeks. My mother actually sounded like my mother. I hadn't heard the sound of life in her voice in over ten years. I'd blocked out so many memories for fear of facing more hurt. Sitting here now, on the verge of something life altering, frightened me. I wiped the tears and forced myself to swallow the rest of them.

"Mom, that sounds amazing. How are Lia and Bianca?" I asked.

"They're great. They're actually out with some friends. They had an overnight and they haven't come home yet. They've been wonderful. We've had so many special moments lately, and the only thing missing is you. We want to see you, Aria."

My heart accelerated at the thought of going back home. Surrounded by reminders of the hurt and loneliness would be too much to bear.

"Mom, it would be great to see you all, too, but I don't think I'm ready to come home. Maybe we can meet and have a family weekend?"

"That actually sounds wonderful, Aria. Do you have any ideas?"

Immediately, a location popped into my head. I smiled. "How about the happiest place on earth?"

"The happiest place on earth? Where's that?" she asked.

"Disney World, Mom!"

We both laughed.

"You know, that would be perfect. The girls and I have never been, and I think we'd all have a wonderful time."

"Check with the girls, and let me know which days would work, and I'll take care of the flight and hotel arrangements. I'll call you in a few days with the details."

"You don't have to pay for this, Aria. I can cover the cost of this trip."

"Mom, it's okay. I want to do this for us."

"Okay, but only if you're sure."

"I am. I'm actually quite excited."

"So am I. I can't wait to tell the girls."

"Okay. Tell them I said hello, and that I love them. I'll talk to you soon."

"Okay, I love you, Aria."

"I love you, too, Mom."

I hung up the phone with a myriad of feelings: hope, fear, happiness, amazement, excitement. For years, I'd run from memories, feelings, and relationships, but deep down the desire to face those demons was there. And now, maybe it was time I made an attempt to restore my relationship with my family. I was somewhat hesitant to admit it, but I really missed them. I needed them...and they needed me.

I grabbed my laptop and searched for info on Disney vacations, feeling optimistic at the sight of those happy families. I sent an email to my travel agent with what I wanted, and possible dates, and then hit send before I could get nervous.

I was more excited and happy than I dared hope, but I quickly found myself wondering if this was a good idea. Was this all going too fast? Maybe I should check in with Lia and Bianca to get a better read on the situation with Mom before committing to anything further.

I was doing it again—overthinking everything. I decided to stop analyzing and just go with it. But then again, the last time I didn't analyze something and just "went with it", I exposed myself to the bullshit that was Aiden Wyatt.

Where the fuck was he anyway, and why had he made not one attempt to contact me? I missed him. I wanted to hear his voice, to see him, to be in his arms...and in his bed. I swallowed those desires and went in search of another bottle of wine.

৯৯   ৯৯   ৯৯   ৯৯

Over the next two weeks, work felt like work again, not the place I went to play games with Aiden. I still hadn't heard from him. It had been three weeks and not one word. If I didn't know it when he first disappeared, I definitely knew now that he was done with me. It hurt, almost unbearably, but I was determined to view it as a learning experience and not give any more thought to him. He was just another broken piece of me, a piece that I sealed away in the box with the others.

I'd been talking to Mom, Lia, and Bianca more over the recent weeks. Mom was still happy and, well, just Mom. It felt really good. I was even considering a trip home later in the year.

We were headed to Florida on Thursday. Due to the state of the company, I couldn't be out of the office for more than two days, and even then I was questioning the timing. We had yet to hear the status of the company's direction—just that Raine's son was assuming some type of leadership that would be formally announced in the near future.

The Disney World trip was amazing! My mom, sisters, and I had such an enjoyable time that we hated for it to end. We said our tearful good-byes at the airport terminal, making plans for them to visit me in Boston within the next couple of months.

I had work the next day and hadn't checked my work email very much over the course of my vacation. I did see one or two emails from Raine Industries announcing that Mr. Raine's son, Wyatt, had assumed leadership of the company. I would imagine that the announcement didn't quiet much of the upheaval. Blake had never met Wyatt but he'd "heard" things, and from what Blake had shared with me, Wyatt was a force to be reckoned with.

Wyatt and his restructuring staff had been visiting several of the Raine Industries' subsidiaries. There was a fragment of worry in regard to that — RPH had been very successful over the last few years, but we were not on target with Mr. Raine's strategic plan.

This was the exact thing Blake had been worried about a few months ago. But we hadn't expected a shake up so soon — clearly things had changed with the son taking over. I wondered if that meant RPH would be restructured, and what that meant for my job.

❧ ❧ ❧ ❧

Walking in to my office, I saw a panicked Raina at her desk. My mind went into overdrive. In all the years Raina had worked for me, I'd never seen her panic, even with the heavy workload I consistently placed on her, which would be overwhelming for anyone, let alone a lady with three kids and an insanely needy husband. She looked up at me with both relief and concern on her face.

"Ms. Cason, finally," she stated, her voice burdened with worry.

"Hi, Raina. What's going on?" I asked.

"Perhaps we should talk in your office."

"Of course."

We were about to walk through my door when Blake called out from behind us. "Aria, there you are! Why have you not answered your phone or replied to my emails?"

"What? I haven't received any calls or emails from you, Blake."

"Well, it's neither here nor there at this point. We need you upstairs now."

"I was about to have a meeting with Raina, can this wait?"

"I'm afraid not. That's what I've been trying to contact you about."

I looked at Raina and saw the worry in her eyes. What in the hell was going on? Why was Blake so freaked out?

"Whatever you were planning to meet with Raina about may very well be moot. Let's go."

This seemed off. Was I being fired? The company restructuring announcement was of concern, but was it really to a point of me losing my job? I placed my purse and laptop bag in my office chair and followed Blake to the elevators. I looked back at Raina and she managed a small smile. I shrugged and looked at Blake — worry was draped across his face as well.

"Blake, what the hell is going on?"

"We were scheduled for a meeting with Raine's son in the next two weeks, but it turns out he and his team arrived this morning. We have no idea what we're dealing with, but an email went out this morning that we were to all meet in my office at nine o'clock." I glanced at my watch; it was five minutes till.

My heart began to race, and my panic must have showed, because Blake said, "Don't worry, Aria. I think we're okay as far as our positions are concerned, but there's something more pressing that I need to share with you."

We stepped off the elevator and headed to his office. "More pressing than this? I can't imagine anything more pressing at the moment. What is it?"

"Blake, there you are." It was Adam and he looked as panicked, if not more so, than Blake. "They're here and he's with them. They're waiting in the executive conference room."

"I thought we were meeting in my office," Blake said.

"We were, but there wasn't room for the restructuring team. Hello, Aria, welcome back. Sorry to hit you with all of this on your first day, but we tried to reach you."

"Uh, thanks Adam," I replied, confused as to why I didn't see any of the calls or emails.

"Come, we're already late," Adam said.

We quickly entered the executive conference room. I was the last to enter and was immediately taken aback by the tension in the room; everyone was exceptionally quiet. I swiftly took note of the six new faces—astute, stern, and unreadable.

Everyone was seated around the conference table with the exception of the man standing at the far end of the room. He was overlooking downtown Boston as he spoke on the phone. Something about his stance was familiar: the confidence, the power, the dominance. No doubt, much like his father, he was a no-nonsense type of person.

I swallowed my nervousness, squared my shoulders, and kept in step with Blake and Adam. We took the three seats on the left side of the table, leaving the chair at the head for Mr. Raine, who apparently was the man standing near the window. He ended the call and turned to face the room.

"Mr. Raine, we're all here and ready to begin when you are." My attention turned to the man seated across and to the right of me. He appeared to be in his early fifties. He was handsome, and his voice didn't fit his appearance. I was staring at him as he glanced at me with a wry smile, which I returned.

"I would like you all to meet the new President and CEO of Raine Industries, Mr. Wyatt Raine," he said.

I looked toward the window and stopped breathing. I was staring directly into the green eyes of Aiden Wyatt.

Wait. What?

◈Chapter Twenty◈

I sat in a trance as Aiden's voice faded in and out. Too many images and thoughts swarmed in my head. Was this real? How did I miss this? Why did he keep his identity a secret? Had he just been using me to get his kicks? Was his internship a ruse to spy on RPH and report back to his father? I wanted to see his eyes, but I couldn't bring myself to look directly at him — staring past him instead. I felt like such a fool. I wanted to crawl under the table and bawl my eyes out. Why would he do this to me?

His words flowed over me like too-hot water. I could barely stand it. I'd missed the sexy baritone richness of his voice. I'd missed the dark beauty of his eyes. I'd missed his touch. And here he was, a few feet away, and he was more of a stranger to me now than he'd been on his first day at RPH.

I caught the word "restructure" and remembered the team he'd brought along with him — someone was being replaced. I knew I needed to pay attention to the words coming from this asshole's mouth, so I listened. I listened and waited on my chance to get the hell out of this room.

He discussed the company's leadership changes and outlined some immediate modifications to the overall plan for RPH and some other affiliated divisions of Raine Industries. He would be at

RPH for the remainder of the week, and would be leaving one member of the restructuring team behind as he continued with his meetings with the key RPH companies.

After his spiel, he opened the floor for questions. Even those I thought would have caused him to give pause, he shrewdly answered. He was very impressive, which I'd seen at every meeting I'd had with him. But today was an entirely new level. The way he spoke with such authority and steely control, it was intimidating. He closed the meeting and we all prepared to leave.

"Ms. Cason, I would like a word with you," he said.

I stopped dead in my tracks. I fucking hated him. As the others made their way out of the conference room, I returned to my seat. It took everything in me to hold back the tears that wanted to desperately run trails down my cheeks.

"Aria."

I didn't reply.

"Aria. Look at me, please."

My breathing accelerated as my heart pounded. I forced myself to turn slowly until my eyes met his. They were hard and impassive. I was not looking into the eyes of the man I saw three weeks ago. I was looking into the cold green eyes of the head of a multinational conglomerate. A multi-billionaire. A huge fucking regret.

"Aria, I know this must come as a shock, but I would very

much like to—"

"If you have asked to speak to me about anything beyond business matters, I will excuse myself."

His jaws tightened. "Very well," he replied. "There will be a significant change in RPH's executive management team," Aiden began.

I *was* being fired. How fucked was this? This man had pursued, fucked, and reduced me to tears on more than one occasion. Now, here he was to humiliate me even further. Did it have to be him to deliver the blow? Couldn't he have had someone else fire me? Maybe he didn't want to forgo the pleasure of doing it himself. Fucking asshole.

"Oh? What type of change?" I asked.

"I can see you mistook what I said. Maybe I should present this differently. After having worked alongside you and reviewing your professional accomplishments and contributions to RPH, I would like to offer you the position of CEO of Raine Publishing House."

What the fuck?

"Excuse me? Surely I misheard you."

"I'm certain you heard me correctly. I want you to run this company."

"Me? What about Blake?"

"Blake is being replaced, obviously," he stated very

nonchalantly, as if Blake was of no consequence.

Who was this man? Obviously, I didn't know him as well as I should have, but did I ever know him at all?

"I don't understand. Is that why you're here?" I asked.

"That is one of the reasons. Yes."

"Dare I ask the other reasons for this absolutely nightmarish day?"

"Oh, so I'm the object of your nightmares, am I?"

"I didn't say that."

"Perhaps you should tell me exactly what it is you *are* saying, Ms. Cason."

"I'm not saying anything that you don't already know." I glared at him and felt pure hatred.

"One thing I am *not* here for is to play games with you."

"I'm sure. You've already done that," I spit out.

"Aria—"

"Don't bother replying to that," I said.

"I won't." He sat back in his chair and tapped his finger on the table. "Are you going to accept the offer?" he asked.

"And work for you? That would be laughable, if I didn't know you were actually serious. To be honest with you, I've been seriously considering moving on from RPH."

"Have you?" he asked. He stopped with the tapping and leaned forward.

"Yes." I crossed my arms over my chest, shielding the remaining pieces of my heart.

"Interesting. What are you considering moving on to? I seriously doubt you'll be able to easily obtain a job comparable to this in the publishing industry, or any industry, if it was deemed best you remain at RPH."

He was threatening me. "What are you doing?"

"I'm doing what's necessary."

"And you find blackmail necessary? Because this appears more like extortion than a fucking promotion!"

"Careful," he warned. "Aria, term it however you wish. The facts remain the same. I've hand-selected you, as I know you're more than qualified to assume this role. Meade is out. So if it isn't you, it will be someone else. Either way, the decision has been made."

"Unbelievable! Do you honestly expect me to take Blake's job, just like that?"

"You're not taking anything. He's earned the opportunity to move on from RPH, just as you've earned the opportunity to assume this position. He's had five years to prove himself. As I see it, if he hasn't done that yet, he won't. This is a business, not a place for practice runs. This discussion is over."

I couldn't say anything. I just stared at him, angry and hurt. I could feel tears about to spill over. The first time I'd seen him or heard his voice in weeks, and this was what I got? I rose from my seat and headed toward the door.

"I'll expect your answer first thing tomorrow morning," he said.

I slowed as I reached for the door, my hand on the doorknob. "This is not a side of you that I particularly care for."

"Is that so? Why don't you tell me what side of me you do particularly care for? I'll be more than happy to oblige, Aria."

I exhaled the shock and disappointment as I opened the door and walked out of the conference room. I headed back to my office in a daze, confused and deflated as I tried to wrap my brain around all that had just happened. I slowly stepped from the elevator and my eyes immediately fell upon Raina. I saw guilt in her eyes that I didn't quite understand.

"I'm sorry, Ms. Cason."

"Excuse me?" *What did she have to be sorry about?*

"I wanted to warn you before you attended that meeting."

I looked at her, even more confused, trying to understand what she meant. She couldn't possibly know what just happened. Before I could make sense of what she was saying, Adam was behind me, asking to speak privately.

I left the office that day with so many thoughts running through my head that I could've screamed. The thought of Blake and his impending departure was weighing heavily on me. I remembered when Aiden first arrived at RPH, Blake had mentioned that he suspected that the powers-that-be would send someone to analyze RPH, but neither of us thought it would be in the form of Aiden Wyatt, or whatever the fuck his name was. He'd been spying and conspiring this entire time. How could he have done something like that to Blake? To me?

I went home again as distraught as I'd ever been since meeting Aiden. This was, by far, the worst. The tears flowed without ceasing. I pulled over to the side of the highway, seeking the composure that had somehow eluded me.

I just didn't understand how he could have done this to me. He knew. He fucking knew how reluctant I was to be in a relationship of any sort with him. He knew how incredibly difficult this had been for me. Yet he pulled me in — kicking and screaming. He told me so many things that I honestly believed, with everything in me, were true. We'd spent countless hours sharing. I gave myself to him in a way that I never thought I ever could give myself to anyone. And today he was so cold — it was as if we were strangers.

I hated him. I desperately hated him. I hated myself for being so naïve as to let him in. I hated myself even more because I still wanted him.

A steady flow of cars passed by as I sat there, on the side of the road — sobbing. Several minutes later, I eased back into the flow of traffic, crying the entire drive home.

✎Chapter Twenty-One✎

Walking into my building, my eyes were cast downward, hoping to avoid the inquiring eyes of the doormen. I saw Silas and turned away, too slowly, I realized, as I saw his expression morph into one of concern. He'd never seen me like this in all the time I'd lived here. Another fucking first! I pressed the button for the elevator and was thankful to find it empty.

As I stepped into the condo, I was taken aback by the change in its appearance. In the far corner of my living room, near the bar, was a baby grand piano. I dropped my purse on the floor and looked around to see if anyone was there.

"Hello?" I called out. No answer. I walked to the wall intercom to call downstairs.

"This is Silas. How may I be of assistance, Ms. Cason."

Fuck, it would be Silas. I cleared my throat. "Silas, there's a piano in my living room. I didn't order this, and I didn't give anyone permission to enter the condo."

"It was delivered today, ma'am. We attempted to reach you on your office and cell numbers as the delivery man requested. We were routed to a Mr. Raine, and he said you were in a meeting, but that you had left a message that it was okay to let them in."

"Oh, I see." I stared at the piano, wondering why Aiden had done this.

"Is everything okay, Ms. Cason?"

Facing the intercom, I replied, "Yes, everything's fine. I simply forgot is all. Thank you, Silas," I replied, releasing the intercom button.

I turned around and glanced across the room. With a heavy heart, I walked over to the piano. There was a beautiful bouquet of orchids displayed in an intricately patterned crystal vase situated in the middle of the lid. Lying beside the vase was an envelope. I knew it was from Aiden. Part of me wanted to rip it and toss it in the trash, but the part of me that longed for him wanted to open it. I ran my fingers across the envelope, wondering what he could have possibly written that would make any difference at this point. I wouldn't throw it away, but I also didn't want to read it yet. I stood there staring at it until the vibration of my phone severed my fixation.

After grabbing my purse from the floor, I pulled out the phone. Seeing Aiden's name on the display wasn't surprising — he'd be equally unsurprised when I didn't answer. Pressing ignore on the call, I placed the phone on the table and headed to the kitchen. There were only two bottles in the wine cabinet. I knew both of those would be empty before I went to bed tonight. I opened one and, forgoing a glass, drank directly from the bottle.

My phone was vibrating again as I flipped through the TV channels. I glanced at the display. Four missed calls from Aiden and two texts. I read the first.

I know the timing of my surprise was less than ideal, but I hope you liked it. Please answer the phone.

And the second.

Aria, we need to talk. Call me.

I took a swig of wine and dropped the phone beside me on the couch as I continued channel surfing. I had no intention of speaking to that fucker. I happened upon an episode of *Modern Family* and was glad to see that it was a marathon. I hadn't watched this show in ages. I loved Eric Stonestreet's character, Cameron. I needed a friend like him around, especially now.

I fell asleep on the couch, only to be awakened by the steady vibrations of my phone. I'd missed five more calls and several angry texts—all from Aiden. Sighing, I turned the TV off and dragged myself to the bedroom. I didn't have an appetite at all, and I didn't want to be awake. I was asleep almost as soon as my head hit the pillow.

Rolling over in bed the next morning, my eyes slowly opened. I wondered what time it was. Since I'd forgotten to turn my phone back on, the alarm hadn't woken me. Aiden had texted and called all night, and not wanting to be bothered, I'd finally turned the phone off. Why would he try so vehemently now when he'd done absolutely nothing for weeks?

Turning the cell back on, I was greeted by ping after ping — texts from Aiden and April. I quickly read April's texts.

What's going on? Call me back.

Are you okay? Call me!!

Aiden called me. I'm so sorry about all of this. Call me!

Why did he involve April in this? How did he even get her number? Oh, I forgot — he was Aiden *Raine,* which meant he could do whatever the hell he wanted with the many resources he had at his disposal.

My thoughts immediately flashed back to St. Barts when he claimed to have made a call to the concierge to locate my villa. It dawned on me that he'd been able to obtain information on my whereabouts because of *who* he was. He'd said that his father owned property there, and I conveniently assumed it was a timeshare of some sort. He didn't bother to clarify. Now I was certain I knew why. If his father owned that whole property, it would be as easy as breathing for Aiden to find the name and location of my villa.

Everything had been a lie. How much of a fucking idiot was I? Why didn't I ask more questions? Better still, when I saw things didn't add up, why did I continue to go along with his demands?

Sitting on the edge of the bed, a new day's flood of tears

began to flow. It hurt to even breathe. I was such a fool. I prided myself on being such an intuitive person, being able to read people, but somehow I let all of the warning bells fade into the background. All of the weird intense exchanges between him and his dad—now it all made sense. He never wanted to talk to me about the issues with his father. And the subliminal messages and questionable glances between him and his family when I was around—they were in on it, too. But why? Why would they go along with something so insane? It made no sense!

Wait! His father's name was Connor. So who the hell was Wesley Raine? I went to my computer and googled Wesley Raine and was overwhelmed with image after image of Connor. On Wikipedia I typed in "Wesley Raine." I looked at the right side of the screen and saw his full name—Wesley Connor Raine. His children were Victoria Sloan Raine, Nicholas Carter Raine, Aiden Wyatt Raine and Allison Sophia Raine. *Son of a bitch!*

Rage. I was overwhelmed with rage! Of course, the other feelings were there, extremely close to the surface, but I was actually grateful that fury was now overshadowing those. I angrily wiped my tears and went to reply to April's text.

I'm sorry Aiden contacted you about this. Everything's fine. I'm running behind schedule for work, but I'll be in touch soon. Love you.

I scrolled through the other texts from Aiden. *Was he fucking kidding me?* He was angry with *me*? I tossed the phone on the bed and rushed to take a shower and dress for work. *Work.* The one place I had looked forward to going to every day was now like walking into a nightmare by choice.

As I started toward the kitchen for a granola bar and a bottle of water, the piano whispered my name as I passed. I looked at the beautiful instrument and my eyes flashed toward the note. Part of me knew I shouldn't, but I wanted to read it.

Aria,

I'm sure you now realize that I've been less than truthful with you. I have reasons for that, and I hope you'll allow me the chance to explain.

I had selected this piano the afternoon after breakfast with my family. It was custom made — especially for you. I hope we have the chance to make beautiful music together.

-A.

I placed the note on the piano lid and walked around to sit on the bench. On the back panel above the keys was an inscription, *Kingston and Virgini ...Making beautiful Music Since 2014.* My tears flowed, my chest feeling as if it would collapse. I sat at the piano as pieces of my inner being shattered around me. How was I going to survive this? Survive him?

As I dressed for the day I was dreading, I gave myself reassuring pep talks, all the while, Aiden-filled images and conversations teetered in the periphery of my mind. Although my stomach was in knots and my head didn't seem to want to stop pounding, I knew I'd get through this, somehow. I'd been broken before. I'd actually never reconnected the damaged parts—I'd only hidden them. But at any rate, I did it before, and I damned well would do it now.

I took a deep breath and opened the door of the condo, ready to face another day of the hell my life had become.

Walking into the RPH building was menacing. Although they couldn't possibly guess, I felt that everyone knew what was going on. My heart tightened as I stepped out of the elevator onto the floor of my office. My eyes settled on Raina—she looked uneasy. *Really? I just got here!*

"Good morning, Raina. Is everything all right?" I asked, approaching her desk.

"Good morning, Ms. Cason. I'm not sure. Mr. Raine was just here, and he's called twice since I arrived. He said that it was urgent that he speak with you, and I was to alert him when you arrived."

I didn't want Raina in the middle of this, and quite frankly I was upset at Aiden for behaving in such an unprofessional manner, even more so given his new position.

"It's okay. I'll check in with him as soon as I settle in."

The phone rang and she nervously looked up at me. "It doesn't seem as though you'll have time to get settled. It's Mr.

Raine."

"It's fine, Raina, please forward the call to me," I said, walking into my office.

I closed the door and prepared myself for what I knew would be an unpleasant conversation. Sitting at my desk, I took a deep breath and lifted the receiver.

"This is Aria."

"Good morning," he said.

"That remains to be seen. How can I assist you?"

"Did you receive my texts?" he asked.

"I'm not sure that I did. Were they of a business nature?"

"I can assume you aren't sure you received my voicemails either," he said, his irritation flowing through the phone.

"I actually haven't had a chance to check any voicemail. As soon as I walked into my office, I was bombarded with a rather large nuisance."

"Oh. Is that so?"

"It would seem. I really have a full day, so if you can enlighten me as to the purpose of this urgent conversation, I would appreciate it."

"Aria, we need to talk."

"Isn't that what we're doing now?" I propped my forehead in my palm and looked at the patterns in the wood of my desk.

"We need to talk like two mature adults, without the fucking attitude."

Fine. He didn't like my attitude? I gave him only silence.

"When is the first break in your schedule? And before you say you don't have any, I know that you do."

More silence.

"We can do this the easy way or the hard way, princess. It's your choice. But either way, we will do this."

I knew he would do whatever necessary to make this happen. Maybe the faster we got this over with, the faster I could extricate myself from this bullshit.

I sat back in my chair and looked at the time on my phone. "Give me an hour. Should I come to you?" I asked.

"Yes, that would be best, as I have back to back meetings scheduled, and every minute is crucial to my day. I'll expect you promptly at nine-thirty." He hung up.

I fucking hated him. My eyes stung as the tears tried to force their way to the surface, but thankfully, they were halted by the knock at my door.

"Yes."

It was Raina, her face overflowing with compassion. She'd never witnessed this behavior from me, and I had no idea of how much was visible on the surface. I felt like shit.

"I thought you could use a cup of tea, Ms. Cason."

Hell, I need something a lot stronger than tea. "Thank you,

Raina," I replied as she placed the cup on my desk.

She turned to leave and closed the door softly behind her.

I took a sip and closed my eyes, wondering how I was going to make it through a face-to-face with Aiden.

I sipped my tea as I worked through the ton of email. It was a quarter after nine when the phone intercom beeped.

"Ms. Cason, a Mr. Dane Patrick is here to see you. Should I send him in?"

I spit tea all over my desk. *What the fuck?*

I reached for my phone and quickly texted April.

Dane is here at my fucking office! Did you ever hear anything from him or his wife?

Placing the phone on my desk, I hurriedly replied to Raina.

"Please send him in." I needed to get rid of him as soon as possible.

Raina walked Dane into my office and closed the door behind her. There he stood — a large regret that should've stayed in Venezuela. Dane was leanly built with dark hair and soft hazel eyes. He was a handsome man. Too bad he was a jerk. I motioned for him to have a seat.

"Hello, Aria. You look beautiful, as always. How are you?"

"What are you doing here?"

"Wow. No hello?"

"Not for you. Liar!"

"So you know about my, uh…"

"Wife? Uh, yeah! What the hell have you gotten me mixed up in?"

"That's why I'm here."

He explained that his marriage was ending and that his wife was trying to get everything on the grounds of infidelity, and she planned to have her lawyer call me in to testify.

"Look, you'd better find a way to fix this. Don't bring me into the middle of your shit."

"Aria, listen—"

My door abruptly opened, and Dane stopped mid-sentence.

It was Aiden, and he wasn't happy.

He looked at me, and then at Dane, who stood to face him. I didn't know what to do or say.

"This is Mr. Raine," I offered.

Dane reached out to shake Aiden's hand. Aiden returned his gesture with an ice cold glare.

"And you are?" Aiden asked.

"Dane Patrick," he replied, confused by Aiden's immediate disregard for him.

"And what's the nature of your business with Ms. Cason?" Aiden demanded.

"Well, that's between me and Ms. Cason."

Oh shit! What a way to fan the flames idiot.

Aiden moved toward Dane, who seemingly took an involuntarily step back.

I quickly stood and cornered my desk, grabbing Dane's arm.

"Dane was just leaving," I said. "Let me walk you out." I led him to the door as Raina stared at us. I leaned in so that only Dane could hear.

"Don't you fucking dare come back to my office. If you do, I guarantee you'll be arrested," I whispered.

"If it were only that simple. I'll be seeing you soon, Aria."

Fuck! Why was all of this happening? Now I have to deal with Aiden's inquisitive, demanding bullshit on top of trying to figure out how to handle Dane!

I turned and walked past Aiden to my desk. "Can I help you with something?" I asked, my impatience and frustration coming through loud and clear.

"Is there something going on that I should know about?"

"No, I don't think so."

"Was that personal?" he asked.

"And if it was? Never mind. You of all people know I don't do personal at work. I made that mistake once. Trust me—I don't intend to repeat that huge lapse in judgment."

"Am I supposed to take that personally? Because I did."

"So what?"

"Aria—"

"And don't ever walk into my office intimidating my guests."

"I don't think I did that at all. I merely questioned his intentions."

"As if you have the right?"

"I have every fucking right," he said, his eyes blazing.

"No, you have no right to dictate to me in any capacity besides RPH business, and that's still up in the air."

"Aria, I don't know what you want me to say here. Do you honestly think I'm going to sit by and watch as you invite some asshole into your life while you ignore me?"

"I expect exactly what you've shown me over the last few weeks—*nothing!*" I exclaimed.

"You've ignored my calls and texts. How long do you expect that to continue before I force you to communicate with me?" he asked.

"I'm not doing this with you. I assume you're here for the answer to your blackmail offer?"

I saw a glimmer of irritation on his face as he walked to sit in one of the chairs in front of my desk. "Yes, I would like to know what you've decided."

"Well, it's not like I have much of a fucking choice. Either I succumb to your threat, or I risk career suicide."

"I'm really disappointed you view this opportunity with such malice, Aria."

"Oh, you're disappointed? Ha! We don't want that, do we?"

He sat back in the chair and crossed his leg, his ankle positioned on his knee.

"I'll accept, but with conditions," I said, meeting his gaze.

"You will accept, and there will be no conditions. The contract was emailed to you a few moments ago. Review it and send the e-signed copy to HR as quickly as possible, as Blake is being told today and the announcement and press release will be going out this afternoon."

Unbelievable. Who is this man?

"I have some pressing matters to attend to, so we'll not be able to discuss much more at the moment, but I'll see you at your place at seven o'clock. I'll bring dinner. Don't bother refusing—this has gone on long enough. We're talking this out tonight."

My heart was racing. I was angry and confused, but so fucking turned on by this man and his dominance that I couldn't fight.

"I need to talk to Blake," I said.

"No, you don't," he countered. "Once he's relieved of his duties, he'll be escorted from the building. All of that is happening within the next twenty minutes. I expect you to keep quiet until then. Understand?"

"Look you arrogant—"

"Aria, I don't have time for this. I'll see you this evening." He stood and walked over to my desk and kissed me softly on the forehead. He then turned and casually strolled out of my office.

He smelled so good.

I fucking hated him!

❧Chapter Twenty-Two❧

Within an hour, the announcement of my promotion and Blake's departure was detailed both in interoffice email and on the Internet. I felt like a coward and a traitor. I hadn't spoken with Blake because of Aiden's warning that I shouldn't. This felt wrong, but I didn't want to do anything to upset Aiden at this point, because I wasn't prepared for where that could lead. So I kept quiet as I was told.

This was so not me. I'd changed so much in the last few months. Changes or not, I felt like I owed Blake an explanation. I promised myself I'd reach out to him as soon as some of the dust settled. I owed him that much. Blake was responsible for my having a job at RPH, and here I was replacing him. I didn't like this, but after considering my options, accepting the job was the only move that made sense for me.

My head was still throbbing, and I just wanted to go home, fall into bed, and bury myself under the covers until everything felt right again. My phone rang, and I glanced at the display and saw that it was Raina.

"Yes?" I answered as I rotated my thumb and index finger on my temples.

"Ms. Cason, do you have a moment?"

"Yes, of course," I replied, wondering what other shock I needed to absorb today.

"May I come speak with you?" she asked.

"Sure, give me a couple of minutes and show yourself in."

I'd received a text from Aiden just as my phone rang, and I wanted to read it before meeting with Raina.

I'm anxious to speak with you this evening. I've missed you terribly.

I was weak for him—I wanted to reply, letting him know I felt the same, but I knew I shouldn't. I placed the phone on my desk just as Raina walked in and closed the door behind her.

There it was. That same guilty look I noticed yesterday. Confused, I motioned for her to have a seat at the table as I stood to join her.

"Is there something wrong, Raina?"

"Ms. Cason, I have something to tell you, which I wanted to share with you weeks ago, but I wasn't able to because I was afraid I would lose my job."

"Raina, what is it? I highly doubt you've done anything that could result in that happening."

"After you hear this, you may think otherwise."

She glanced down at the carpet. This was not a Raina I'd ever seen.

"Does this have anything to do with what you wanted to

speak with me about yesterday?"

"Yes."

"Okay, let's hear it. I'm sure it's not as bad as you think."

"Well, I wanted to warn you about Mr. Raine."

"What?" I asked, confused.

She sighed and placed her hands on the table, nervously twisting them before looking at me. "I knew some time ago that Mr. Raine and Aiden Wyatt were the same person," she said, hesitantly.

I was quiet, caught off guard by her disclosure—and also wondering how it was possible she knew something like this, and I didn't.

"I knew he'd be arriving yesterday to meet with you, and I didn't want you to be caught off guard, but just as I was about to tell you, Mr. Meade came and rushed you off to the meeting with him."

"I don't understand. How is it that you knew about his identity weeks ago?"

"The week he resigned, he contacted me. He told me who he was, and he wanted to speak with me about you."

She looked at me, nervous as she took in my reaction. I wasn't sure if she saw anything beyond anger, as that was the only emotion I could display at the moment.

"Maybe I should back up a little. I strongly suspected

something romantic was going on between the two of you. The others may not have noticed, but being as I work so closely with you, I was able to pick up on it. Besides that, I've worked with you for years, so I think I am pretty attuned to your mannerisms and such. There were some obvious changes in your personality and overall behavior, especially when Mr. Raine was around. I knew that if my assumptions were correct I should keep it to myself, for obvious reasons."

Could this be any more humiliating?

"Evidently he knew of my suspicions, or maybe by the time he contacted me he didn't care if I knew or not. He'd called on my cell phone one evening. He told me his identity and what had happened to his father, and that he would more than likely be assuming control of Raine Industries. He didn't go into great detail about the two of you, but he did tell me enough to confirm my suspicions. He was concerned about you, but knew he couldn't come to you with any of this."

I sat there taking in everything Raina had revealed, but I was still quite confused. Why would he take her into confidence? Why had he not paid me the same courtesy?

"Why would he tell you this Raina? I don't understand, and why didn't you immediately tell *me* about it?"

Raina sat twisting her hands in her lap. She looked at me apologetically as she continued her story. "My theory is he knew his abrupt departure would hurt you. He regretted the dishonesty and knew he couldn't come to you with this any other way than in person. Since he didn't know when he was returning, he wanted me to keep an eye on you — to know if you'd moved on, and if you did, he wanted to be made aware of it as quickly as possible so that he could intervene."

"So he wanted you to spy on me and report back to him?" I asked, incredulous. Though, after seeing him in action these last couple of days, this really wasn't as shocking as it would have been three days ago.

"Ms. Cason, I feel horrible about this, and I've told him so. When he alerted me to his arrival, I literally begged him to allow me to tell you before you walked in and discovered it alongside everyone else. He reluctantly agreed, but obviously the opportunity to warn you passed before you found out yourself."

I sat quietly absorbing this news, soaking in yet another wonderful tidbit of information about Aiden.

"Raina, I'm not upset with you, and I appreciate the fact that you didn't want to be involved with this. I can certainly understand why you followed his instructions. Believe it or not, he gagged me, too." Immediately I was embarrassed at the use of the word *gagged,* as visions of Aiden fucking me, gagged across my desk, flashed in my head. "I wasn't able to alert anyone, even Blake, of his being fired and my replacing him."

"I threatened to quit, you know," she said. "I told him you'd been an amazing employer and I refused to betray you in this way. But after he convinced me of his intentions toward you, I agreed. He told me that he knew how highly you thought of me, and that he didn't want to put you though losing both of us within such a short time."

"Well, how thoughtful of him," I replied sarcastically.

"You're upset, understandably so. Ms. Cason, I know it isn't my place to say, but don't be too hard on him. I think you should give him a chance. He's an extremely intelligent and powerful man, who has experienced more than I can fathom, but the communications I've had with him have revealed that he's walking in uncharted territory when it comes to you. All of the intelligence and power in the world mean nothing when it comes to affairs of the heart, and it would appear you have his. While I disapprove of his tactics, I think his heart was in the right place."

I sighed and offered a smile. "Thank you, Raina. I'm sorry you were placed in this position. I'll take it from here."

"I think he makes you happy," she said.

I couldn't reply to that. Had someone said that a few weeks ago, I would have agreed.

"Are we okay?" Raina asked.

"Of course we are," I assured her.

"I was so worried you'd think I'd betrayed you."

"I don't think that at all, Raina."

She stood to leave. "Congratulations on your promotion. I know you'll take this company to heights unknown. "

"Thank you, Raina."

She turned, but I stopped her before she could leave. "Thanks for your loyalty, and I'm relieved you didn't quit. Who would I have taken along to the top floor to help me run this place?" I asked, smiling.

Raina returned my smile, and as soon as she was gone, I hurried back to my desk for my phone. I reread Aiden's text then quickly typed a reply.

Fuck you. Don't you dare come to my place tonight or any other fucking night!

After powering off my phone, I hit the speaker button and told Raina to forward all office calls to the answering service for the remainder of the day. I then began reviewing the recent e-publishing report. Upon noticing some discrepancies, I later called Raina in to work on some revisions.

We'd barely started when my door flew open to reveal an extremely angry Aiden Raine.

❧Chapter Twenty-Three❧

He stared at me and I easily returned his heated glare. Raina looked at me, obviously startled and confused by Aiden's sudden appearance. He briefly glanced in her direction. "Leave us," he instructed and slowly returned his furious gaze towards me. "And see that we're not disturbed," he ordered, his eyes not leaving mine.

As soon as Raina closed the door, he stalked toward me, reaching me in a few strides. He grabbed my arm, yanking me out of my chair. "I don't have time for your bullshit, Aria."

"Just as I don't have time for yours! Hence my text." I jerked my arm from his grasp.

He stalked closer, making me crazy, so I took a step back. Without warning, his hands cupped my face, pulling me into a kiss. I resisted, but he continued, his tongue demanding access to my mouth. When he finally pulled away, his hands were still on either side of my face, his piercing green eyes willing me to surrender to him.

"Stop fighting me," he whispered.

He placed his lips on mine once more, and as if I had no choice, I responded to him. We kissed as if we were starved for each other.

He broke the kiss, breathing harshly. "I've missed you. Every day."

"Oh, I never would have guessed. What, with all of the attempts to contact me over the last several weeks," I spit out.

"I know I owe you an explanation, but I also knew it shouldn't be something I communicated in a text or email, or even a phone call. Don't you think I understand what you gave to me when you allowed me to get close to you? I never took that lightly. Not for one moment. I simply wasn't in a position to speak to you face to face."

"Oh my God! Do you think I'm that much of an idiot? You're Aiden Wyatt Raine, multi-billionaire. You have access to private planes and whatever else you want. If you wanted to see me, you very well could have, so save the bullshit."

"Yes, I did have access to you, but I was not in a position where I could leave my mother. She was distraught when Dad had the heart attack. She was hospitalized shortly afterwards, and I literally didn't leave the hospital for two weeks. I actually had the hospital convert some space into an office, which is where I worked when I wasn't sitting with one of my parents."

"I hadn't realized," I said sympathetically.

"Don't you think this has been difficult for me? Keeping all of this from you? Wondering what you must think of me?"

"I don't know what to think. You're different. You've been so cold with me. You're shielded — I barely recognize the person I thought I was getting to know."

"I'm a different person when it comes to work, Aria. I always have been. There's an immense pressure on me. My father has groomed me my entire life to one day take over his company. I never wanted it, which is why I often assumed a slightly different identity so that I could be me and do what I wanted. I know it sounds fucked up, but you didn't grow up the son of Connor Raine — the constant scrutiny, the expectations, the misery of it all."

His issues with his privileged life were inconsequential to me. "You lied to me, Aiden. Every day, every moment, was a lie!"

"No. I just didn't tell you the entire story. People who I'm *not* trying to date treat me differently when they learn who I am, so just imagine how you would have responded had you known my true identity. I wouldn't have stood a chance with you. I thought about this from every angle, and I didn't see any other way."

"Oh really? You have what? Three, four degrees — and you couldn't think of a way to tell me the truth? It appears the educational system also fails the most elite society members."

"Aria, listen to me, please. You have this thing with power and control. Here I am with both. You wouldn't have given me the time of day, and you know it."

"Well, I guess we'll never know."

I finally came to my senses and tried to push him away. He reluctantly released me.

"Tell me you understand. Please," he said, his fluid green eyes pleading my acceptance. But I couldn't give it to him.

"I can't believe you—although, I don't know why I'm surprised. Since the day you darkened my door, you've flashed nothing but audacity and expected me to just go along with whatever you threw at me. But this—this is a whole new level of fucked up. One day everything was fine with us—hell, more than fine, more than I would ever have thought I would go along with—and then nothing! Now you want me to understand when you didn't even have the decency to pick up a fucking phone!"

"What was I supposed to do, Aria? Call you and say, 'By the way, everything I've told you up to this point has been a lie?'"

"You could have said something. Anything. It would have been better than thinking you didn't care! That you fucking used me and tossed me to the side when you were done! You said nothing for weeks, Aiden. For weeks! And now you come back and what? What did you expect to happen? Did you think I would just fall into your arms and say 'Hey, don't worry about it. Would you like to fuck me now?' Well, it's not happening, and I don't fucking understand it! I don't want to understand. I want you out of my life. You didn't seem to have any problems staying away then, so you shouldn't have a problem doing it now! Go away!"

"Aria, don't do this. I know I fucked up. If I could go back and do things differently—"

"Blah, blah, fucking blah. Do you have any idea how many times I've heard that lame ass line in the movies? At the very least, come at me with some original bullshit that I just may have a small chance of falling for!"

"Aria, I'm only saying what I feel. I don't give a shit if it sounds like a line. Just tell me what I need to do. Tell me, and I'll do it."

I didn't understand how someone who seemed so sincere could have deceived me and left me in misery for weeks. Just the thought made my heart hurt. I couldn't go through this with him again. I wouldn't. "There's nothing you can say or do, Aiden. I'm done."

His face was twisted in pain as if he were being tormented. "I miss you, princess. I love you."

I stopped breathing. Those words had only been spoken to me by one other man—my father. Hearing Aiden say them now, it was like someone had punched me in the stomach. They weren't filled with elation or contentment; they only evoked feelings of fear and pain. They awakened images of the agony I'd seen on my mother's face every day for over fourteen years. I didn't want it. I never wanted it.

He hurriedly walked over to me, ignoring the look of

resistance in my eyes, cradling my face with impatient hands. As deeply as I wanted to reject him, as soon as his lips met mine, I was there with him. His kiss didn't start off with the sweet exploratory softness; this kiss was one of such fierceness that it literally took my breath away.

Desperate for his touch, I instinctively wrapped my arms around his unyielding body, giving into him. Giving him what he — what *we* — so desperately wanted. Our connection was a poignant reminder of our irrefutable need for each other. My body surrendered, nearly going limp in his arms. His soft lips were rough on mine, but I wanted this, needed it in a way that I could never say aloud. So I gave in, letting him remind me of what he felt — remind me of what I made him feel.

Just as suddenly as he initiated the kiss, he ended it. He drew away, breathing as heavily as I was — still grasping my face between his hands. He looked at me, searching my face, staring deeply into my eyes. It was as if he could see everything I'd stored inside — the pain, the fear, the want, the insecurity — all of the shattered pieces.

His penetrating gaze revealed his desperation, the longing and need he had for me. His beautiful face briefly betrayed him as it revealed a glimpse of his own pain, adding validity to what I saw in his dismal green eyes. He was hurting as much as I was, and it was deep…and it hit me. The realization was exactly like his kiss—rough and deep. It was the kiss of a man letting go. No sooner did the thought enter my mind than he turned and walked away. I stood there, watching him exit my office...knowing that it was finally over.

THE END

Epilogue

I opened my laptop and accessed my email account to start a new message. Once I finished, I read it and desperately wanted to hit *send*, but something inside me just wouldn't allow me to do that. Instead, I read it over and over.

Aiden,

I don't regret you. I thought I would. I knew I would, but I don't. Loving you made me realize that I can have a life outside of my fear — that I don't have to omit part of life. For that, I thank you. And even now as I say good-bye, my heart is overflowing with love for you. I'm pretty sure that I will always love you, but I have to let you go. I won't stand in the way of you and your family. I won't force you to choose, and I don't want to be the person who destroys your family.

Family once meant so much to me, and I forgot that. I pushed it aside because of the hurt of my childhood, which I now know was not torn apart because of a lack of love, but because there was so much of it. You have a responsibility to your family and thousands of others. Yes, I know you have just as much of a

responsibility to yourself, and when you come to terms with that, I
know you will find me.

All my love,
Now and forever,
Aria

I read it again. And again. I couldn't send it, but I couldn't delete it either. I printed the email and saved it in my drafts and turned off my computer.

Discussion Questions

1. Aria is firm in her stance of keeping men at arm's length. What is it about Aiden that causes Aria to lose herself in him?

2. Do you think Aria views her isolation from others as dysfunctional or necessary?

3. Do you think Aiden would have been able to allow Aria to dominate him? Why or why not?

4. Were Aiden's reasons for keeping his identity a secret forgivable? Do you think there is more to his story?

5. Do you think Aria needs counseling and if so, do you think she realizes the need for counseling?

6. What are your thoughts on Aria's decision to reconnect with her family?

7. Do you think Melena (Aria's mother) is still in contact with Matteo (Aria's father)?

8. If you were Aiden and wanted a life from under the cloud of the Raine name, what would you do?

9. Both Aiden and Aria are very driven. Aria loves her job. Although Aiden is a very astute business man, he

doesn't seem to have the same passion for business as Aria. Where do you think Aiden's passion lies?

10. Do you think Aria has seen the last of Dane Patrick?

AIDEN AND ARIA'S STORY CONTINUES

IN THE UPCOMING SEQUEL OF THE UNTOUCHED SERIES

TOUCHED

Coming Soon from Lilly Wilde!

Connect with Lilly Wilde

Facebook at Lilly Wilde

Twitter at @authorlilly

Good Reads

Google Plus

Linked In

YouTube

Pinterest

Instagram

Thank you for reading *Untouched*. If you enjoyed it, I would love to hear from you! Please take a moment to leave a review at your favorite retailer.

Thanks!

Untouched is available as an eBook and in print edition at most online retailers.

Please subscribe to *Letters with Lilly*, a monthly newsletter from your author and friend, Lilly Wilde. You can subscribe on the newsletter tab on Lilly's website: www.lillywilde.com

If you would like to join the street team, please contact the author on Facebook or by commenting on Lilly's website: www.lillywilde.com

Books by Lilly Wilde

Untouched—Book One of The Untouched Series

Touched—Book Two of The Untouched Series

Touched by Him—Book Three of The Untouched Series

Only His Touch, Part One—Book Four of The Untouched Series

Only His Touch, Part Two—Book Five of The Untouched Series

Forever Touched—Book Six of The Untouched Series

What readers are saying about Untouched:

"Simply Exquisite!! This book is amazing! The description of the characters is so vivid and extremely catching. I felt like I was actually living the story. I was so drawn to Aria, Aiden, and April. The communication between Aiden and Aria is so touching... I laughed throughout the book and cried at the end. Cannot wait to read more... I love the sensuality of it all. One of the best breathtaking books I have read so far. Can't wait for the next one. Great writer! Awesome Job Lilly!"

~ *Review from Amazon*

"Lilly Wilde gives you the same excitement we got from 50 Shades and The Crossfire Series. Except Lilly delivered it to us in a whole new way. It was so much more realistic than the others that you not only finished it yearning for your own Aiden, but you actually think it's

possible to find him. You are captured from the beginning to the end. You fall in love with this couple. This couple is so sexy, and your mind takes you away to forbidden places and feelings. It's a great story and a sexy read. You don't want to miss out on this!!!!!"

~ Review from Amazon

"I loved your book! Aiden was a perfect cross between Christian Grey and Jesse Ward...The perfect man."

~ Review from Amazon

"LILLY DEFINITELY BLEW ME AWAY WITH THIS! Aiden and Aria made me fall in love from the beginning. Their story is so similar to 50, Crossfire, Driven, This Man, but at the same time it holds some unique individuality that really makes it stand out."

~ Review from Amazon

"I've read a lot of books, many from this genre—50 Shades, Crossfire Series, This Man, etc.—and in a word this book is AMAZING. You immediately become invested in the characters and take this emotional roller coaster ride with them. I found this book to have more real life undertones than some of the others I've read, making the characters more relatable. It has been said that every story has been told. Well, that may be, but definitely not in this fashion. It's a must read!"

~ Review from Amazon

"What else can be said about a phenomenal writer who brought to life two amazing people in a story that is not only emotionally charged, but is realistic? Aria and Aiden will capture you from the beginning and won't let you go. I can't get enough of them. Reading this, I had every emotion possible. I was happy, pissed, sad, and curious, but mostly I was captivated by their story..."

~ Review from Amazon

What readers are saying about Touched:

"Once again author Lilly Wilde has delivered an amazing story of love, lust, romance, intrigue, heartache, and suspense. From the first sentence of Touched *to the last, the author's way with words pulls you right into the story and leaves you wanting and wondering...craving more. Great job Lilly Wilde. Looking forward to the next step in Aria's and Aiden's journey."*

~ Review from Amazon

*"Lilly Wilde, you are truly AMAZING. I couldn't and wouldn't put this book down. I fell in love with Aiden and Aria in the first book of the trilogy (*Untouched*) and I fell in love with them even more in* Touched*. I had probably every emotion a person could have. It had twist and turns in every chapter. I could see Aiden and Aria in my mind and hear them talking in my head. I want* Touched by Him *out NOW. I can't wait to see how all the twist and turns play out. I can't believe you just started writing not long ago. I am a HUGE fan of yours now and for life. Your books have me shocked and amazed. Thank you for writing these books*

and taking me away. I will be searching for my Aiden while I wait for Touched by Him"

~ *Review from Amazon*

"*After reading* Untouched *(Book 1)...I was hooked and (Book 2)* Touched *certainly didn't disappoint me... Wow, the story line is amazing and so real. Lilly Wilde has smashed it again. Personally I now think 50 Shades is rubbish! (Sorry to you 50 Shades lovers; yes, I used to be one myself.) Touched is way more realistic, and has so much more to offer. The main characters are brilliant, the story line is so gripping. Loads of drama, and as for the hot sex, this will not disappoint you. I couldn't put my Kindle down! Seriously this is a must read!"*

~ *Review from Amazon*

"*ABSOUTELY LOVE THE UNTOUCHED TRILOGY. I love every detail about Aiden and Aria, who are both strong, confident, career-driven people with a love and passion so strong it's unbreakable. I was so entranced from beginning to end that I didn't want to stop reading. I enjoyed* Untouched *so much, and I knew would fall in love with* Touched *as well. The story unravels detail by juicy detail, and I love it...A LOT! This book will have you crying, screaming, and begging for more, all in one chapter. I haven't cried after reading a book since I read FSOG and this book did it.... The water works flooded my sheets. If you're looking for a book that has a great story line and some steamy scenes...then look no further. This is the book for you.*"

~ *Review from Amazon*

"Wow, I knew this series was good but I'm floored by just how good. I could hardly put Touched *down; each chapter is like candy. Aria and Aiden are hot as lava together, and you'll be on the edge till "The End." I can't wait for the third book. I will read anything written by Lilly Wilde. Anything!"*
~Review from Kobo

"I am absolutely in love with this trilogy! Lilly Wilde wrote one HOT, steamy little number. She definitely has an amazing talent to draw you in from the first paragraph and leaving you begging for MORE!"
~Review from Barnes & Noble

"I don't know where to begin. I guess that I will start by saying that Lilly Wilde has ruined me for other authors. Her style draws you in from the first sentence. The story of Aria and Aiden is one that I just cannot get enough of. Touched *and* Untouched *(the first book in this trilogy) had me experience every emotion possible. I feel like I am part of this story. Part of these characters' lives. And that is what a great book is supposed to do. The heat and passion in this book is intense. Once I started it, I found it difficult to put down. I simply cannot wait to read more of their story. I need more of Aria and Aiden in my life."*
~Review from Barnes & Noble

"Wow, Lilly, I just want to say how amazing this was. I was hooked after book one, but now I can't wait until book three. You grab the reader and don't let go. Please hurry with #3!!!"

"I cannot believe it!!!! I never thought a book could leave me in such a state! I'm an emotional wreck, but Miss Lilly, you have done this to me with Aria and Aiden's story. I'm forever changed. I fell in love with Aiden and Aria within the first few pages of Untouched. *In the beginning, I thought this typically would be a hot, kinky, sex-craved story, but boy was I wrong!!!! It's soooooo much more than that. I was instantly hooked. Lilly pulled me deeper down the rabbit hole, curious to know more. I couldn't stop myself!!!! I had no control to put this book down. I felt like I was living in this story and feeling every emotion with it. I laughed, I really cried, my jaw dropped as to how much I was turned on, and I do mean a lot!!!!! I've been exposed to all things that are Aiden and like a starved, crazed woman I want more. I need more Lilly. I'll be pulling my hair out waiting for the next installment to be released. This is one trilogy you'll want in your collection, ladies! This is one trilogy I will never forget, and I know a group of ladies that never will either. I applaud you, Lilly, on a fantastically awesome job. I'm sooooo happy that I got to experience this. You truly are an amazing writer. I'll be waiting for what's to come next!"*

"Lilly Wilde did it again! The second installment of Aiden and Aria's story was even more emotional than the first. I cannot wait for the third. This book will have you laughing and crying all on the same chapter. Lilly is an amazing writer with a talent for telling a story that is a steamy and fun to read. She makes you feel like you are a part of the story and the characters are long-time friends."

~Review from Smashwords

"This book series really makes you feel like you are a part of the action. I cried, I laughed, I got mad. You will fall deep into this series and will not want to come back to reality. Lilly Wilde takes you on a rollercoaster of emotions, and you will forever love it. To be so entwined with them is great. You will not want to put the book down, and when it's over you will literally be begging for more. I can't wait for the release of the last book." **~Review from Smashwords**

About the Author

Lilly Wilde is the Author of The Untouched Series (Untouched, Touched, Touched By Him, Only His Touch and Forever Touched). She is a wife and mom who loves to fill each day with happiness and laughter. Lilly loves to dream, get lost in fantasy and create alternate worlds in which we can escape ever so often. She's down-to-earth, engaging and compassionate with a great sense of humor. Her laughter is one of the first qualities that you'll notice; you'll become instantly drawn to her witty and fun-loving spirit.

Lilly spent a lot of time daydreaming as a child which led to numerous hours of reading and eventually the writing of poetry. The first story Lilly began writing was entitled *He Lied To Me*, a novel she plans to complete in the near future. After years of starting and stopping several novels, she eventually set a goal to complete her debut novel, *Untouched*.

Her stories are of strength, growth, facing demons and stepping outside your comfort zone. They often surround topics of family and love and the beauty of both.